THE ARTIST

By Ryan Anderson

—

This book is a work of fiction. The characters in this book have no existence outside the imagination of the author and have no relation whatsoever to anyone bearing the same name or names. Any similarity to real persons, living or dead, is coincidental and not intended by the author. No part of this book may be reproduced, stored in a retrieval system, or transmitted by any means without written permission of the author.

ISBN: 978-1-4357-1622-3

Printed in U.S.A.

For more information visit: www.lulu.com/ryananderson

I dedicate this book to Melissa Edwards Conway, a very special person in my life. Thank you for your friendship. Also, I would like to thank everyone who has supported me in my endeavors.

-Ryan

The Artist

In the early morning hours of August 29, 2005, one of the worst known natural disasters in the history of the United States hit the Gulf Coast with such crippling, devastating vengeance that the world sat watching with their mouths open in horror, speechless at what Mother Nature had deemed necessary. Hurricane Katrina blew into New Orleans from the Gulf of Mexico with such an awesome force of winds and water that some of the levees holding in the contents of Lake Ponchatrain broke, drowning houses, cars, buildings and people who either couldn't or wouldn't heed the warnings and flee to higher ground or evacuate. This unforgiving fury of wind and water left behind an endless stream of debris and damage that would take years to clean and repair. Its impact on the current American way of life affected everyone, in all states. Human suffering reached phenomenal records. For those people who were not fortunate enough to find a way out of town in the days before Katrina made landfall, or at least manage to gain access to the Superdome which was designated as the number one shelter, death by flooding or life by clutching the remnants of rooftops became their only options.

The Big Easy would no longer be the same, in more ways than one. Not only did it destroy lives, property, and historical buildings, but it also unleashed an evil that the Gulf Coast wasn't totally aware of, not to mention the least prepared for. Katrina flushed this evil out of his hiding hole, the one he had relied on to feed his wicked hunger and desire for two decades. He couldn't swim. He never tried to learn. He knew the consequences of staying in his small house east of Bourbon Street, but didn't care. He knew he would survive. All the years he had spent in New Orleans had been a hell of a lot more dangerous to his life than a hurricane could ever propose, so he had made his mind up to hunker down and take all of the ripping abuse that Katrina could give him. By the time the hurricane had passed, seventy five percent of his own beloved city of endless sin was under water, including his house. When it had become too much for him to handle, he had calmly climbed out of the upstairs window and pulled himself and a red waterproof duffle bag onto his roof. There, for quite some time, he hugged and dug his fingernails into the shingles that were blowing off by the minute. After the winds calmed down just enough for him to look around and let go of the roof with one hand, he quickly dug into the red bag, and brought out a plastic bag that contained an assortment of severed decomposed fingers, credit cards and driver's licenses, locks of hair, and several undergarments. These things were very dear to him; they were his collection of favorites, the ones that had really made a difference in his life. Gazing upon each item one last time, he remembered every detail of his collection, and how he had obtained them all. Then, he threw one by one, into the wind. He chose to treat this as a sacrificial ceremony. Hurricane Katrina had washed him completely clean, giving him a brand new life, and he was extremely thankful.

Over the hours he had spent on the roof top, he had plenty of time to think about his next move. He had made his mind up about something that had been a pressing issue for sometime. He had decided to leave town. His darling New Orleans would not be the same for a long time, maybe ever, and besides, with all of the damage, police and security would be everywhere, imposing curfews, rules and regulations. He wouldn't be able to get done what he needed to do, so he decided to leave and make a new home for himself.

For several months the need to flee town had weighed heavily upon him. Years ago, he had exhausted the whores and prostitutes of Bourbon Street, and had carefully and methodically turned to the young established, but lonely young women of the Big Easy to feed his hunger, finely tuning his art. Although these women had been a more fulfilling hunt and catch than the prostitutes in his early years, they brought along a far worse liability than he had first imagined.

People missed them and searched for them. They were loved; the prostitutes were not. Over the years, the police caught on to similar patterns of several of the murders, formed a profile with the help of the FBI, and hunted him desperately. So far, he had been able to evade their grasp easily, simply by being the private man he had always been and also by killing in different ways and patterns. No one really knew him, liked him, disliked him, or thought about him. However, the media coverage of his work had become, in the last year, too public for his comfort. Months before Hurricane Katrina hit, he researched many small towns and cities across the Southeast, looking for a new place to live, and one place, in particular, seemed perfect for his plans.

There on his ruined rooftop, in the midst of one of the worst hurricanes to ever hit the United States, he had watched the dead bodies float by as he made his final decision. He would wait until his rescue, and move to Orange Beach, Alabama. Not too far, not too close, not too small, and not too big. It was perfect.

Hours later, rescue teams arrived by boat and helicopter. Ignoring the stares and questions of the rescue team, he laughed out loud maniacally when they harnessed his body and lowered him from the roof into the safety boat below. The rescuers figured that his close encounter with death and the drowned and bloated bodies that were floating down the flooded street of the poverty ridden residential area were probably enough to make this lone man laugh with hysteria. They never gave him or his large red waterproof bag a single thought as they whisked the boat away in the direction of another rooftop that housed another family of five in need.

Chapter Two

Fifteen months after Hurricane Katrina massacred the Gulf Coast, Detective Hank Jordan found himself fishing on the bay near Fort Morgan instead of his beloved pier in Gulf Shores. The pier had been completely destroyed, and the politics of the state of Alabama had so far made it impossible to rebuild. He could always fish at the Pass in Orange Beach, but it was usually too crowded for his comfort. He was dreaming of the days when he would hook some live bait, and cast it out into the calm waters circling the end of the Alabama State pier, when suddenly he realized a Redfish was tugging at his line. While he was reeling it in, his cell phone started to ring. The ring tone let him know that his partner, Hillary, was calling him with urgent news. Unable to reel in the fish and answer the phone call at the same time, he cut the line quickly letting the fish go, and picked up the cell phone.

He sighed in disgust as Hillary told him the bad news. "Hank, this is pretty ugly down here. A couple of teenage kids found a body in the dunes behind the Pelican Perch condominium complex. She is around 30 years old, wearing a wedding band on the only finger she has left, and ligature marks all the way around her neck."

Hank put his hand up to his forehead and gazed at the horizon. "Is the one finger left printable?"

"Of course not. The pad was sliced off."

"Is she wearing any clothes?"

"Well, she is wearing a white sheet now, but, no, she was found naked."

4

"Alright. I will be there in about twenty minutes, Hill. I am down Fort Morgan fishing, so it will take me a couple of minutes to get down there."

Hank sat down on the bank and began to gather up his equipment. It had been several years since the Morrison murders had claimed almost an entire family in Orange Beach, and since then, all had been silent, except for the occasional bar fight between a drunken tourist and even drunker local. A couple of illegal Mexican migrant workers had died on the rigs, but other than that, the sleepy little fishing village had been just that, sleepy and content. Now, Hank had the dead body of an unknown naked woman in the dunes of a condominium complex packed with tourists. Whoever the killer was, he wasn't stupid. He had made the effort to stall the identity of his victim by removing all but one finger, then slicing off the pad of the remaining one. They would have to use dental records to identify her, and that would take longer.

Hank loaded up his fishing rods and tackle box, threw out the rest of his live bait, and headed toward Orange Beach. On the way, he called the manager of the Pelican Perch to let him know that he was on his way, and to ask him if he or anyone at the complex had reported anything or anyone unusual in the past twenty four hours. The manager had no information to give him, but he was desperate for the removal of the body. His vacationers were calling his office every second, demanding to be moved to Pelican Perch 2 in Gulf Shores, about ten minutes away, which was already packed. The local media was swarming the lobby of the office, and people were packing the beach, rubbernecking through the dunes and the police tape for a glimpse of the dead woman.

When Hank arrived at the scene, the teenagers who had the misfortune of finding the body were still being questioned by the police. There were four of them, a brother and sister and two guys; they had made friends while on vacation. They had been throwing a Frisbee when the wind caught it and blew it into the dunes. The girl had run after it, and while searching, tripped on the dead woman's left arm. She now sat in the sand, shaking and crying hysterically while her parents and Hillary tried to console her. Her brother and his two friends were trying to appear unaffected and tough, but everyone knew they were all horrified as well.

Hank passed the entourage, stepped over the police tape and knelt down beside the dead woman. Making sure no one could see in, he removed the white sheet to see what she looked like. She was beautiful, even in death. There was dried blood caked around the stubs of what used to be her fingers, around what appeared to be stab wounds, and also between her thighs. He wouldn't know for sure until after her autopsy, but it looked like she had been stabbed, raped, and strangled to death. He shook his head in disgust at what a human could do to another human, and thought about Judith, his fiancée. Shuddering slightly at the morbid vision of something like this happening to her, he blocked her from his mind, finished examining the body, and stood up to turn.

He was heading out of the dunes when something a couple of feet away caught his eye. It looked like a leather strap sticking out of the sand, maybe from a belt or a purse. Hank tugged on the strap and pulled out a purse that had been buried only three or four inches in the sand. On closer glance, it turned out to be a satchel rather than a purse, made of soft suede. He opened the flap and peered inside. The satchel contained nothing but a single sheet of paper labeled "picnic" with a list of items. All of the items but three had been circled. Hank stared at the sheet of paper for a couple of minutes, trying to make sense of it, then finally waved over some officers to show them what he had found. It was no coincidence; the satchel had to be either the dead woman's or the killer's.

Hank walked down to the beach as the coroner took pictures and loaded her body into the back of an ambulance. The sun had already started going down, so the stifling heat of the day began to cool slightly, carrying a breeze in from the Gulf waters. Two dolphins were playing in the distance. He dialed Judith, who answered on the second ring.

"Hey, Hank! I was just getting ready to call you. A nurse from the ER just came in to the cafeteria and said that an unidentified body of a woman had been found on the beach. What is going on down there?"

"Well, you heard right. I am here right now, just finished looking at her. It's pretty bad, not real sure what to make of it yet. They are loading her up right now." Hank paused for a second to watch the waves ripple and to think of Judith's face. "I just wanted to call you and tell you that I love you."

6

"You are thinking about the Morrisons, aren't you?"

Hank sighed into the cell phone. "No, not really, I was just thinking of you. This woman is wearing a wedding band, so I guess she is married. It makes me shudder to think of how her husband will feel when he finds out. I can't imagine what I would do if it were you."

Judith smiled on the other line at the tenderness in her fiancée's voice. "Baby, don't worry about me. Nobody is going to get me. Go find the killer. I love you, too."

Hank smiled and flipped the phone shut. Tearing himself from the sun's burnt orange reflection in the ripples of the Gulf of Mexico, he headed back to the crime scene to help disperse the on-looking crowd.

Chapter Three

His name was Roy Fontaine with no middle name or initial. He was the product of single parenthood and grew up in the swamps of Southern Louisiana. Roy's mother's name was Irene Clover Fontaine. At the young age of sixteen, she became pregnant. She had suspicions about who the father was, but couldn't tell for sure, so she never fingered anyone. It never mattered anyway; all of the prospects were migrant trappers drifting through looking for temporary work from her father. Although she longed for a daughter, she birthed a boy instead. Irene raised Roy the best way she could by illegally trapping alligators and selling her body to local drunks. She never once openly sold herself in front of her son, but by the age of twelve, he knew exactly how she paid the bills. He never cared. He never really even felt any true love for his mother, or anyone else. After Irene gave birth to her son, she would marvel at how quiet he was and thank God for giving her such a sweet and calm baby. However, as he grew, she noticed that he was extremely shy, keeping to himself more than a child should. She could never afford to take him to see a doctor, and always hoped he would grow out of it. Roy never did. He would spend hours in the swamps by himself, only to return quietly to his bedroom where he would paint and draw morbid scenes of a disturbed fantasy life that was forever changing and morphing into deepening darker images. Irene was politely declined access to his drawings as he became older. In a way, she was grateful for the decline so that she would not see the nightmares of her son's creations, though, every now and then she would get a glimpse of his latest works, and it would always make her

8

cringe. She suspected that he allowed her to catch the glimpses just so he could watch, out of the corner of his eyes, her face slightly distort in horror at what he had painted. He never directly acknowledged her peeking, but there was something about his strange aloof behavior that let her know that he knew she had seen them, and in some way, her repulsion gave him much pleasure. She was the only person that had ever seen his artwork, and she made sure she kept it that way, not that she had to. Roy was very secretive and kept a close watch on his creations. They were the only belongings that he cared for, and they were not for others to enjoy. Over the years, she grew accustom to his nature, and accepted his private ways, justifying it by telling herself that it was just the way God made him. After all, he had never caused her any trouble, and always did what he was told. But most nights, right before Irene would fall asleep, she knew in the back of her mind that there was something cold and evil about the nature of her son.

On the night of his thirteenth birthday, Roy gave her a gift wrapped in a taped up bloody bath towel. On top he had placed a bow crudely made from the flowered sash of her favorite nightgown. Holding the gift in her shaking hands, scared to open it, she stared for a few seconds at her son, who never smiled nor frowned but steadily met her stare with uninterested eyes. Finally, she opened up the blood bundle he had bestowed upon her. In it were two eyeballs covered in sticky crimson blood. Every hair on Irene's body stood straight up, and she took a quick deep breathe before she spoke, not quite knowing how to handle this situation. After what seemed like an hour had passed, when really it was only thirty seconds, she placed the towel on the table and firmly took her son by both arms. Roy never flinched. She asked him in a quivering voice where he got the eye balls and why he gave them to her. Never looking away from her eyes, he shrugged nonchalantly, and told her he found them in the swamp, and that he gave them to her because they were blue. Blue was Irene's favorite color. Irene took no comfort in his answer. His words were poison, and she knew that there was no sweet sentiment in his actions. He wanted to hurt her, simply because he was bored. After Irene let go of his arms, he had once again become bored with her and began watching the television, leaving her with the sorrowful eyes staring up at her, as if pleading with her to find their owner.

Irene knew that they were not alligator eyes. She told Roy to go to bed, which he promptly did after politely saying goodnight. Then, Irene went to the kitchen, grabbed a bottle of whiskey, and drank herself to sleep. In the morning, a neighbor woke her with a frantic phone call, desperately searching for her dog. Irene's stomach churned with a sick feeling that was not from the whiskey, although it didn't help the situation. She knew that the eyes her son had gifted her the night before belonged to the neighbor's dog. Not knowing what to do, she woke Roy and asked him to help in the search for the dog. She hoped for a second that he might break down, feeling humiliation and remorse for his actions, and confess to her what he had done. Her spirits rose slightly when he eagerly got out of bed and agreed to the search, but as he walked out of the door, he stopped on the porch, turned to his mother, and gave her the most evil grin she had ever seen in her life. Irene froze in the doorway, and watched in disbelief as her son joined the search party already formed by the mailbox on the side of the road.

Two days later, the dead dog was found lying on its side with his head tucked under some bushes about a half a mile away from their house. At first, the dog appeared so mangled that he looked like he had been hit by a car. Upon second glance, the dog had clearly been partially burned, stabbed multiple times, and skinned in some places. When the man who found him finally rolled him over to inspect him further, he immediately jumped back in horror. The dog's eyes had been crudely cut right out of his head. A small buck knife had been left behind, savagely lodged into the dog's chest.

The day that Irene received the news about the dog was the day that Irene became an alcoholic which quickly led to an array of drugs that included a serious addiction to methamphetamine. She never said a word to her son about the dog or the eyes again. She did not have to. She knew that he knew she would always know what he was, and there was nothing she could do to help or save him. Irene wished that she could have killed herself immediately, but she chose to attempt to kill herself slowly, subconsciously in hopes that she would watch her son grow up to be a good person. Eventually, her meth addiction took over her life, and one day, she simply was never seen again. Roy did not kill his mother. He could have, and he would have, but he just never cared to. He never cared whether she lived or died. He was seventeen when Irene went missing, and he has been on his own ever since, calling himself an artist.

Chapter Four

Roy Fontaine resided at 1456 N. Pine Street in Orange Beach, Alabama. It took him approximately six months to finally settle after being rescued from his rooftop in New Orleans. During those six months, he traveled all over the southeast, biding his time, and laying low, just to make sure that his house was ruined enough not to alert officials. He had taken great pains to clear out any evidence of his life. However, he wanted to make completely sure that he didn't leave anything behind. The day before the hurricane hit, Roy had purchased cans of black paint and hastily covered up the murals that covered almost the entire inside of his house. He had been painting these murals for over fifteen years, adding to them every day. It had pained him immensely to cover these masterpieces up, but he knew that not everyone would appreciate their value, as they were obviously a macabre mosaic of his life's best work.

The mural in the dining room had been his favorite. Covering all four walls was a painted collage of every female face that he had ever had criminally intimate contact with. Not all of the women who he had come in contact with were from New Orleans. Each face was painted in full detail, approximately three times larger than life. There were beautiful golden blondes with unbelievably tanned faces, tempting brunettes with perfect olive skin and rosy pink lips, several-raven haired Asian beauties, and countless fiery redheads of different varieties. Around each face was a custom painted picture frame that lent some description of their backgrounds. Around the face of a woman he had briefly kidnapped from a ranch in New Mexico was a painted frame of lasso ropes. The face of a piano teacher from Vermont was encircled by rows of black and white piano keys. Trina's face, a prostitute who went missing from New Orleans ten years ago during Mardi Gras, was captured in painted Mardi Gras beads in shades of purple, gold and green. There were one hundred and forty seven of them in total; those were just the chosen ones.

Roy had always chosen his victims very carefully and methodically, taking pictures of them while he stalked them. After he was satisfied with at least one head shot, he would burn the rest of the pictures and keep the one he favored best. Then he would capture the woman, do whatever he wanted to her, then return home and add her face to the walls of his dining room, where forever they would be his dinner guest. Not all of the women had been killed. There were dozens of faces of women who had been kidnapped, molested, raped, tortured, and set free. Others had been killed swiftly after just one kiss; many others had not been so fortunate. But, they were all painted with exquisite detail, peering down at the dinner table, smiling eagerly, as if waiting for their dinner date to arrive. They were his harem, his wall of beauties.

One face in particular was painted larger than the rest, and had been painted on the wall at the head of the table opposite from where Roy sat every night. Her name was Sharon. Sharon had been Roy's first victim, from the neighboring town where he grew up. Roy used to watch Sharon all over town, obsessing over her until he could handle it no more. One night, at the age of sixteen, Roy kidnapped her, blindfolded her and took her into the swamps, where he raped her, and slit her wrists to make it appear to be suicide. Sharon was found several days later in the swamps half eaten by an alligator, not far from where he had killed his neighbor's dog. The case was never really investigated. Roy still thought about her at least once a day. She was his favorite, his first piece of artwork. He had painted Sharon with her gold lustrous locks, seductively smiling, with a rose stem between her lips. One of the thorns on the stem had pierced her bottom lip, and droplets of blood were trickling down her chin. He had even painted his own mirrored image into her eyes, so that he could see his silhouette in her gaze as he ate dinner. Her frame was painted in gold leaf, thick and ornate, fit for a queen. She had been his pride and joy, but not his love; Roy didn't love.

The other murals in his house were not so beautiful, but to him, they were masterpieces. Winding through the dark hallways leading into the living room and open kitchen, he had painted, both from memory and fantasy, the scenes of his crimes in a modern art fashion where the bodies were twisted into each other, swirling in and out of the bloody backgrounds, morphing into different crime scenes along the walls. The small bathroom was painted in dark colors with blood swirling and dripping. In his own mind, he referred to the bathroom as his "bloodbath". It had been one of his very seldom attempts at humor, and one that he knew would be lost on everyone but himself.

His bedroom was the only room that did not have anything painted on the walls. In fact, there was nothing on the walls, except periwinkle blue paint. He painted it blue because it had been his mother's favorite color. He would have painted it his own favorite color, if he had had one, but as a true artist, he favored each color as much as the next. He would have painted her face on the wall, but her body was never recovered. And in Roy's mind, true art was only seen through death. So, he had decided to paint it blue until he knew for sure his mother was dead.

Before he had painted over the murals with black paint, he had taken pictures of each one in detail. On the day that Hurricane Katrina hit, he had packed them, along with the head shots of all of his victims, inside his red duffle bag. Now, inside his new house on Pine Street, Roy Fontaine gazed upon his pictures, trying to decide the layout of his first mural inside his new home. The house had been purchased from an elderly couple from Minnesota who decided that they no longer wished to spend their retirement years in a hurricane zone. They had had enough after Ivan, and then Katrina had come. They sold their two bedroom modest home to Roy for $250, 000. It sat in the back of a two acre lot which was covered with dense foliage and palms, creating a perfect setting for Roy to go unnoticed. The neighboring houses were owned by once a year, maybe twice, residents who came usually on the Fourth of July to celebrate and enjoy the beach.

After four hours of meticulously spreading out all of his pictures on the living room floor, Roy picked up a new photo, and added it to the makeshift collage. The headshot was of a beautiful Alabama blonde

13

named Jillian Brannon. She was so beautiful that Roy decided that she would be his new Sharon. She was, after all, his first in his new life, and, she had begged him to take care of her. Jillian would be painted on the wall opposite of where he sat in the dining room, peering across at him shyly from the sand dunes, larger than life.

Roy sat Indian style, admiring his mural plans, when his cell phone rang. It was his agent in New York. She had sold ten of Roy's paintings this month, and had an order for fifteen more at two different galleries. Roy snapped the phone shut. It was time to work.

Chapter Five

Detective Hank Jordan walked into the medical examiner's office and sat down in a chair, waiting to be briefed on the status of the dead woman. After five minutes, Dr. Edward Foster, stepped into the room, shook hands with Hank, and ushered him into the autopsy room. There on a stainless steel table, she lay, uncovered, and cleaned from the sand and the blood.

Dr. Foster leaned in to her body as if studying something he missed, and then turned to Hank. "She definitely was killed by strangulation, Hank. The stab wounds were not sufficient enough to kill her, and although she was raped, she would have survived wounds from that as well."

Hank nodded his head while staring down at the dead woman. "Does she have a name yet?"

The doctor continued, "No, not yet, we have to go by dental records, of course, and that is going to take some time. Hopefully we will know who she is in a couple of days. Also, I believe that the ligature marks around her neck were caused by the strap of the satchel you found partially buried in the sand. It matched perfectly, and I found strands of her hair stuck in the metal studs where the straps meet the bag. Looks to me like she was killed with her own satchel."

Hank intently studied the dead woman's face, but nothing registered as familiar. She was probably a tourist. "Ok, Dr. Foster, let me know if you find out anything else."

Doctor Foster shook Hank's hand once again and then covered her body with a white sheet. "Will do, Hank. I thought we had seen enough of murder in this little town over the whole Morrison/Czech thing."

Hank turned from the doorway and sighed. "Yeah, me too."

Outside the sweltering morning sun beat down with a July vengeance, steamy and heavy. Sweat immediately beaded upon Hank's forehead as he walked to his truck. The doctor's office was right across the street from the bay, and Hank stared out into the calm water, watching pelicans dive into the blue to catch their breakfast.

It had been a little over twelve hours since the body was found in the dunes with no leads yet as to who she was. Watching the pelicans, Hank wondered if she was a mother. Her wedding band had indicated that she was a wife. He hoped that she had left no children behind. Waiting for the perfect time to dive in for the kill, the pelicans circled intently on some unfortunate fish swimming happily beneath them. When the moment approached, one of the pelicans dove swiftly into the water to catch his prey. Hank watched closely at the scene, trying to see what kind of fish it was that the bird had chosen, and jumped slightly when his cell phone interrupted his focus.

It was Hillary. Hank flipped the phone open and answered the call.

"Hey Hill, got anything yet?"

"Maybe. I am down at the station right now. Dispatch just got off the phone with a man named Ed Brannon who called in to report his wife missing. They got into an argument early yesterday afternoon at the Flora Bama Lounge, and he took off. Left her there. He said he told her to get a taxi back to their condo. They are here on vacation from Birmingham, Alabama, staying at the Lagoon Landing on the canal. And, she's blonde, and thirty two years old."

Hank jotted down some notes while she talked. "Ok, is he there now? At Lagoon Landing?"

"Yes, there should already be a unit there, condo number 205. Are you on your way over? I can go, but I have some errands to run and paperwork to finish first."

"Yeah, I am about five minutes from there, so don't worry about coming. I will call you if I need you. Thanks, Hill."

"No, problem. Call me later."

Hank ended the phone call and got into his truck. The pelicans had already moved onto better hunting grounds, or perhaps, shade from the sun. Four minutes later, Hank pulled into the parking lot of Lagoon Landing where he was met by two police cruisers. An officer leaned into Hank's window as he pulled the truck up, and informed him that there were two other officers in the unit taking notes from Ed Brannon, the man whose wife was missing.

He pulled into a shaded parking space and walked up the flight of stairs to the second floor. When he reached unit 205, he was met by a very worried and hung-over husband. Ed Brannon stood up from the couch and shook Hank's hand with one hand, and wiped the tears from his face with the other one. After the introduction, Hank asked Ed to tell him everything that happened yesterday. He wanted to hear all of the details before he showed him a picture of the dead woman.

Ed took in a deep breathe and started the story all over again. He and his wife Jill had been having some problems lately so they decided to come down the beach for a two week vacation to try and patch up their problems. They had both had affairs, and just recently, everything that had transpired in their separate lives had come to light. They fought all the way down Interstate I-65, several times threatening to turn around and go back home, and after a couple of silences, decided to makeup and keep driving. As soon, as they got to the beach, the fighting and making up continued. Over the past week, they had drunk way too much, spending their days at the Flora Bama Lounge and the beach in front of the bar, and their nights fighting or passed out. They had met several other couples who were also on vacation, and had been drinking with them every day. According to Ed, around two o'clock, he asked Jill if they could leave the lounge and go back to the condo for the rest of the afternoon. She had told him that she was having fun and didn't want to leave, but Ed had persisted. It made her so angry that they started to argue again. Jill had accused Ed of not wanting her to ever have any fun and always wanting to control her. They were both drunk, having done several tequila shots over raw oysters at lunch with their new vacation friends. Ed had finally had enough of fighting and told her that he was going back to the condo by himself, and that she could come back whenever she wanted to, but that he wouldn't pick her up. Ed told Hank that he came back to the condo around 2:30 in the afternoon, and started to drink heavily by himself. He didn't remember when he passed out, only that he woke up this morning, and Jill hadn't come back to the condo. He had tried to reach her on her cell phone several times, but it had been turned off.

Hank listened closely to every detail, and when Ed was finished, he asked him if he had a current picture of his wife. Ed thought for a second, leaned over from the couch, and fished his wallet out of the pants he had thrown down on the floor the night before. The wallet contained two pictures, one of the couple and the other of Jill by herself. Hank stared down at her face, and knew immediately that it was the face of the dead woman who was found in the dunes late yesterday afternoon. She was absolutely beautiful; blonde hair, piercing blue eyes, and a smile that would capture any man's heart.

As Hank pulled out the file folder containing the photos taken from the beach, he steadied his eyes on Ed who was staring down at the floor. Ed wasn't paying attention to what was unfolding until one of the officers sat down beside him and placed a hand on his shoulder. Then, he snapped to attention as he began to study Hank's face and sudden mood change. He opened his mouth to say something, but no words would come out as his attention was diverted to the open file folder in Hank's lap. Captured forever in time, was a picture of his beautiful wife Jillian Brannon lying in the sand, naked, bloody and dead. Hank moved the open file folder just in time before Ed vomited and phoned the station immediately to inform them that their first lead had just fallen into his lap.

Chapter Six

With a paintbrush in his right hand, and a palette full of paint in his left, Roy Fontaine sat in his chair with his canvas staring back at him. He hated more than anything painting the happy scenery that had made his living, but he had to make money somehow. He was an artist after all, and his paintings had become quite valuable over the years, especially in the North East, where there was a high demand for southern art. After Hurricane Katrina hit, the market shot straight up, especially for his creations. He mostly painted scenes from his childhood, not the morbid ones, but ones he could remember growing up in the swamps in rural southern Louisiana. When he first started to paint for the public, he would occasionally get his kicks by painting one of his beauties into the painting. He had used Trina first, his favorite of the prostitutes from New Orleans, because he figured no one would recognize her. Gradually, he began to use different ones for background people, painting their faces so small that nobody would even think about studying their faces for recognition. Over the years Roy had become more and more daring with his work, and the more he painted the women of his past into the scene, the more he enjoyed his work. Although he was a talented artist, he could tell how much he had improved, even in the last five years, just from the sheer fact that he was enjoying it more. He felt a heightened sense of pride knowing that the beautiful faces of his victims were hanging on someone else's wall, and that he was the only person in the world that knew it.

Over the past two decades, Roy had used a number of different agents to market his artwork. His newest agent, Melissa Edwards, was from Manhattan. She was so good that he had decided to drop all other agents, and work exclusively with her. Although he had never met her in person, or even given her his real name, she had proved in the last two years to be the best agent he had ever worked with. She held the record for selling two hundred and two of his paintings in a year, at the average price range of around fifteen hundred dollars a piece. When he had first contacted Melissa, he expressed to her his desire for complete anonymity. Having seen his work in other galleries and knowing the value of his paintings, Melissa jumped at the chance to work with him and granted him all the anonymity he desired. She felt honored to represent the man who signed his paintings "The Artist". She knew that she would probably never meet the mysterious man, but she didn't care as long as she was getting a commission from his work.

The naked canvas sat on the large wooden easel, waiting patiently to be clothed in color, while Roy envisioned his scene. Above the canvas he had taped a picture of Jillian Brannon and also one of Sharon. He stared at their faces intently, as if he were wishing that they would suddenly speak to him from their photographs and instruct him on how to bring them together for the first time. After about twenty minutes of staring, he decided to make them sisters in a row boat drifting through the Manchac swamps under moss covered cypress trees. He favored painting sisters because he never had one, and he noticed that people enjoy the serenity that they lend to a painting. They both had long blonde hair, and resembled each other slightly, so it was only natural that they become sisters. After making that decision, Roy then began to envision what they would be wearing, and got lost for several minutes in the fantasy.

Roy's ego was mostly to blame for not worrying about any recognition of Jillian Brannon's face in his painting. The other factor that Roy considered, and one that was the main reason for his move to Orange Beach, was the fact that it was a tourist town that relied solely on its annual beachcombers. The city of Orange Beach went to desperate measures to keep crime from hitting major media so that its reputation wasn't injured nationally. During his research, Roy had run across articles on the internet about the investigation of several murders in connection with an illegal Russian/Czech business supplying immigrant workers to businesses across the Gulf Coast. The investigation into the case, which had ultimately involved multiple gruesome murders, had been huge, and even that didn't get great national attention. As long as he was careful not to kill in a pattern or in the same area, Roy was confident that he could continue to create the artwork he lived for.

His attention snapped back to reality, and he looked away from the canvas before him down to the dinner plate on the small table beside him. Choosing the one with the least chipped red fingernail polish, Roy gingerly picked up one of Jillian Brannon's fingers and used it to mix up a batch of burnt sienna, titanium white, mars black and a couple of drops of blood for the background base of his painting. Each of the nine fingers that Jillian had given him were skewered through the stubs with six inch long metal rods with a cork base; Roy had learned that fingers were easier to use this way, and less messy, even after the blood had already dried. He swirled the finger around and around through the paint, using the fingernail to scrape out paint that was lodged in the corners of the mixing cup, then whisking them into the center of the mixture. After he was satisfied with the color, he removed the finger, wiped all of the excess paint from under the fingernail with a paint brush, and placed it, fingernail down, inside a mason jar of water. Instantly, the water turned murky from the excess brown paint still lodged in the folds of the knuckles on the finger, but Roy was pleased that he removed most of it when he could still see the red fingernail polish through the glass; he never liked to waste paint. With long wide brush strokes he covered the large canvas with the fingered acrylic mixture, and smiled politely up at Jillian for her extended help with their first masterpiece.

Chapter Seven

At the police station in Orange Beach, Hank was joined in the conference room by several other officers, Hillary, and the Chief of Police Daniel Whittaker, who was fondly referred to by all as Big D. Big D clapped his hands loudly to bring every one to attention, and when everyone was settled in their chairs, he pointed to the enlarged pictures of Jillian Brannon on the wall behind him. Two of them had been confiscated from the wallet of her husband Ed and the rest were shot by the coroner the afternoon they found her.

Big D was big, and carried a big voice to match his size. He looked at the officers and asked, "What I want to know is how in the hell could someone have killed here during the day in the dunes of a crowded beach and walked away with nine of her fingers without anyone seeing anything? Hank, where are we on this?" Big D focused in on Hank.

"I just left the Brannon's condo about fifteen minutes ago, and, although, Ed Brannon is being kept for questioning as a viable suspect, my gut feeling tells me that it's not him, sir. We searched the condo for any signs whatsoever of blood, bloody clothing, knives. Didn't come up with a damn thing. Plus, he was obviously still drunk from the night before. I mean, it's always possible that he killed her and came back to the condo and drank himself to sleep. He already admitted that they had been fighting for almost their entire vacation, so there clearly are reasons to suspect him, but, his manner, attitude, and behavior after he found out Jillian was dead, just didn't make me suspicious of him. Also, we have a couple of units down at the FloraBama Lounge asking questions to people left and right. Hopefully, they will radio back soon. According to the husband, the Brannons had joined up with several other couples and became drinking buddies every day now for a week down at the lounge, so maybe they saw her leave with someone. We are still waiting."

Big D nodded, "Ok, let me know as soon as you hear anything. We all remembered what a nightmare that whole Russian and Czech thing was down here, so let's get cracking on this thing so it doesn't blow up in our faces like it did the last time. Keep away from the local press as much as you can, and don't give out any details. Clear?"

Everyone nodded, and Big D left the room to deal with the phones. He had been fielding calls left and right from condominium complexes worried about their guests' safety. The rumors were starting to quickly spread, as they always do in a small town, and, suddenly, it seemed like everyone had Big D's personal cell phone number, including the Sheriff of Escambia County. He had made his mind up to change his number that afternoon. If his own town breathing down his neck wasn't enough, then Escambia County Sherriff's Department was enough to tip the scales. Since FloraBama Lounge was located right on the border of Florida and Alabama both jurisdictions were present any time there was a problem. It usually caused major headaches for all who were involved. Hopefully, The FloraBama would not be considered a crime scene in this investigation, so a tug of war would not ensue between the two states. Big D could only hope. He called Hank's cell phone to let him know they would be there as well.

After jotting down some notes in the file, Hank walked out of the police station and drove down the beach highway toward the FloraBama Lounge. As soon as he walked into the bar, an employee spotted him and gave him a huge grin. Jessica Horne had been the head cashier for the night shift for as long as he could remember. She had just clocked in several minutes before Hank had arrived, so she hadn't been questioned by the police units or Escambia County deputies who were currently roaming around the two story lounge. Jessica ran over to Hank and gave him a big hug. "Don't tell me you are stepping out on Judith, now! Where is she?"

Hank laughed at the very thought of the idea and pinched Jessica on the arm. "No, no, no, never. She is probably walking out of the hospital as we speak." Hank looked down at his watch and then back up Jessica. It was 5:30 in the afternoon, and he realized how fast the day had flown by. "No, I am here on business. Have you spoken with the police yet?"

Jessica shook her head. "No, I just got on. I saw them in the back bar. What happened? Some idiot get clocked in a bar fight?"

Hank laughed. "No, not this time. You haven't heard anything yet, obviously, or you would have already been asking me questions. So, before you do, I am already going to tell you that I can't answer them. But I need you to answer mine."

Jessica cocked her head to one side and raised her eyebrows in anticipation. "Whew, sounds serious. Ok, shoot."

Hank opened his briefcase and took out the file folder containing the pictures of Jillian. He chose the two he had taken from Ed Brannon earlier that day, being careful not to expose the ones of her laying in the sand, and held them up so Jessica could see them,. "Have you seen this couple or this woman in the past week?" Not wanting to cloud or taint her memory, he didn't inform her that the woman was dead.

Jessica focused in on the single picture of Jillian and rolled her eyes, laughing. "Yeah, I have seen her, and so has everyone else in here. She is quite the flirt, I can assure you. She got on stage the other afternoon and tried to organize an impromptu bikini contest. The crowd was all for it, but the band was irritated with her; they get paid by how long they play, and they were on a time schedule, so they booted her off the stage." Jessica noticed the somber mood change, and looked at Hank. "I know I am not supposed to ask why, but I am. Why are you asking me this?"

"I promise I will tell you in a second, but first, can you remember the last time you saw her?"

Jessica thought for only a second and nodded, "Yeah, yesterday afternoon. I came in early, around three o'clock in the afternoon. And she was leaning into the counter buying a bottle of gin and some cigarettes from the front store. I asked her if she was going to try and start up another bikini contest today."

Hank was taking notes. "Did she respond?"

"No, she waved me off. She was shitfaced." I didn't see her leave, but I assume that she did. You can't brown bag in the lounge." Jessica thought for a minute. "You know, Hank, you should ask Chuck. He is

24

the day bartender at the back bar, where that girl usually hangs out. Hold on, I will go get him. He is in the back, counting his tips." Jessica disappeared through double doors and moments later returned with Chuck.

After wiping his hands down with a bartender towel hanging from his waistband, Chuck shook hands with Hank and looked down at the photos of Jillian and Jillian with her husband, Ed. He laughed like Jessica had when he saw her face. "Yeah, the last time I saw her was yesterday afternoon when she was walking away from the bar down the beach. A little after 3 o'clock, I think. But I don't know if she came back. Her and her husband got into a fight in front of my bar and he left her here. I gave her a shot on the house. The guy was a real asshole. She was just trying to have some fun, and he all of a sudden, just wanted to leave."

Hank wrote everything down and asked, "Was she alone or with someone when she was walking down the beach?"

Chuck responded, "No, she was by herself."

"Do you remember what she was wearing at the time?"

Chuck whistled and Jessica rolled her eyes at him. "Hell yes, I remember. That's why I was watching her walk away. She had on a yellow thong bikini, and believe me; you don't see that much down here. She probably got a ticket for it."

"Was she carrying anything?"

Chuck thought for a couple of seconds and nodded his head. "Yeah, she was carrying a big brown purse." He hesitated, then asked, "Hey, what's all this about anyway?" Jessica chimed in too, but before Hank could tell them that she was found dead, Chuck remembered something. "Oh yeah, I did see her talking to a man in the distance. I glanced back a time or two to see if she was still walking away, and I remember seeing a man approach her, but it was too far away to see who it was. I am pretty sure he was white with dark hair, but that's about it. It wasn't her husband, though. That guy was damn near bald, and the guy on the beach had a head full of hair. The next time I looked, I couldn't see her at all. So, what gives?"

Hank radioed into the other officers who were roaming around the bar, and asked them to come to the front. He looked at Chuck and Jessica, who waited for his answer and said, "Well, this woman was found in the sand dunes about a mile down the beach behind Pelican

Perch condominiums." Jessica's mouth dropped open, and Chuck's eyes grew wide. Hank continued, "Look, both of you have been a huge help. I just asked a couple of officers to come up and take some more notes from you guys, and I would appreciate it if we could count on you to come down to the station and make an official statement if it comes to that."

Chuck and Jessica both nodded in compliance and said, "Yeah, no problem." Chuck walked away to talk to an officer on the side, and Jessica gave Hank a hug goodbye. "Damn. That's terrible! I hope you find the person who killed her. All we need down here is a media circus. That would really suck, well, maybe not if they all drink." Jessica laughed at herself. "Tell Judith I said a big hello. Hey, when are you two going to tie the knot anyway?"

Hank folded the file under his arm and shrugged, smiling sheepishly. "I am not sure, but I promise you I will let you know as soon as we decide." He turned to walk out of the front door and yelled back at Jessica waving, "Thanks, Jess, I appreciate it!"

Jessica smiled and waved back.

Hank's cell phone rang. It was Judith. "Hey babe," Hank said into the phone. "Just get off work?"

Judith replied, "Yes, just now. Want to meet at my place for dinner? I am cooking. I just left the grocery store, and I figured you would be stressed from today, so, I bought you the biggest lobster they had. And I named him Larry."

Hank laughed out loud then licked his lips at the thought of eating a big fat lobster for dinner. Then, it dawned on him that he hadn't eaten anything all day long except for a pack of peanut butter crackers from the vending machine at the station. He was starving. "Well, thank you, and yes, I will meet you and Larry in about an hour. I have to stop by the station first and do some quick paperwork, and then I am all yours. And Larry's."

Judith laughed too. "Ok, babe, I love you. Bye."

Hank closed his phone and drove to the station to inform Big D that Mrs. Jillian Brannon had met an unknown white man with dark hair on the beach before she died. Hank thought sarcastically to himself, "Yep, that's one hell of a lead you got there, Hank." But, so far, it was all he had.

26

Chapter Eight

The aromatic candles burned slowly, generously supplying rose scented smoke plumes to the living room and kitchen. Inhaling the calming bouquet Judith stood at the kitchen counter tearing lettuce for a dinner salad while Larry the lobster played with ice cubes in the stainless steel sink. After the salad was made, and the water set to boil, Judith sat down on the couch and watched an afternoon rainstorm set in over the Gulf of Mexico through the glass doors leading out onto the deck. She had not been able to stop thinking about Hank since the body of Jillian Brannon had been found on the beach.

Judith had met Hank in 2005, right after Hurricane Ivan slammed into Gulf Shores and Orange Beach, Alabama. One of her best friends, Tammy Morrison, her husband and twin sons had been brutally murdered by two illegal Czech immigrants, and Hank had been the lead detective in the case. The only survivor that fateful night had been Tammy's daughter Anna, who had heroically fought to live after being raped and partially strangled. Judith, being the family's pediatrician, had fallen into the painful role of her caretaker, nursing her back to health so that she could help Hank identify her family's murderers. Judith and Hank had fallen in love with each other during the investigation and high speed criminal chase across the southeast. After the criminals were caught, and a huge illegal Russian/Czech owned employment operation that covered the Gulf Coast and Southeast beaches, had been exposed and brought down, Judith and Hank's whirlwind romance quickly evolved into a beautiful long term relationship which eventually blossomed into an engagement for marriage.

She had fallen in love with Hank for many reasons. One of the main reasons had been his sensitivity to the child survivor Anna, and his strong unfaltering determination to solve the case and bring her assailants to justice. She had watched Hank struggle with painful emotions that had been unfamiliar to him. It had been particularly difficult for Hank, as he was also linked personally to the murder victims and their extended families. He had told Judith many times throughout their relationship that if hadn't been for her support and love, he probably would not have been able to handle the gut wrenching emotions involved in the case. She had believed him. Now, she sat watching the rain begin to fall and the lightning strike the water, preparing herself to once again be a rock for her fiancée, worrying that the body of Jillian Brannon would bring up painful memories for him.

Judith also wondered if she should cancel the beach trip she had been planning for a couple of months with an old friend from college, who had planned to stay with her for seven days. Melissa Edwards, her roommate during her freshman year, was due to arrive in one week. She wanted to be open to devote as much time to Hank as possible over the upcoming weeks, and even though they didn't live together, Judith did not want to make Melissa or Hank feel uncomfortable, especially not knowing what turns this case could bring.

Melissa had dropped out of nursing school after her first year, learning quickly that she did not have the stomach for the job. Instead, she chose to chase her love for art, returned to her home state of New York and eventually became a very successful art agent in Manhattan. They had remained quite close over the years, and she knew that Melissa would completely understand the situation and either find somewhere else to stay or postpone. The only problem was that it was such late notice, and right in the middle of tourist season. She had chosen to wait until Hank arrived so she could ask him what he thought about her predicament before she made the decision.

The water began to boil, and Judith's attention turned to the sound of Hank running up the porch steps to escape the rain. She grabbed a towel and met a soaked but smiling detective at the front door. He was carrying flowers. Judith laughed and traded him the towel for the flowers while pointing at his feet for him to remove his shoes. She leaned into him and gave him a quick kiss on the top of his head as he toweled off. "I hope you are hungry. Larry is a total fat ass."

Hank laughed at her humor and also at the fact that she had not only named his dinner, but that he could tell by the tone of her voice that she had grown fond of the crustacean that she had so carefully selected for him from the tank at the grocery store. Judith was like that with all living things, especially small ones. If she found an earthworm on a sidewalk after a heavy rain, she would carefully pick it up and return it to drier soil, so it would not bake to death on the concrete. If a frog hopped into her pathway, she would gingerly cup it in both hands, without fear of getting warts or getting peed on, and place it in an area that he wouldn't be stepped on or run over. After Hurricane Katrina had come and gone, Hank had helped her nurse a baby squirrel that had fallen from a tree during the powerful winds back to health. Walking into the kitchen, he peered into Larry's play pen, the sink, and whistled, "That is a huge lobster! Larry? What's up man? How's it snapping? You cold in there?"

He imagined Larry trying to wave at him despite the rubber bands that wound around his pinchers and he knew that he could not eat him. From the corner of his eye, he watched Judith try to ignore the conversation and smiled softly, walking slowly up behind her to hold her around the waist. Nestled beneath her hair was the soft spot on the back of her neck that he loved to snuggle his face in; it always smelled so good. Softly parting her hair, he found the place with his lips and inhaled her scent. Judith felt his warm breath and relaxed back into his chest. They lingered together by the sink, watching Larry attempt to climb the walls of his confinement. After a moment of silence, Judith turned around to face him, kissed him on his mouth and walked to the refrigerator to remove the salad and steaks that she purchased as a back up plan for dinner. She knew herself only too well, and Hank too, like the back of her hand; she had suspected that they would end up freeing Larry into the Gulf of Mexico, ultimately wasting twenty five dollars. Hank settled himself on the couch and watched her place the roses he had brought into a crystal vase on the kitchen table. He noticed her silence, and wondered what was on her mind. "What's up babe? Something on your mind?"

Judith finished arranging the roses and joined Hank on the couch. "Yeah, a couple of things, no big deal really. Mostly, I am just worried about you and how you are handling everything. Second, I wanted to talk to you about my friend, Melissa, coming down to visit. You know she is supposed to be here in seven days, and she will be here for a full week. I think maybe it would be better to cancel it, or rather postpone it for the time being."

Hank shook his head and picked up one of her hands, playing with her fingers. "No, no, no, Judith. Listen, honey, I am just fine. Thank you for being concerned. I really appreciate that. I know you are thinking about Tammy and her family, but seriously, I'm ok. I won't lie and say I didn't think about them today, but there aren't too many days that go by that I don't think about them. And, about your friend; I will not allow you to cancel this. You have been waiting too long for your vacation with Melissa, and I am looking forward to meeting her for the first time too. This case is strange, to say the least, so I am not going to have much time to be hanging out anyway, so, please, don't cancel it. Have fun with your friend; you deserve it. It's the first vacation time away from work you have had in a year."

Judith nodded and sighed in relief. "Ok, ok, I won't cancel it. But, if you need me, for anything at all, I am here. I want you to know that. I can leave Melissa at a drop of the hat, so, I want to make sure that you know that you can count on me, and you will not be breaking up my fun in any way. So, if you need me, you had better call me. Or then I will be mad at you....."

Hank listened to Judith rattle on and just fell in love with her more and more. She was forever on the move to fix things broken, to mend people's bodies and hearts, to provide a safety net for someone who felt insecure. When she realized that she was rambling and saw the way he was admiring her, she promptly stopped talking, and sheepishly smiled back at him. "Well, you get the point."

Hank nodded that he did. "So, what do you say we take Larry for a walk in the rain and show him his new home?" He knew that the temperature of the water was not exactly an ideal habitat for Larry who hailed from Maine, but he did it for Judith, because she was the sweetest woman he had ever met in his entire life. They walked the fifty yards through the drizzle, cut off Larry's rubber bracelets and threw him into the waves. The sun finally broke through the clouds and the afternoon showers were over.

Back at the house, Judith phoned Melissa to confirm the time of her arrival. Melissa answered on the first ring with a big squeal of delight, and Judith listened to her friend's strong New York accent on the other line. "Hey! I was going to call you tonight. Oh my God, Judith Estha, I am so excited about coming down there. You have no idea how badly I am in need of some sun, girl. I look like I could be the long lost daughter of Johnny Winter. I mean, seriously, I could get moon burned I am so white. Only one week to go. I am so excited!"

She loved to hear Melissa pronounce her last name as Estha instead of Esther. Judith giggled at her friend's strong Northern accent and excitement, and allowed herself to join in her enthusiasm. "I know! I am excited as well. This will be so much fun! Ok, so I am supposed to pick you up at the airport at two o'clock, correct?"

"Yes, that is correct. Oh, and also, before I forget, I hope you don't mind, but I am expecting a new shipment of unframed paintings, and if I do not receive them before I leave, I instructed my secretary to overnight a few of them because I wanted to show them to you and possibly some galleries in the area. If they arrive at my office before I leave, I will bring them with me, but just in case they don't, is it ok with you if I have them delivered to your house?"

"Of course it is ok with me. I would love to see them! Who painted them?"

"Oh, that's the best part, girl! Have you ever heard of the anonymous painter who signs his work as "The Artist"?"

Although she certainly admired art, Judith was not as enthusiastic about art as her friend was, and did not know many artists names. Shaking her head, Judith replied, "No, sorry, I do not, but you know me, I don't even know who painted the paintings in the hospital corridors that I see every day of my life. Is this painter a big deal?"

"Oh, yeah, especially after Hurricane Katrina! Girl, he actually sought me out and contacted me a couple of years ago, and believe me, I jumped at the chance to represent him. He is known for his anonymity; hell, even I have never met the guy or seen his picture after two years! I have only talked to him by phone. Kind of cool, huh? I have been selling his paintings like mad crazy, and he is mailing me a new shipment of his latest work. Anyway, I appreciate you letting me mail a couple of them to your house. And I promise I will not take too much time working the galleries while I am there. I am so looking forward to just relaxing."

They talked back and forth for several minutes until Hank returned to the kitchen from the back deck with two perfectly cooked medium rare Black Angus filet mignons. Judith ended the phone call with Melissa, and repeated the conversation with girlish excitement to Hank over a bottle of red wine and a perfect dinner.

Chapter Nine

After five long days, the case of the mysterious and brutal murder of Jillian Brannon seemed at a stand still. Not one single suspect had been brought in, and after having insufficient evidence as a suspect of her murder, the Orange Beach Police Department was forced to release Ed Brannon. The toxicology reports from the autopsy had shown absolutely nothing but alcohol intoxication, and from the resulting interviews of everyone who had seen her last at the FloraBama Lounge, the report came as no surprise. Hank was irritated every time Chief Big D breathed down his neck for news he could not give; anyone who could have been interviewed and questioned had been, all saying the same stories with nothing new to offer. Although five days is a short period of time, it had passed by so slowly to those who were trying to find the killer. Everyone prayed for a break in the case, as the media quickly moved onto the next story of a bull shark that had attacked a small boy in Mobile, Alabama.

Roy Fontaine delighted in this, taking small breaks from his painting to watch the small town media quickly pack its cameras to trail another story of fresher interest. Over the past five days, he had completely submerged his entire being into his creations, sleeping and eating little, breaking only to watch the local news and use the bathroom. His diet had primarily consisted of his favorite food, which he kept in large quantities in the pantry so he would not have to leave the house until his work was done. Sardines and crackers. He called it his painting food. From childhood, his mother Irene had fed this to him so many times from the sheer lack of money to buy anything else, but Roy had always enjoyed them. Although he could definitely afford to enjoy it, even after entering adulthood and becoming a successful painter, Roy had never been interested in fine cuisine. He recognized that one must eat to survive, and that had always been the reason he did, but he also recognized that he enjoyed the small fish out of a can, and that they were cheap and easy to find. In fact, seldom did he ever go to the grocery store for food, when everything he was comfortable eating could be found in any convenience store or gas station. His main staples were sardines, canned meat, beanie weenies, and sugar of all forms; he loved candy. Roy absolutely detested eating anything green, and could not remember the last time he had eaten a salad or vegetable that was green unless it was diced up bell pepper in a frozen microwavable burrito from the 7-Eleven. However, to help counter his bad eating habits, Roy had always been an avid vitamin and supplement user, which he purchased via the internet. His only food weakness that would necessitate going to a grocery store was beef, and one trip would carry him through for months; he preferred filet mignon cooked rare with no seasoning, seared in a skillet on the stove. He would purchase an entire filet, carefully cut each steak with great precision, shrink wrap them and freeze them for later. This was his only culinary treat.

Tonight, he ignored the sardines and crackers and treated himself to two of the steaks after finally completing ten exquisite paintings. With great pleasure and self satisfaction he carefully sliced each piece of steak and slid them into his watering mouth while staring at his works of art. Nine of the paintings had been created for his agent. Seven of those were lovely scenes of life on the bayou and swamps of Louisiana, and the eighth painting was a festive yet sorrowful scene of Bourbon Street after Hurricane Katrina. It depicted a scene of locals cleaning up the debris and carrying on the celebration of a Friday night street party that had made the street so famous. This painting boldly included three faces of prostitutes that Roy had the pleasure of killing a long time ago. Nothing about them had changed. They were still prostitutes in the paintings, hanging out on the streets, seductively smiling and waving down the few tourists who had joined in the aftermath celebration, looking for free beads and a five dollar cup of the mixed cocktail called Hurricane. He had placed Jillian Brannon in the scene as well, as a tourist waving for beads with outstretched hands to the partiers on the balconies above the street.

The ninth painting was the painting of Jillian and her new sister, Sharon, lazily winding through the Manchac swamps. It was the painting that had taken him the longest to complete. He had enjoyed painting it so much that he almost decided to keep it for himself, but after much consideration and a huge burst of energy, he had decided to send it to Melissa after all, and create a painting for his eyes only.

The tenth painting was his favorite masterpiece. Relying solely on his memory, he reconstructed the perfect way he had left Jillian Brannon laying naked in the dunes. He had enjoyed her company tremendously, and thought she was one of the prettiest girls he had ever killed. He admired his painting, thanking Jillian once again for her help in this creation of art, and also taking the time to thank her husband Ed for his stupidity and carelessness. Roy had been watching the couple closely for four days, and if not for Ed leaving her at the FloraBama by herself, then he might not have had the luxury of getting to know Jillian as well as he did. It was out of sheer luck that she had chosen to take a drunken trek down the beach instead of trying to ask for a ride, which he been prepared to offer. Making sure she was determined to leave the lounge by foot, Roy had driven approximately three hundred yards down the beach road, parked across the street from the Pelican Perch condominiums, and walked into the sand dunes, cutting her off. He had made a short attempt at small talk, and when she began to cry about her argument with her husband, he offered to take her home, which she accepted.

Roy was a skilled hunter and fast killer. The entire rape and stabbing took approximately two minutes. The removal of her bikini and fingers, with the help of a double guillotine-style cigar cutter and a small razor-sharp buck knife, took a swift minute and a half. In a flat fifteen seconds, her satchel had been emptied into a small bag of his own, and buried lightly in under ten seconds. He was putting his car into drive only seven minutes after he had lured her into the dunes. Although he had preferred a longer amount of time with Jillian, he wanted to get it over with as soon as possible before anyone saw anything. He hadn't created art since before Hurricane Katrina had hit New Orleans, and his burning anticipation was more than he could handle.

After the last bite of his steak was swallowed, Roy rolled each painting, except for his personal gift to himself, and stuffed them into a prepaid mailing tube addressed to Melissa Edward's office in Manhattan. Early tomorrow morning he would drive to somewhere random in Mississippi about three hours away and overnight them to her office. Tonight, he would rest while digesting the rich Angus beef that swam in his stomach.

Chapter Ten

Hank chose his favorite button up blue polo shirt from the closet and laid it on the bed next to a pair of jeans, and quickly jumped in the shower. Another day had passed without finding any more clues to the murder mystery, and the Orange Beach police station was beginning to wonder if they were ever going to find Jillian Brannon's killer. With no witnesses to anything that took place, and a whole new batch of tourists filling up the area for the weekend, the chances of finding any new evidence on the beach was growing slimmer and slimmer by the minute.

He peered down at his watch as he toweled off, and noticed he was running late. Judith was probably already at the FloraBama by now, waiting patiently for him to join her for the drink he had promised earlier that day. He picked up his cell phone and dialed Judith's number.

She was already at the bar, and the music was playing so loudly that she almost missed his call. Right before the voicemail picked up, she heard the ring and answered. "Hello? Hello? Hey, hold on a second, Hank. Let me walk outside so I can hear you?" She grabbed her purse from the bar and quickly headed out to the front parking lot where all of the motorcycles were parked. On the way, she bumped into a man entering the bar, tripped over the door stop, and almost dropped her cell phone trying to catch some of the contents of her purse as they spilled out. Embarrassed she looked up at the man to apologize, but he was already walking away. Finally, after she composed herself and put her purse back together, she returned the phone to her ear. "Hank? Are you still there?"

"Yes, I am here. What happened?"

Judith laughed, "Oh, nothing, just being my usual klutzy self, and I haven't even ordered a drink yet! I tripped going out the door and bumped into someone in the process. I think I might have stepped on his foot; either that or it was the door stop. I am not quite sure. Anyway, where are you?"

"I am walking out of the door as we speak, just wanted to call you and let you know that I was running a little bit late, and didn't want you to worry."

"Oh, ok, well, I will be sitting at the front bar. Jessica Horn is working tonight. She said she spoke with you the other day when you were questioning people up here. I had just sat down when you called."

"Ok, well, save me a seat and I will be there in a few."

Judith swung her purse back onto her shoulder. "Ok, babe, I will be right here waiting. Love you." She snapped the phone shut, and walked back into the front bar and grabbed two seats beside Jessica's cash register. It was her and Hank's favorite place to sit because from these two seats, they could people watch all night long, and at the FloraBama Lounge, a night couldn't be more entertaining than spent watching people. Behind the front bar was a swinging wooden door that led into the main bar where the bands played and where people lined up shoulder to shoulder to drink and dance. Beside this door stood, at all times, at least two bouncers who checked identifications. One of the most entertaining things to watch had always been the college kids who tried to get into the infamous bar with fake driver's licenses. Very few of them were ever successful. The bouncers kept a huge photo album that contained hundreds of fake ids that had been confiscated over the years, and Judith laughed every time she was allowed to look at it. Her favorite id was a Caucasian kid that looked no more than sixteen, posing in front of what appeared to be his mother's kitchen curtains, boasting that he was thirty one. The kicker was that it also stated that he was African American. Year after year, teenagers would try anything and everything for the chance to party at the FloraBama.

As she sat waiting for Hank, she and Jessica thumbed through the pages of the album, laughing at the new ones that had been added since the last time she had come in for a drink. She had forgotten all about the man she had tripped into moments ago. The man, however, had not. He had entered the main bar and now sat in the dark corner to the left of the stage, peering in at Judith through the window behind the bouncers. The waitress approached his table and asked him if he wanted anything to drink. Roy Fontaine thought about his choice of beverage for a second, and settled on a Heineken. As the waitress wove her way through the tourists back to the bar, he focused again on Judith. She was prettier than any of the other women he had seen floating around the bar, and he wondered who she was. Noticing that she knew that bartender well, and at least one of the bouncers, he would be careful not to let anyone see him openly stare at her; he would bide his time patiently, sip his beer and continue to watch her, and anyone else that caught his attention. The lounge would be packed tonight with a fresh batch of tourists just itching to chase the country and southern rock songs with shots of whiskey and tequila, and Judith was but one woman, and definitely not a tourist. Whoever she was, thought Roy, she was beautiful when she laughed. The waitress returned with his beer, and Roy paid cash. The crowd in front of the band began chanting and shouting, and he turned his attention to a woman in her forties who was already drunk and taking off her bra so she could add it to the countless dusty other ones hanging from the rafters. He watched as the woman successfully removed her undergarment without taking her shirt off. She flung it high into the air, while the crowd cheered her on with new rounds of shots as the band began the intro to Johnny Cash's Ring of Fire. The bra finally wrapped around one of the beams, and the crowd went wild.

Hank entered the front bar and smiled at Judith who was laughing so hard with Jessica that she was holding her stomach and wiping a tear from her face. He new immediately that they were looking through the picture album, which had been named the FloraBama's Chronicle of Idiots. Judith saw Hank standing at the entrance and waved him over while Jessica poured him a scotch and water and Judith a Crown and Diet Coke. She poured herself a shot of tequila, toasted them, and left to tend to the other patrons so Judith could update Hank on the new entries.

Roy Fontaine sat in the corner and watched the man join the woman. His face was so familiar, but he could not remember where he had seen him before. He stared intently at the couple through the window, waiting for a full shot of the man's face to come into view, when one of the bouncers stood up to stretch and blocked his view entirely. Roy began to scan the crowd instead of staring into the bouncer's backside, and settled his gaze back on the drunk woman who now had another woman with her. They were teasing the band with the prospect of them flashing their breasts. The crowd knew that they wouldn't do it, but cheered on anyway as the women delighted in all of the attention they were receiving.

After an hour had passed, Roy became bored with the crowd and the obstructing backside of the body building bouncer who stood firmly with his meaty tattooed arms crossed. He checked his watch and decided to go home, hopefully being able to sneak a peek at the face of the man who had joined the woman that tripped into him at the entrance. He exited the swinging door into the front bar and casually looked around the bar as he exited. He was able to see the man's face clearly, but it still didn't register in his mind. Something about the man bothered Roy, but he couldn't put his finger on what.

As he drove home, excited about seeing his creation again, the name of the man suddenly popped into his head; he realized in a split second that the man seated at the bar was the detective who had worked that Russian/Czech case several years back. The case had been on every news station across the Gulf Coast for weeks. He remembered his last name, Jordan. He was also the detective currently working the unsolved murder of Jillian Brannon. Roy cursed himself for being so careless; even if the police had no evidence, it had been careless not to recognize the detective and leave immediately. On the other hand, he thought to himself, sitting so closely and admiring the woman of the man who was hunting him was exciting. Earlier, when the woman had tripped into him, he noticed that she was wearing an engagement ring, but no wedding band. He had also noticed during the night, that the detective wasn't wearing a wedding band either.

He drove home with more purpose than to admire his new painting. He wanted to know who this woman was, and he hoped that they had put an engagement announcement in the local newspaper. If so, Google would provide her name for him. For some reason unknown to him, he felt drawn to her, and fantasized killing her, knowing that it could be the most daring and dangerous of all of his artwork. Shivers of wavy delight ran through his body as he pulled into his garage, entered his house and sat down in front of the computer.

He clicked on the internet explorer and typed Detective Jordan Orange Beach engagement into the Google search bar. The third result on the search list paid off with a picture and engagement announcement in the online newspaper of Gulf Coast Times. Her name was Dr. Judith Esther. Roy smiled back at her and steepled his hands together under his chin.

Meanwhile, Judith and Hank were finishing their drinks, and winding it up for the night. She leaned over to him and whispered into his ear, "You know, tonight's the last night for a week that you will have me all to yourself."

Hank cleared his throat and quickly asked for the check, which made Judith laugh. "My place or yours?" he asked.

"Mine. I don't want to have to get up in the morning and drive home and then drive all the way to Pensacola and pick up Melissa at the airport. I was hoping to sleep in on my first day off."

Hank nodded as he signed the credit card slip. "I have no problem with that. You probably wouldn't be able to drive home anyway."

Judith slapped him across the arm, laughing, "Hank!"

Chapter Eleven

Melissa Edwards accepted the overnighted UPS package just in time before she left the office for her flight to Pensacola. She was in such a hurry that she didn't even have a chance to open the mailing tube that contained the latest works of The Artist. She already knew they would be absolutely beautiful, and sell quickly, and as much as she would have liked to view them, she had to wait until she got to Alabama. When she arrived at the airport, she checked her bags and the mailing tube of paintings and called Judith while waiting to board.

Judith was sunbathing on her deck when the phone rang. She saw Melissa's phone number on caller id and answered. "Hey, chica! Are you all ready to fly?"

"Yes, in just a few minutes. I cannot wait to get there! Oh, and the paintings I told you about? Well, they came! I just got them right before I left the office. I haven't even seen them yet! Anyways, I will be there in about four hours. I have a small layover in Atlanta, so that will put me in Pensacola around six o'clock your time."

"Ok, have a safe flight, and try not to eat too many peanuts or you will be bloated in your bikini."

"True, true," Melissa laughed. They said goodbye and ended the call.

Judith baked in the sun and daydreamed about her date with Hank last night. She had had a great time at the FloraBama, and an even better time after they returned to her house. The sex had been phenomenal, and he finally left her house around eight a.m. with no more than four hours of sleep. He had slipped quietly out so she wouldn't wake, and Judith slept until ten a.m.

The merciless sun beat down on Judith until she could stand being dry no longer. She donned her Bob Marley flip flops and walked through the soft white sands of the Alabama beach until she felt the cool waves of water envelope her ankles. She lunged into the next wave and swam a couple of feet into the Gulf, soaking her hair and face with the salty water. It had been too long since she had taken a vacation, but she had absolutely no excuse for not swimming in the ocean and lying in the sun. When she had originally purchased her home, Judith had envisioned herself swimming everyday, taking long walks on the beach at sunset, and taking advantage of the beach life in general. But, with work, and stress, and everyday life, she had grown use to living right on the water, and lost her surprise and wonder of it. As she floated on the shimmering water, she realized how lucky she was to have it and made a mental promise to herself to stop ignoring the beauty of her own backyard and enjoy it more often. She wished that Hank was here with her in the water, but she knew he was at his office, desperately searching for any clues that would help him find out who murdered Jillian Brannon. Thinking about the dead woman sent shivers through Judith, and she felt guilty for wishing that he was there with her. It soured her carefree mood, and she returned to her deck for a late lunch.

As she walked back from the beach, something sent shivers up her spine yet again. At first she though it might be the cool breeze that came from the Gulf, but the more she walked, she sensed something else, like she was being watched. Judith stopped and scanned the surrounding beach, searching for anyone who might be staring at her, but found no one. After a few seconds, she shrugged her shoulders and kept walking, but looked cautiously around her until she arrived at the deck. By the time she got inside her house and checked all of the rooms, the feeling had subsided; she finally resigned herself to the fact that it had just been her imagination. After all, moments before when she was floating in the water, thinking of Hank, she had a mental picture of the dead woman lying in the dunes.

She ate a salad and a bowl of clam chowder, and began tidying up the house for Melissa's arrival. Hank had planned to meet them when he got off work for dinner at her house, and she wanted to make sure everything was spotless. By the time she finished cleaning and showering, it was time to drive to the airport in Pensacola. Forty five minutes later, she pulled her car up to the curb where Melissa was already waiting for her. It had been so long since she had seen her, but she hadn't changed a bit.

Judith and Melissa hugged each other briefly and quickly loaded the luggage and mailing tube into the trunk before the airport police told them to get moving. During the drive to Orange Beach, Melissa marveled out how much the area had changed since she had last visited. The damages of Hurricane Ivan were still very visible, especially along the Perdido Beach coast in Florida. Houses sat empty and condemned right along side new constructions of high rise condos that dwarfed everything around them. As Judith crossed the state line, Melissa gasped at what was left of the FloraBama.

Judith nodded her head and said, "I know. It's sad, isn't it? It's still fun to go, but it's not nearly what it used to be. They have come a long way in rebuilding, though. You should have seen it right after the storm! This entire area was demolished."

Melissa shook her head. "Wow. You know, I have seen many pictures and watched news coverage, but it's not the same until you see it for yourself! And poor FloraBama! It looks like a tent city!"

"Like I said, you should have seen it a couple of years ago. This is nothing! "

They continued across the state line and entered Alabama where even bigger high rises were being built left and right. The height restrictions on buildings and condominiums had once been no more than fourteen floors, however, greedy slick construction companies had somehow found a way to sucker the city of Orange Beach into updating the restrictions to a whopping thirty floor maximum. Before anyone had time to protest the change, the companies had swooped in and quickly built the behemoths that now towered both sides of the beach road. They were an eye sore, especially when they were stuffed into small places in between older shorter condominium complexes. As they passed the Pelican Perch condominiums, Judith decided to tell Melissa about the Jillian Brannon case. It hadn't made national news, so Melissa would not have heard about it.

When she finished the whole story, Melissa sat horrified in the passenger seat. "Judith, this is terrible! And poor Hank! It seemed like only yesterday when the Morrison family was murdered, and I totally remember all the phone calls you made to me about all of that. Why didn't you tell me all of this while I was in New York? I mean, I could have postponed this trip, you know that!"

"I know you would have, Melissa, and I did think about it. But Hank wouldn't let me do it. He assured me that he was fine, and that he wanted me to enjoy my vacation. So, I am going to. I just wanted you to know in case he needs to come over and talk, you wouldn't feel uncomfortable."

Melissa rolled her eyes and flicked her friend in the arm. "Judith Estha, please! Me feel uncomfortable? I have known you forever!"

Judith laughed at her friend's New York accent. It never failed to amuse her. Finally, the ride was over and Judith pulled her car into the driveway. After they unloaded Melissa's luggage into the spare bedroom and settled in, Judith popped the cork from a chilled bottle of Monkey Bay Sauvignon Blanc and poured two glasses; the two sat on the deck watching the dolphins play in the waves, and reminisced about their old college days. They were having so much fun that Melissa had forgotten about the paintings still rolled up in the mailing tube.

Chapter Twelve

After watching Dr. Judith Esther on the beach, Roy had returned home and feverishly began working on his new murals. Her address had been easy to find via the internet, and the fifteen minutes that he had allowed himself to spy on her had rewarded him with a huge burst of energy that flowed faster than he could paint. For months he had mapped and coordinated the new walls of his home, strategically placing the photos of his dead beauties throughout the house so that he could recreate their faces in new murals. His starting point had been the dining room wall, opposite of where he sat, and just like before, in his house in New Orleans, he painted Sharon, his first kill, larger than life, captured in an illustrious golden frame. However, this time, he had not painted her in the center, but to the left of the center; it had taken three hours to paint her.

To the right of Sharon, Roy had chosen to paint Jillian Brannon the same size, captured in an ornate silver frame intertwined with red and orange hibiscus flowers. In her painting, she was holding one of the flowers in her right hand while her left was open and raised palm out, as if waving to him. He had once again used Jillian's fingers to mix the paint, and now sat at the dining room table cleaning them, while admiring his work from across the room. The red fingernail polish was almost completely gone from each of the fingernails, and the flesh that had been skewered had withered and blackened. After meticulously cleaning each one, he wrapped them in aluminum foil and returned them to the freezer, trading them for a small package resting in the freezer door.

Roy returned to the table with his package and placed it beside a can of clear shellac which had already been opened. He slowly and carefully opened the package and left it to thaw on the table while he walked through the house and studied his layouts for the rest of the murals. Roy had never been one to start a mural and finish it completely before moving on to the next one. Instead he chose to sporadically paint along the way, wherever he felt the most creative, adding things here and there. To the public's eye, they would have appeared completed, however, in his mind, the murals in his old house in New Orleans had never really been finished and never would have been. And now, in his new house, he would repeat the process over and over again. He would just keep adding, painting, and creating along the way, as if keeping the walls alive by feeding it more paint. In the hallway leading back into the dining room, a picture of a woman's body that he had taped up months ago caught his attention, and for several minutes, Roy lost himself in a fantasy as he reminisced about decapitating her in New Mexico; she had been a fighter to the end. Lying in the desert underneath a cactus, her body was headless in the photo. A picture of her severed head was taped in the bathroom, along with several others. The hallway mural, Roy had decided, would be a countless pool of bodies swimming in and out of each other, morphing into scenes of bloody reality and fantasy, much like it had been in his old home.

Tracing the headless body in the photograph with his finger tips, Roy snapped back to attention and returned to the dining room table to finish his artwork. The thawing process had taken less than thirty minutes due to the fact that it was so thin. Roy swaddled the softened fleshy finger pad with a paper towel to soak up any moisture left on it and placed it back on the table while he stirred the shellac with a paint brush. The thawed finger pad belonged to Jillian Brannon; it had been sliced from the one finger that he had left Jillian with that day in the dunes. He had taken it home and carefully cleaned away as much of the meat as he could with a razor blade, tweezers, and a magnifying glass, under which he had noticed that her fingerprint resembled a small rose bud directly in the center. It was then that he had decided that he would shellac it into her painting.

When the shellac had been stirred enough, Roy picked up the small piece of flesh with a pair of tweezers, and walked towards the painting of Jillian. On her painted outstretched waving hand he applied a tiny amount of adhesive at the end of her ring finger, where he had originally cut it from, and pressed the finger pad into it. Then he quickly shellacked it into place so it would not slide down the wall to the floor below. It was a morbidly proud moment for him, and one that he would enjoy more after the shellac completely dried. Then he could actually caress the finger pad with his own, and still feel the ridges of her rose bud finger print through the thin layer of shellac. He had never added any other mediums to his paintings before, except for occasionally mixing in some of the victim's blood with the paint, so this was, in Roy's mind, extremely creative and artistic. He sat back and stared in complete silence into the eyes of the two women forever watching him from across the room.

Chapter Thirteen

At the Orange Beach police department, Hank Jordan sat at his desk and poured over the contents of Jillian Brannon's file, searching for any clues or signs that he might have missed. There was absolutely nothing. The interviews taken from various people from the FloraBama were basically all the same, and shed no light on the mysterious murder. The photographs held no secret clues left behind in the dunes, told no story of how Jillian's came to rest there, and Hank was irritated. Leaning back in his chair, he scratched his head and closed his eyes, going over every detail in his mind, wishing he could see the killer's face. His cell phone rang and jerked him back to reality. It was Judith. "Hey babe." He could hear Melissa's laughter and MC Hammer's "Can't Touch This" playing in the background, and it made him smile to know that Judith was having fun.

"Hey detective!" Judith laughed. "How long will it be before you come over for dinner? Melissa is dying to meet you! Anything new on the case?"

Hank shook his head and closed the file on his desk. "Nope, I have absolutely nothing. It's so irritating, waiting like this for something to pop up." He realized that he sounded negative, and didn't want to bring Judith down, so he stopped himself immediately. "Something will come along though. I can feel it." Hank cleared his throat and asked, "So, am I correct in that you and Melissa are actually listening to MC Hammer?"

Judith laughed into the phone hysterically, "Oh yeah! That's not the best part though. You should see Melissa in the background actually trying to do the MC Hammer dance, you remember? From the video? Where he is wearing those stupid pants with the long crotch?" She stopped talking to catch her breath, and then started laughing again.

The laughter was contagious and Hank chimed in, visualizing what Judith was talking about. "I haven't seen that video in years. Have you two gotten into the wine already?"

Judith responded, "Uhmm, what do you think?"

"I figured as much," Hank laughed. "I am leaving here in about thirty minutes. What are we having for dinner?"

Judith composed herself finally and was able to catch her breath as the song ended. "Whew, that was funny. Ok, so, we went to Lartigue's seafood store and got five pounds of royal reds, some corn and new potatoes, and Melissa made a key lime pie for dessert. How does that sound?"

Hank was all but salivating from the corners of his mouth. He could never turn down royal red shrimp or key lime pie. "I am leaving right now! I'll be there in a few minutes."

"I thought that would grab your attention. Hurry up so you can be here for the unwrapping of Melissa's newest paintings of her best selling artist. She just got them in today before she left New York, and she is dying to open them. The painter calls himself 'The Artist', and no one has ever met him before. His paintings are quite valuable. She wanted to wait until you got here to open them."

"Wow! Sounds pretty interesting. I am walking out of the door as we speak. Oh, do you guys need more wine?"

"Yeah, go ahead and get some. Monkey Bay Sauvignon Blanc."

Twenty minutes later, Hank showed up with two bottles of wine, and finally got to meet Melissa Edwards for the first time. The smell of the shrimp and vegetables boiling held everyone's attention, so they decided to eat dinner before they unwrapped the paintings. The air was as festive as it could get; Hank listened to the women trade funny college stories back and forth while he dipped the steaming royal red shrimp into garlic butter and chased them with bites of buttered potatoes and buttered corn on the cob. After a full thirty minutes of gorging themselves on all of the food, the feast was finally over, and the table cleaned of the spilled butter and messy shrimp shells. Hank offered to do the dishes while the girls went to the spare bedroom to retrieve the mailing tube of paintings.

Moments later, Judith and Hank sat on the couch and watched as Melissa rolled each painting out onto the floor and dining room table, like a makeshift gallery. They were beautiful renderings of life in the Louisiana swamps and one of a festive night on Bourbon Street. Hank admired them one by one and asked, "How much are these worth, Melissa?"

Melissa pointed at the largest painting across the room. "That one over there will sell for at least five thousand, if not more."

Hank whistled at the price and turned to walk to the canvas that she was pointing at. It was absolutely beautiful; two women cruising through the Manchac Swamps of Louisiana on a romantic wooden paddle boat. The Artist had captured the scene perfectly, shedding the sun's rays through the mossy covered cypress trees onto the faces of the girls in the boat. The painting was titled Sisters and signed front and back "The Artist." Judith commented on the excellent use of the artists colors, and broke away from a smaller painting on the table to join Hank at the larger canvas. As they studied the painting together, Melissa spoke of the mysterious painter. "This guy is extremely talented, and I could not believe my fortune when he sought me out to represent him. Even before Hurricane Katrina hit, his paintings were popular up North, but now, after the storm, it's like people can't get enough of him."

Hank stared at the canvas. "So, Judith said you have never even met the guy? Do you even know his name or where he lives?"

Melissa smiled and shook her head. "No! Nobody knows who he is. He is extremely secretive and all financial transactions are anonymous or through accounts under different names. Before he signed on with me, he made me promise to respect his privacy. The whole mystery behind this guy is exciting enough for me, and I was dying to work with him. I have a cell phone number that I call when I need a quick order, but that is about it. He always uses UPS; these paintings were mailed from a UPS store in Mississippi, but he uses different locations every time he mails them. Some are in Louisiana, Mississippi, Alabama, Georgia, even Florida. The shipment before this one was mailed from Fort Walton, Florida, I think. Pretty cool, huh? So mysterious!"

Hank was staring at the painting intently as Melissa spoke. He had been listening to every word she said but slowly became engrossed with the women in the boat, and Melissa's voice was muffling in the background. The longer he stared at the faces of the women, all sounds around him were drowned out by his own heartbeat; he couldn't look away. He suddenly realized why, and felt his heartbeat race; he turned to look at Judith who was holding onto his arm, and for a spilt second, feared that he couldn't speak.

Melissa stopped talking and she and Judith watched Hank's face turn white as a sheet. Judith pulled on Hank's arm and said, "Hank! What's wrong? Are you ok?"

Hank pointed at the canvas and touched one of the women's face and said, "That is Jillian Brannon! This woman right here is Jillian Brannon!"

The two women slowly walked closer to the painting and Judith gasped. "Surely not! But my God, Hank, that is a complete copy of her face!"

Hank ran to his truck to retrieve the file folder, and returned with the pictures of Jillian. Holding them up against the canvas, all three stared in silent disbelief.

Melissa spoke first. "You really think it's her? The dead girl from the sand dunes?" Stunned, she sat down at the dinner table and nervously shook her head. "This has to be coincidental! I mean, surely it's not her. I mean, maybe he saw her picture in the paper and used her face."

Hank responded, "I don't know, Melissa, but I can sure as hell tell you that they have the exact same face. There is no denying that!" He compared photos again to the woman in the painting and turned to face Melissa. "I need to find out who this guy is."

Suddenly, Judith called out from across the room. "Oh my God, Hank, here she is again!" She was staring down at the painting of Bourbon Street, and there Jillian was, waving for beads.

The three poured over each painting, looking for more scenes in which Jillian's face might appear but found no more. The festivities of the night were over, and Hank called the police station with a sick feeling in his stomach. He wanted to find out who "The Artist" was and why he was painting pictures of Jillian Brannon.

Melissa and Judith sat horrified on the couch and waited for the cops to show up as Hank took pictures of the paintings. They felt as if they were surrounded by death. Hillary arrived at the house first, then a police unit arrived along with Chief Big D, and Judith welcomed them all into her living room and dining area where the paintings were displayed around the room. Hank walked Big D and Hillary over to the painting named Sisters and pointed out the face of Jillian while holding up a picture that he had confiscated from Ed Brannon the day after her murder. Big D nodded and said, "That is certainly not a resemblance. That is definitely her face painted in perfect detail. Didn't you say there was another painting?"

Hank led them to the other painting of Bourbon Street and pointed at the woman waving for beads. Big D and Hillary studied the face and both agreed that there was no question of mere resemblance. Even though the face in the painting was significantly smaller than the one in the painting Sisters, it was clearly the same woman painted with exquisite detail. Big D opened his cell phone and dialed the number of Marcus Donnarumma. Marcus was a crime scene investigator who had signed on with the Orange Beach Police Department several months after the investigation into the Morrison's murders. He was only in his early thirties, but had trained and worked in Mobile, Alabama before coming to the island, and had helped solve several large homicide cases in his short career. He was also responsible for taking the pictures of Jillian Brannon's body after it was discovered. Marcus answered the phone. "Hey chief, what's up?"

Big D said, "Sorry about it being so late, but I think Detective Jordan may have stumbled on something to do with Jillian Brannon. Can you meet us over at Judith's house? We got some paintings we want you to look at."

"Paintings? Uh, sure, what's the address?" Marcus asked.

Big D gave him the address, and the phone call ended. Five minutes later, Marcus knocked on Judith's door. He was shown the paintings, which he examined thoroughly. He also examined the others, and agreed that there were no other faces that resembled or looked like Jillian Brannon. Hank and Melissa briefed him on "The Artist", and Marcus listened intently while taking notes. Finally, he reached in a bag that he had brought with him and began mixing up a strange solution in a spray bottle.

Melissa watched and wondered what he was doing. She was the only person in the room with absolutely no background in crime solving knowledge, and was embarrassed to ask. Hank noticed the puzzled look on her face and said, "He is mixing up Luminol, Melissa. Ever heard of it?"

Melissa shook her head, "No."

Hank responded, "Luminol is a chemical that when mixed with blood, lights up a bright blue color."

That struck a familiar note, and Melissa remembered seeing something about that on an episode on television of Law and Order. Then, she realized that they were getting ready to spray the paintings to look for blood, and she placed her hand over her face. Judith held her other hand; together, they watched the entire process. Marcus Donnarumma sprayed the paintings with the Luminol, grabbed his camera quickly, and instructed an officer to switch off the lights.

Everyone gasped together; the room lit up like the Fourth of July as the camera flashed quickly to capture the thirty seconds of bright blue light that illuminated from every single painting in the room. If not Jillian's, someone's blood had been mixed into the paint that covered each painting; the room was filled with death.

Chapter Fourteen

There was a moment of heavy silence after the lights were turned back on in Judith's house. The glow from the Luminol had faded, returning the paintings to their original beauty although no one in the room could appreciate them anymore after having just witnessed the secret bloody light show. Melissa was shaking and crying silently on the couch while Judith tried to console her.

Finally, Chief Big D broke the silence by walking to the center of the room and asked for everyone's attention. "Ok, folks. Looks like we have a big big problem here. As your chief, I will ask each and every one of you to keep your mouths shut about this. Talk to no one but each other until I say otherwise. That means, no press, no family, not even your preacher or priest. We have nothing but to assume that this artist is in someway connected with Jillian Brannon's murder; if not the sole killer, and since she was killed here, then I would safely assume that he is in this area or has been recently."

Everyone nodded in agreement and listened intently as the Chief continued. "Hank, I need to meet with you and Marcus Donnarumma back at the station. Those paintings need to be rolled up, and taken with us. Somehow, between now and tomorrow, we need to put our heads together and form a plan on how to find out who this guy is and where he lives. Let's pray to God that he doesn't live here. Miss Edwards, we are going to need your help on this." He stared down at Melissa who was still sobbing on the couch. "But for tonight, why don't you get some rest, and we will talk more in the morning, ok?"

Melissa wiped a tear from her eye and managed to compose herself enough to answer Big D. "Yes, thank you for allowing me to sleep on this. I will do anything to help, although I don't have the faintest clue where he is. He has always been such a mystery; I wouldn't even know where to begin."

Big D replied, "That's alright, Miss Edwards, just leave that up to us. But for tonight, try to think of any ways you could possibly link us to him, and we will start in the morning. Good night Judith. Hank, I will meet you, Hillary and Marcus back at the station. It's probably going to be a long night."

The officers in the kitchen walked to the paintings and carefully began to roll them up one by one and place them back into the tube that they had been mailed in. After he walked Big D out along with the other officers, Hank returned to Judith and Melissa on the couch.

Melissa had stopped crying, and sat staring down into her shaking hands that were wrapped inside a tissue that Judith had given her. Hank knelt beside her and patted her on the back. "Melissa, I am truly sorry that all of this is happening. But I am also amazed at the coincidence of all of this. I mean, of all the people in this world whom you could ever be best friends with, it's the woman engaged to the detective searching for your biggest client who is a mystery to even yourself. If that's not proof that everything happens for a reason, then I don't know what is. I know you are horrified, but I have to say, I am sure glad that you came when you did. We really needed a break on this case, so, thank you."

Melissa smiled down at Hank and nodded her head. "Well, I appreciate that, Hank. I really do. I am just sitting here, drowning in guilt, not knowing how many paintings I have sold that could have blood on them. I mean, what if this guy is some sick serial killer, or something. It makes me want to vomit just thinking about it. And that poor girl! I mean, what if he is here, right now, in Orange Beach? What if he knows that I am here?" Melissa shook slightly at the thought of Jillian Brannon.

Hank asked quickly, "Melissa, did you tell him you were going on vacation? Did you tell him that you were coming to Alabama?"

Melissa shook her head quickly, "No! Absolutely not. He doesn't like small talk, and made it very clear a long time ago that he doesn't want to get to know me personally at all. The last time I spoke with him, I gave him the order requests, and that was it."

Hank was already taking notes as she spoke. "Were these personal requests from a specific buyer?"

Melissa shook her head again. "No, I just needed to fill some empty spaces in a couple of galleries that showcase his work. He doesn't paint by request, so I never know what I am going to get until I get them."

Hank thought this was a good start, but didn't want to pump Melissa for anymore information until the next morning. He stopped questioning her and returned the pad of paper to his pocket. "Alright, ladies. I have to get to the station. Are you two going to be alright?"

They nodded and Judith walked Hank out to the car to speak with him privately. By the roadside, Judith leaned into Hank's chest and hugged him tight, to which he responded even tighter. "Judith, are you positive that you two will be ok tonight? I can come back here after I leave the office."

"I think we will be fine. I am just in shock right now. What are the odds of all of this happening? Go back to your place and get some sleep; I'm sure you will need it for tomorrow. I am going to stay up with Melissa for a while, and then give her something to help her sleep if she needs it."

Hank leaned down and kissed her quickly before driving away in his truck. Judith watched as his tail lights faded in with all of the tourists on the beach road and returned to the house to take care of her friend. Her vacation had just begun.

Chapter Fifteen

By the time Hank reached the police station, the place was buzzing as fast as a downtown New York police station on Friday night. Sometime during the night, a nasty fight between two groups of bikers had broken out in the parking lot of the FloraBama, and the ones who weren't en route to the hospital for broken noses and cuts were being booked and escorted to the detox tank to nurse their drunken states to morning hangovers and regrets. Hank slipped past all of the commotion and headed straight for Big D's office where he and Marcus and Hillary were already waiting for him. He sat down in the empty chair next to Marcus and took out his notepad and pen.

Big D sighed and asked, "Ok, guys, where do we go from here? Anybody got any ideas?"

Hank spoke first. "Well, before all of this happened tonight, Melissa talked to Judith and me at length about this guy. She mentioned that he always uses UPS stores to ship his paintings to her, and that he rarely uses the same ones twice. She told us that the paintings are always mailed from the south; she has in the past received shipments from Louisiana, Mississippi, Alabama, Georgia, and Florida. And, she thinks that the shipment before this was had been mailed from Fort Walton. So, what I propose is this. We tell Melissa to call this artist for another shipment of paintings. Meanwhile, we contact every single UPS store within a three hundred mile radius in all directions from Orange Beach, and warn them about any shipments to Melissa Edward's office. When he comes in with his paintings, the store will be asked to immediately call local law enforcement who will then pick him up and detain him for us."

Big D thought about Hank's idea for a couple of seconds, nodding his head and taking notes. "Well, that's definitely a start. But what if this guy goes to a UPS office outside of the three hundred mile radius, and we completely miss him?"

Hillary spoke up. "Maybe there is someway that one single UPS store could flag an address and enter it into a database that would go to every store in the country."

Hank nodded and wrote on his pad. "Yeah, that's always a possibility. I didn't think about that. I will check with the local office tomorrow and ask if that's possible."

Big D pushed himself away from his desk and leaned back into his chair. "Ok, but be careful what you say. One slip of the tongue here and we'll be swimming up to our necks in panicked tourists and media. Do not under any circumstances tell them why you are asking, and call me as soon as you find out if they can flag Melissa's office address. In the meantime, I am wondering if we should put Melissa in another condo, and provide her with some temporary police protection until we get some answers about this guy. She is the only link that we have to him, and I am not willing to lose her this early in the game. Hell, this guy might know that she is in town for all we know." Big D thought about everything for a second and then looked at Hank again. "What do you think about taking a flight to New York with Melissa? I am not sure where this investigation is going yet, obviously, but do you think it might be a good idea? You could check out her office, gather up any paperwork that you think might link us to this guy, and if you find anything, we can then notify the police department there about all of those other paintings. I will be willing to bet that there are more paintings with blood on them."

"Talk about the media! I mean, yeah, I would fly up there in a heartbeat, but, if this guy is some sicko killer on the loose, and there are more paintings with blood on them, the press would eat us alive!" The room was silent as the four pondered what to do. Hank stumbled upon an idea. "Ok, what about this? Why don't I take the first flight out in the morning with Melissa, and look around her office like you said. While we are there, she can call him from her office to order more paintings. That way, her number will come across his caller id, placing her in Manhattan at the time of the order. That way, if this guy suspects anything, or thinks that she may be here, it will put his mind to rest. Meanwhile, I will check everything out, gather up what I can, and fly back with her in a couple of days. We won't notify the Manhattan police about the other paintings until we either find out who he is through whichever UPS store he goes to next, or we miss him. Hillary can cover for me while I am gone." He studied Big D's face for approval, and seconds later he received it.

"Ok, sounds good. Go ahead and book two flights and see what you can come up with. Hillary, cover for Hank while he's gone. Marcus, how fast you can have DNA samples taken from these paintings? We need to find out as soon as possible if it matches Jillian Brannon's."

Marcus was already on his feet. "I will do it right now, sir, and take them to the lab first thing in the morning. I'll make sure to put a rush on it. Oh, and Hank, don't worry about going by UPS. I will take care of that for you in the morning."

Hank held out his hand to Marcus and shook it in appreciation. "Thanks, man. I will call you as soon as we arrive."

Hank and Big D remained in the office for another hour, talking about The Artist, and fine tuning their preliminary plans to try and catch him. After an hour had passed, Hank checked his watch; it was almost midnight, and suddenly he realized that he hadn't even called Melissa to tell her that she was flying home in the morning. He excused himself from Big D's office and walked outside to get some fresh air while he made the call.

Judith answered the phone, "Hey! We were just getting ready to go to bed."

Relieved that he did not have to wake them up to tell them the news, Hank informed Judith of his plans to fly to New York with Melissa. "I would very much like for you to go with us. Do you want to come? You are on vacation, after all."

Judith sighed heavily into the phone, "No, Hank, I think I am probably going to just go back to work and postpone my vacation time until the fall maybe. Maybe we can go some place special together. Go ahead tomorrow with Melissa and see what you can dig up, and I will be waiting for you guys in a couple of days. Oh, and I can take you to the airport in the morning, too. Hold on for a second so I can get Melissa on the phone." Judith knocked on the bedroom door, and handed the phone to Melissa when she opened the door. "It's Hank. He wanted to tell you something before you went to bed."

Melissa put the phone up to her ear, and nervously said, "Hey, Hank. Anything new?"

"Are you homesick yet?" He asked.

Chapter Sixteen

At 4:00 in the morning, Roy Fontaine painted the last strokes of the night on the new mural in the hallway. For two hours he had been lying naked on the floor on his side painting along the baseboards, thinking about the detective's fiancée and fantasizing about all of the evil things he could do to her and the artwork he could create from her. He was unable to think of anything else but her, and finally left his painting position to sleep off his arousal.

As soon as he lay down, Roy knew that sleep for him would not come easily. The burning itch deep inside of him to have Judith was consuming much more of his life than he understood, and he could not ignore it. To kidnap and kill the fiancée of the local detective would be the most daring thing he had ever done in his life, and could also prove to be the most reckless if something went wrong. However, Roy Fontaine's ego had grown so much over the years that it began to cloud his decisions, making him feel invincible. He lay there in the darkness, wrestling with the pros and cons of kidnapping her, and as he thought about her, he slowly realized that it wasn't up for debate anymore. Before he slept, he made a final decision; he would come up with a plan as soon as he woke up. It was the only way to get her out of his head, and he knew it. As he drifted off to sleep, he smiled in anticipation.

Four hours later, Judith pulled up to the curb at the airport to let Hank and Melissa out of the car. Earlier, while Melissa was getting ready for her flight, Judith came close to changing her mind and almost packed a quick bag. But in the end, she decided to stay home and return to work early so that she could reserve her remaining vacation days for a later date. Now, as she helped Melissa and Hank with their luggage, she regretted her decision and wished she had just packed a bag; it was too late now. She would just have to wait for their return in a couple of days.

Hank took her hands in his and kissed them while she hid her regret by smiling back at him. They exchanged I love you's and Judith watched them hurry through the entrance to the check in lane as she slowly exited the terminal. On the way home, she stopped by her office and made a visit to the hospital so she could reschedule her upcoming week; it wasn't difficult. Over the past month she had weaned her schedule down to nothing but emergencies, which another colleague had agreed to respond to in her absence.

By noon, she was emotionally exhausted from the events that had taken place and physically drained from lack of sleep; she had tossed and turned for most of the night after Hank ended the phone call with Melissa, resulting in about two hours of sleep. When she realized that she was dozing off in her office, Judith decided to return home and take a nap. The fifteen minute drive back to her house took a full hour. The beach town was bustling with shopping tourists and teenagers surfing up and down the beach highway in their hot rod cars. Stuck behind a red mustang with the words "Beach Bound" written with shoe polish on the rear window, Judith almost fell asleep at a red light. The horn of a pick up truck full of teenagers startled her back from dozing off, and Judith pressed the accelerator. By the time she pulled into her driveway, Judith could hardly keep her eyes open. She took a couple of steps into her house and quickly chose her plush oversized couch over the bedroom; she was fast asleep in less than a minute.

Roy Fontaine's van was parked in the parking lot of a hotel across the beach road. Through a pair of binoculars, he had watched Judith park, exit the car, walk into her house. The blinds were drawn on the front windows, so Roy had waited several minutes to see if Judith would leave again, then crossed the beach road to the driveway of the empty beach house next to Judith's. At the end of the driveway was a passage through the sand that led to the beach. After carefully checking to see if anyone was watching him, Roy casually walked the down the passage way and found a clear view into the sliding glass doors on Judith's back deck. For several minutes, he pretended to search the Gulf of Mexico through the binoculars; there were tourists playing on the beach, and he didn't want to bring attention to himself. Finally, when he felt secure that no one was paying any attention to him, he swung the binoculars around to the sliding glass doors and peered inside. There she was, asleep on the couch. Roy smiled briefly and returned his gaze once more to the water.

After several minutes, he returned to his van and drove to a nearby abandoned souvenir building that had been destroyed during Hurricane Ivan. Parked behind the building, he quickly removed a magnetic sign of a fake carpet company from the back of the van and placed it on the outside of the passenger door. From a bag in the passenger seat, he removed a tan uniform and matching hat that had the same logo as the sign, and dressed quickly in the back of the van. He owned dozens of different uniforms used to help him blend in when he was on surveillance for his next victim. These items had been purchased online months ago, for such purposes as these. At the time he purchased them he didn't know when he would need them, but he had to build up his collection of disguises after leaving them behind in his old house in New Orleans.

Roy climbed into the driver's seat of the van and looked into the rearview mirror to make sure he wasn't being watched. Satisfied and ready for the job at hand, he pulled back onto the beach road and drove to Judith's house. He Parked in the driveway of the rental house next door, grabbed a black duffel bag from the passenger floor, and walked quickly to the side entrance of Judith's house. She never heard the door open or the blinds on her sliding glass doors being closed.

Chapter Seventeen

Six months prior to Hurricane Katrina, Roy Fontaine kidnapped and killed a young girl leaving a rave party in an abandoned building in downtown New Orleans. While at the rave, the girl had injected herself in the hip muscle with a small dose of an LSD derived drug named Ketamine, known on the streets and in night clubs as Special K. By the time she stumbled out of the party and into the steamy night, her hallucinations were in full power. It had rained earlier that night and the girl was mesmerized by the street light's colorful shimmering reflections in the puddles of rainwater still on the road. From behind a dumpster Roy watched her hallucinate on her hands and knees in the alley for several minutes to make sure that no one was coming to join her. When he first approached her, she was not even aware of his presence, and when she finally realized that he was standing over her, she just stared up at him with a blank expression, as if he was nothing but a statue. Roy simply bent over her, took her by the arm and quickly led her down the alley by her arm to his van waiting at the curb; she never said a word until she saw the murals in his house, and even then, her speech was so slurred that Roy couldn't understand much of what she said. After he raped and killed her, Roy searched through her belongings and found the vial of Ketamine and the syringe she had used, and researched the drug on the internet. Delighted to have stumbled on such a drug after he learned its capabilities and side effects, he decided to keep it for future use on his victims.

Now, approximately one year after discovering the vial of Ketamine, the future victim he had saved it for was right in front of him asleep on her couch. After watching Judith sleep for several minutes, Roy picked up a decorative pillow from a chair in the living room and quietly walked to the backside of the couch where he had already laid the large black duffle bag on the floor. From the bag he carefully withdrew the vial and a syringe, and filled it with five hundred milligrams of Ketamine. He had read on the internet that two hundred milligrams was enough to knock out someone of Judith's size, but he wasn't going to take any chances. When the syringe was full, he placed it between his teeth and grabbed the pillow.

Quickly and savagely Roy sprang over the back of the couch and thrust the pillow hard into Judith's face. The surprise attack shocked Judith awake, leaving her confused for a split second before she realized that someone was pinning her down with a pillow. When she realized she was being attacked, she immediately started screaming and bucking her body. With his left arm and chest he pressed down hard on her bucking body while his right hand removed the syringe from his mouth. Judith had been asleep on her side, and while struggling for air in darkness beneath the pillow and her attacker's bodyweight, her jeans had become loose, leaving her left hip perfectly exposed.

Roy found the flesh within seconds, pushed the needle in hard and pumped her body full of the drug. As soon as Judith felt the needle enter her body, she started kicking and screaming like a wild animal in an attempt to escape her victim; but she was no match for Roy's crushing weight and grip. She fought until she could fight no more, and thirty seconds after the Ketamine was forced into her, Judith passed out.

From his research on the internet, he guessed that the amount of drug that he gave her would keep her out for at least an hour, but he didn't want to push his luck. Working quickly, Roy emptied the contents of his duffle bag, bound Judith's feet and hands with rope, blind folded her eyes and taped her mouth shut. When she was secured, he lowered her body inside the duffle bag, shoving her arms and legs in anyway he could, and zipped it up. After he thoroughly cleaned the area for any clues of his presence, he checked the driveway and the beach through the blinds to make sure he was still alone, pulled down his hat tightly and picked up the duffel bag. Her dead weight was more than he expected, but it certainly wasn't the first time that Roy had carried the dead weight of a woman Judith's size. Roy scanned the room again to make sure he left no signs behind, then hurriedly carried Judith to the back of the van and drove away. Had he spent two more minutes in her house, he could have listened to Hank's voice message on the answering machine that he and Melissa had just safely arrived in New York. Had he spent more time looking around the house instead of being completely transfixed on Judith, he might have noticed the pictures of Judith and Melissa, his art agent, on the television stand.

He drove carefully back to his house, making sure that he did not speed or do anything else to bring attention to himself. As soon as he closed the garage doors, the first order of business was to remove the magnetic sign which he promptly covered with black spray paint and placed in the trash can. The second order of business was to remove Judith from the back of the van. After struggling with her dead weight through the small dark hallway, he finally dropped the duffel bag onto the hardwood floor of the spare bedroom, unzipped it, and checked to make sure that Judith was still breathing; she was.

The spare bedroom had been decorated for a special guest long before he killed Jillian Brannon, but this would be the first time it had ever been used. The walls had been painted black and red, and were sporadically decorated with several of Roy's personal paintings, drawings and pictures of his victims, dead and alive. Chains ending in restraints had been bolted into the floor at each corner of the bed, and a warped mirror, like the ones used at the circus to distort reflections, had been installed on the ceiling. The only window in the bedroom had been masked from the inside with a fake stained glass lining, backed by wooden planks, layered by soundproof padding, and covered with heavy curtains made of heavy red and black paisley upholstery fabric. Hidden behind the curtains was a fairly sophisticated surveillance system that was connected wirelessly to a secret camera in a small hole in the ceiling. Anything that the camera captured could be seen from a live feed from a computer that Roy kept in his bedroom.

He removed Judith's body from the duffel bag and lowered her onto the bed where she was then shackled by the leather restraints on the chains bolted into the floor; she was still out cold from the effects of the dead girl's Ketamine. Roy briefly left the room, and minutes later returned with a video camera and a black ski mask on his face. He pulled up a tripod to the side of the bed, turned the camera on, and waited patiently for Judith to wake up.

Chapter Eighteen

While Melissa hailed a taxi in front of the LaGuardia airport to take them downtown to her Manhattan office, Hank tried to get in touch with Judith again. Twenty minutes ago he had called her at home and left a message for her that they had arrived. When she didn't call back, he tried her cell phone number which went straight to voicemail as well, so he assumed that she had gone straight to her office after dropping them off at the airport in Pensacola, Florida. He pressed Judith's number into the cell phone and waited for a connection, but the call went to straight to voice mail again; this time, he didn't leave another message. If she was seeing a patient, he didn't want to bother her, and she would eventually return his phone call when she got the chance, like she always did. A taxi arrived at the curbside, and Hank joined Melissa in the back seat. On the way to her office Hank dialed Marcus' cell phone number to find out what he learned at the UPS store.

Marcus answered the phone with good news, "Hey Hank. Did y'all have a good flight?"

"Yeah, it wasn't bad at all. We are heading to Melissa's office right now. Tell me you got lucky."

"We sure did, Hank. After I dropped off the DNA samples from the paintings to the lab this morning, I spoke with the manager of the UPS store in Gulf Shores, and he told me that after 9/11, their online system was updated to be able to flag a suspicious address not only in the

States, but internationally as well, so we are covered. When are you going to have her make the call for the paintings?"

Hank had not gone over the plans with Melissa yet; all she knew was that Hank wanted to take a look at the other paintings and any paperwork in her office that might give them any indications of the Artist's whereabouts. She sat clueless in the back seat next to him, so Hank was unable to discuss it with Marcus. "Uhmm. Well, I am not sure about that yet. Let me call you back as soon as I get to her office and get a chance to look around a bit."

Marcus caught the pause in Hank's response. "Oh, ok, I got it. She doesn't know yet." He cleared his throat. "Ok, call me at the station when you know something."

Hank nodded and smiled reassuringly at Melissa who nervously chewed on a finger nail. "You bet! Thanks man. We'll talk soon." He hung up the phone and made small talk with Melissa all the way to the office while craning his neck out of the window of the cab to sight see. It was the first time Hank had ever been to the Big Apple, and he was amazed at how pictures or video footage of the city just didn't do it justice. Everything was just so big.

Melissa's was one of four businesses that leased the floors of a beautifully renovated and restored brick building that dated back to the 1940's. When they arrived at Melissa's office which was located only six blocks from where the twin towers had once proudly stood, Hank paid for the taxi fare and followed Melissa into the building and up one flight of stairs that led to her office. Her secretary was completely surprised to see her walk into the office, and even more surprised when Melissa asked her to go home for the next two days with full pay. Melissa introduced Hank as an old friend, assured the girl that everything was ok, but that some personal matters had come up that she had to deal with promptly and did not want to be disturbed. At first, the girl was hesitant to leave, but after Hank made some small talk with her while Melissa began searching through some files, she finally took up her purse and left the building.

It was the perfect time to tell Melissa about the plan that Hank, Big D, and Marcus had discussed the night before. Hank crossed the room to where Melissa was collecting files that she had kept on the transactions with the Artist, and sat in a chair beside the window.

70

"Melissa, there is something I need to talk to you about. Can you sit down for a second?"

Melissa looked at him, sighed, and put the files down on her desk. "Ok, I knew this was going to happen. What have you not told me? What do you want me to do? I know you were talking about me to that Donnarumma guy on the cell in the taxi."

Hank put his hands in the air defensively, "Whoa, hold on a second! Yes, there is something I would like for you to help me on, but I haven't kept it from you for any reason other than I didn't want you to be nervous about anything on the flight up here. I thought it would just be best to tell you what's going on after we got here and settled in. Nothing but that, ok?"

Melissa sat down behind her desk, and put her face in her hands. "Ok, sorry. Look, I am really really nervous here, and I don't have a clue what to do. I didn't mean to lash out at you. I said before I would help anyway I can. So, what do you need me to do?"

Hank leaned forward in his chair and shook his head. "Apology not needed, Melissa. I can't even begin to imagine how you feel." He paused to smile reassuringly to her. "Ok, here goes. Last night after I left Judith's house, I met with Big D and Marcus back at the station and we discussed some ideas on how to find this guy. Now, I remember you mentioning something about him always using UPS to ship his paintings. Did I hear that correctly?"

Melissa nodded. "Yes, every shipment I have ever received has been through UPS. It's always been a game of mine to try to guess the location of the next shipment. This last time, I guessed somewhere in Florida, but I was wrong. It was Mississippi."

Hank was taking notes as she spoke. "Ok, that leads me to my next question. Didn't you say the shipment of paintings before this last one was from Fort Walton?"

"Yeah, why? What is all of this leading up to?"

Hank stopped writing and looked at her. "Well, what I am thinking is this. The Orange Beach police department can go to the local UPS store in Gulf Shores and flag any packages to your office address as suspicious. This will automatically be entered into an international database, so, if someone tries to ship anything to you, an alert will appear on the computer screen of the UPS worker to call local authorities. Meanwhile, you call him on his cell phone and place another order; maybe tell him that this one is rushed. Make something up, and then, when this artist guy pops into a UPS store, the police will be called and he will be detained. What do you think?"

Nodding slowly, Melissa stared out of the window contemplating Hank's plan. It sounded simple, but she wondered if she would be able to talk on the phone without sounding too nervous. "It sounds easy enough, Hank, but it might take weeks for him to paint another painting. Believe me! Sometimes he is super fast, and other times, it takes days to get a new shipment. Let me get you the files on all of the transactions while I think about it. You want some coffee?"

"Yeah, I would love some, thanks." Hank scanned the office. "Alright, take your time. I am going to step outside for a second and try to call Judith back." Hank walked down the flight of stairs to the ground floor and stepped out into the Manhattan sun. It was definitely warm, but without that suffocating dense humidity on the Gulf Coast, the kind that defies any new brand of anti-perspirant on the market within seconds of stepping outdoors. The busy street captivated his attention for a moment as he watched the taxi cab traffic weave in and out with the messengers on bikes and pedestrians on foot, hurrying to get to wherever they were going; it seemed as if everyone was in such a mad rush, without even a second to break stride. The visual of peering through a glass enclosed ant farm popped into Hank's head. After a while, it became dizzying to watch, and he decided to try Judith on her cell phone again. The call went straight to voicemail.

Standing on the sidewalk, Hank scratched his head and wondered why Judith hadn't returned his calls. He didn't travel very often, and, taking into account the previous night's events coupled with the fact that he was now in New York for the first time, with her best friend, to look for clues on this artist's whereabouts, it was strange that Judith wouldn't have been waiting for his call once they had arrived. At the same time that he worried, he didn't want to bother her at work either, so he would wait a couple of hours for her return call. In the meantime, he and Melissa had work to do. As much as he would love to see the city for the first time, this was certainly not a trip of leisure. Hank placed his cell phone inside his pants pocket, and walked back into the office building.

Melissa was seated at her desk, peering down through her glasses at the paperwork that she had saved on the transactions between herself and The Artist. There were dozens of file folders, each containing UPS signature required receipts dating back two years prior to the very first painting that she ever received from him. She remembered the painting well as she studied a photo copy it from a file on her desk; it depicted a scene of women doing laundry on the banks of the swamp water in the small town of Kraemer, La. The photo copy was only eight inches by ten inches, compared to the actual canvas size of three feet by five feet, so it was impossible to get a clear close view of the faces of the women, but Melissa stared at them anyway, wondering if she was looking down into the faces of actual dead women.

During Hank's absence, Melissa thought about his idea, and after studying some of the photocopies of his paintings in the past, she pondered the right way to approach The Artist. She decided that the best way to coax a quick painting from him had to be to stroke his ego by lying about a buyer offering a large sum of money for a small original. The Artist had let her know very quickly in the beginning that he did not paint commissioned work of a buyers choosing; all of his paintings would be created from his imagination only, so there was no use in asking him to paint something in particular. When Hank walked back into her office, she had put together a plan, and was ready to take action.

Melissa waved him over to her desk and pointed to the chair beside her so that he could see what she was looking at. "Here is everything that I have in this office that is linked to this guy. What you see here in front of me is a photo copy of the very first painting that he sent me. Look at all the women on the bank. I know it's too small of a photograph to really look at the women's faces, but I still wonder if any of them are dead. Gives me the creeps."

Hank took a seat and looked down at the painting in the photo. "Have you thought anymore about calling this guy?"

Melissa took a deep breath. "Yes, I have, Hank. This is what I propose. I will tell him that I sold the painting 'Sisters' to a very wealthy man in Manhattan who was so taken with it, that he is offering double the amount for a smaller painting of the Artist's choosing, to accompany 'Sisters' on his wall at home. I will tell him that the buyer purchased the painting 'Sisters' for five thousand dollars in cash, and so he is offering ten thousand for a new one. I have yet to sell a painting of that amount, and I am positive that it will stroke his ego enough to get him to produce one quickly. We may even get lucky. He may paint Jillian's face in the new painting, who knows? But I think that luring him with a promise of ten thousand dollars will do the trick."

Hank listened intently and thought about Melissa's proposal. "Ok, but what if we scare him away by using the 'Sisters' painting? If he did murder Jillian, it hasn't been that long ago, and if his ego was big enough to paint her into the picture with no worries of it being exposed, then I would not want him to get scared and think someone has recognized her. I think it would be better if we used one of the other paintings instead, as the one that the buyer has purchased, but maybe tell him that he is also thinking of purchasing 'Sisters' as well.

Melissa hadn't thought of it that way, and immediately agreed. "You are right, Hank. Good point. I like your version better. You know, the more I stare at the picture of this first painting, the more I am determined to help find this guy. When do you want me to make the call? I am nervous as hell, but I know I can do this."

"Well, let me make a couple of phone calls to Marcus Donnarumma and Big D first. They have to go back to UPS and flag your shipping address first. Then we can sit down this afternoon on conference call, and put together the final plan. I'll call them right now."

Melissa let out a deep breath and said, "Ok, let's do this. I am ready."

Chapter Nineteen

After Roy had set up the video camera, he crawled into the bed with Judith and spent ten minutes posing her body the way he wished to view her. Her hair was tousled and hanging in her face from the attack, so Roy used a hairbrush that had originally belonged to his lost mother Irene to brush her hair and sweep it from her eyes. After he finished grooming her hair, Roy unbuttoned Judith's blouse to expose her chest and left shoulder, but kept her breasts covered by her bra. Her jeans were still unbuttoned and slightly unzipped, exposing on the waist band of her panties, but because he had already shackled her ankles tightly to the point that her legs were spread wide across the bed, Roy decided to leave the jeans on her for the time being. Returning to her face, he gingerly removed the tape from her mouth with the help of oil and ear swabs, working slowly and carefully so she would not wake. When the adhesive was completely removed, and Roy was finally satisfied with her position, he began to paint the canvas on the easel beside the bed.

Forty five minutes later, the video had recorded nothing but the eerie audio of Roy breathing, mixing up paint and the image of Judith sleeping silently in her drug induced coma. He checked his watch, noting that it had been roughly an hour and thirty minutes since he pumped her thigh full of five hundred milligrams of Ketamine, more than enough to keep her out for more than an hour. The good thing about Ketamine was that it was difficult to overdose anyone with such an amount, so Roy sat calmly beside the bed in front of the easel and canvas.

As usual, he had worked quickly to cover the canvas with background colors, and then painstakingly and slowly painted his victim with exquisite beauty. He had already started painting her into the picture, in the exact way she laid in her leather shackles on the bed. Every five minutes or so, he would pause and reach out to touch Judith's hair, or briefly slide a finger or two inside her blouse or the waist band of her jeans to make skin to skin contact. Then he would return to his easel.

When Roy began to paint her face on the canvas, Judith stirred for the first time, moaning softly while moving her hands. He painted faster to capture her face the way he had placed it, but thirty seconds later she moaned again, this time slowly rolling her head in the opposite direction, covering her face with her hair once again. Roy quietly stood over the bed and took Judith's head in his hands to turn it back towards him. He smoothed her hair from her face once more and turned away from her to sit back down at the easel. With paint brush in hand, Roy looked back at Judith; she was blankly staring back at him with glazed unblinking eyes. At first he was startled, but quickly realized that she was not in the least bit coherent of her surroundings, and probably in the beginning stage of hallucinations. There was no expression on her face, and no attempt to move or talk, so Roy continued painting for ten more minutes while Judith stared back at him.

Without warning, Judith began screaming and wailing at the top of her lungs, thrashing her bound body violently on the bed and pulling so hard against the restraints that her left ankle began to bleed. Abandoning his painting, Roy jumped from his chair and joined her in her screams, enjoying the insanely fun moment while running around the bed to watch her from different view points. Judith was still clearly drugged throughout her tantrum, and calmed down only when she saw her reflection in the mirror above. Roy fell silent and observed her. Not realizing it was her own at first, she appeared puzzled and frightened at the reflection in the warped mirror. Then she began laughing like a maniac at the dwarf on the ceiling, as the warped mirror had shrunk her legs and arms and distorted her face, bucking her forehead in the process. Laughter quickly turned to bitter bouts of crying and screaming out with fright as she slowly realized that the dwarf on the ceiling was her own reflection. In her hallucination, she truly believed that somehow she had morphed into a dwarf, and she quickly closed her eyes to shut out the reflection. Delighted at her reaction, Roy hid in the shadows of a corner in the room, watching the effects of the drug play out.

When Judith finally opened her eyes again, her reflection had morphed again from the change in her position, elongating her legs and arms and pinching her face inwards. She cried silently at her reflection for several minutes while the room around her spun out of control, rolling in and out of her view in red and black everywhere, until she became nauseous and vomited. Roy leapt quickly from the corner and sprang onto the bed, twisting her head to the side so she wouldn't choke on her own vomit. Even though she had woken from her sleep to the sight of him painting beside the bed, this was the first time she really saw him. She fell silent, wondering who this strange man was in a black mask standing in a rotating room full of red and black swirling colors and dwarfing mirrors. The longer she stared at the silent masked man, the clearer things became, and the room stopped spinning so fast. Suddenly, the room stopped spinning at all, and Judith lifted her head slowly upward from the bed to glance at her surroundings, taking great pains to ignore the mirror above. For only a moment, Judith was totally aware of herself for the first time, but it was a fleeting moment. It was during this moment that she saw her restraints and the video camera. She jerked her head towards the man again, and tried to say something, but nothing would come out; panic and hallucinations set in once again, and Roy was enchanted.

Chapter Twenty

Hank Jordan used Melissa's office phone to call the Orange Beach police station, so that everyone could participate in the phone call by speaker phone. When Chief Big D and Marcus Donnarumma were finally connected to the call, Hank introduced them to the plan that he and Melissa had settled on, and after twenty minutes, the plan was set into motion.

After the phone call ended with Hank and Melissa, Marcus Donnarumma and Chief Big D drove to the local UPS store in Gulf Shores, Alabama, to meet with the manager, a well known local named Jiles McGhee. Jiles was born and raised in Gulf Shores, and Big D had known him and his family his whole life. On the way to the store, Big D phoned Jiles to let him know that they were on their way. An employee answered the phone and put Big D on hold.

Jiles answered, "This is Jiles. How may I help you?"

Big D answered jovially, "Jiles! Big D here on the phone! How are you, man?"

"Hey, D! I am good, just fine. It's been a while since I've seen you! How is the family?"

"Oh, they are doing real good, Jiles, thanks for asking. Hey, uhmm, Jiles, I am on the way over to your store right now with one of our investigators, Marcus Donnarumma; I believe he spoke with you earlier this morning, and we need to have a talk in private if you're not too busy. "

Jiles cleared his throat. He had been expecting this phone call since Marcus had shown up asking questions about flagging addresses through their systems. "Absolutely D, come on over. I kind of figured you would be calling. I am not too busy right now, and my two employees up front can handle everything on their own. Just come on in, and walk straight back to the office. I'll be waiting for you."

"Thanks, Jiles. We'll be there in about ten minutes."

Big D and Marcus pulled up to the UPS store and walked to the back office where Jiles was waiting for them. The men shook hands and made quick small talk, then sat down to take care of business. Even though he trusted him to keep his mouth shut, Big D was very careful not to expose the details of the case as he explained to Jiles what he needed from him. "Ok, so here's the deal, Jiles. First, due to the extremely sensitive nature of this case, there is going to be very little that I can tell you at this point, so I am going to go ahead and ask that you not ask me any details."

Jiles nodded in agreement while shutting his office door for more privacy, and Big D continued. "Secondly, we are trying to figure out a way to track someone who is, up until this point, nameless. We are looking for a man, we think, that is a very talented and mysterious artist. This artist periodically mails paintings in a mailing tube to an address located in Manhattan. This office is the office of a woman named Melissa Edwards, who is his art agent. Following me so far?"

Jiles nodded his head, "Yes, go on."

"Now, according to Miss Edwards, this Artist is completely anonymous to the public, even to her, and always has been. He uses fake names and accounts each time he mails her a shipment of his paintings. The only way she can get in touch with him is by cell phone, which changes numbers often." Big D paused for a moment and leaned forward into Jiles' desk. "We believe that this Artist may be connected to a serious crime, and we need to find him immediately if not sooner, and we need your help and promise that you will not say anything to anyone."

Before Big D could even finish the request, Jiles was in complete compliance. "Hey D, man, we go way back! You have my honest word, and I will help you in anyway that I can. You can trust me. I will do exactly what you tell me to do."

Big D smiled at his friend and shook his hand. "Ok, here it goes. Marcus here asked you earlier this morning about flagging an address. Can you explain that process to me?"

"Sure thing, D." Jiles swung the monitor of his computer around so that Big D and Marcus could see what he was explaining. He picked up a pen and pointed at the screen. "After 9/11 happened, our company decided to invest in an updated security system that can allow us to flag an address or shipment that may be linked to terrorism or crime. It took a while to get it going, because it not only covers the United States, but all of the countries that we carry to. See this red button here?" Big D and Marcus leaned in to look at what Jiles was pointing to. "This button, if pressed, will direct me to a field that we can fill out as much information as needed to flag an address. Once this field is complete, the information goes straight into an email format, and is immediately sent out to every single UPS store across the country. The offices are alerted by a warning chime that continues until the email is opened. It does take a little longer to reach the offices in other countries, but no more than a day, depending on that office's internet connections."

Big D interrupted for a second while Marcus took notes. "Ok, so, every store will be notified of the warning email as soon as we flag the address. What happens then?"

Jiles punched a couple of keys on the keyboard and accessed a manual for their system. "If you read here, it explains the process. I will make a copy of it while I explain it to you." Jiles used the mouse and clicked on the print option. "Ok, so, if someone comes into a UPS office and tries to mail anything to the flagged address, an alert window pops up on the employee's computer screen with several different options. For example, if someone has an account with UPS, and hasn't paid their bill, then their address would have been flagged. For that person, the alert window would advise the employee to get the manager, who would in turn speak with that person about their account. Strictly UPS business. However, in your case, the address in question is not a sender but a recipient. This address, as you say, would be flagged in connection with crime, and in the information field that I told you about a second ago, I would type in that if anyone should attempt to mail anything, especially a mailing tube, to that address, then, local authorities should be called immediately."

Marcus stopped taking notes and put a hand up to stop Jiles. "Well, what if this Artist guy gets spooked when the employee refuses to mail it? Or what if it takes too long for local law enforcement to get there? What then?"

Jiles smiled. "Well, I was getting to that. When this new system was implemented, every single UPS employee had to complete an in house class, provided by UPS, on how to use the system, how to be aware of suspicious mailing activity, and how to react to such, especially if the police had to be notified. Now, when that security warning pops up, all an employee has to do is click on the ok button at the bottom of the screen. When that happens, the warning goes away, the original window freezes, and an email, with a warning chime, is sent immediately to the manager's computer, the regional manager's computer and to the UPS security offices, who in turn sends out a 911 call to the local authorities of that store. In such cases, employees are taught to explain, to the customer that the computer is frozen, and there will be a couple of minutes of delay until the order can be processed. Because the warning window disappears, the employee can actually turn the screen around and show the customer that it is frozen, without indicating to him that there is a problem."

Big D whistled in response. "That's genius. I had no idea!"

Jiles continued. "Now, I, of course, cannot promise you that he won't just walk away, but even if he does, each store has several security cameras, that will at least get an image of this person if he shows up. At least, if he runs, you will get a picture of the person you are looking for. And trust me, since this new sophisticated security system was implemented, the security cameras have been a big issue. They are checked on a regular basis by the manager of the store, to make sure that they work properly. I checked mine just yesterday and sent in the report to regional." Jiles leaned over to the printer and removed the copy of the security manual, stapled the pages together and handed it to Big D.

Clearly impressed, Big D was extremely thankful for the knowledge that there were security cameras in each store; if the plan failed and the Artist ran, they would still get a picture of his face. "Ok, Jiles. Marcus and I are going to step outside for a minute to make some phone calls. Then we can get started on this."

Jiles opened the office door, and Big D and Marcus walked out to their unmarked SUV so they could call Hank back with the details.

While waiting for the phone call from Chief Big D, Hank and Melissa looked through magnifying glasses and poured over the photo copies of the Artist's painting, looking for any other scenes in which Jillian had been painted into; they found no one who resembled Jillian, but looked at the faces of many other women, all different. One of the most romantic things about his paintings, to Melissa and most of the buyers, was not only the lovely Louisiana scenery that he painted, but the remarkable beauty and exquisite details of the people, both men and women, who the Artist painted into his creations. Before now, they had always been considered the beautiful faces of time forgotten or the picturesque products of the imagination of a talented painter; but not anymore.

Although the photocopies were too small to see any exact details, even with the help of a magnifying glass, each face that Melissa looked at made her think of the back of milk cartons, or the posters of missing people on the entrance walls of Wal-Mart. To Hank, visions of amber alerts, police bulletins, and cold case files in cardboard boxes stored in dusty basements of old police buildings came to mind. Even though they had nothing that linked him to any other murders, the suspicion was there in both of their minds, and rightfully so, after witnessing the Luminol show in Judith's house less than twenty four hours ago.

Hank checked his watch. It had been a little over an hour since he last called Judith, and she still had not returned his phone call. When he grabbed his cell phone from his pocket to try her again, Melissa's office phone rang. It was Chief Big D. Melissa answered the phone and punched the speaker phone button.

Hank leaned into the phone, "Do we have a green flag?"

Big D's voice boomed through the phone. "Not only do you guys have the go ahead, but Marcus and I just found out that every UPS store has several video cameras. If this guy runs for any reason, we will get his picture. We just wanted to confirm everything with you before we flag the address. Is Melissa ready for this?"

With the faces of the nameless women still swimming in her head, Melissa answered for herself, "Yes, Chief, I am here, and I am ready." She inhaled deeply and began to write on a sheet of paper what she was planning to say to the Artist.

Chapter Twenty One

Judith knew that she was shackled to the bed, but she felt like she was floating in midair, far away from her own body. Although she could wiggle her fingers and toes, she couldn't feel them. Her attacker, the man in the mask, had once again disappeared into the shadows of the room. She tried to follow him with her eyes, but in between trying to escape the reflection in the mirror, and ignoring the spinning room, she lost track of his movements. Since her vision was distorted, and sense of touch was anesthetized, Judith closed her eyes and tried to concentrate on the sound of the room. Hoping to hear some movement that would indicate her attacker's position, she tried to mentally drown out the sound of her own rapid heartbeat. Behind her eyelids was a constantly morphing kaleidoscope view of gold stars and vivid colors. Judith focused at the rapid movement for several minutes before it stopped and faded to complete blackness. In this blackness, Judith felt a great weight of despair and helplessness creep slowly through her body, and realized for the first time that she had been drugged. Being careful not to stir her attacker, she accepted in complete silence the fact that she was experiencing severe hallucinations; she would have to wait until the effects of the drug had run its course, and only then would she open her eyes. She needed perfect lucidity to deal with her situation.

After five minutes of complete silence and no movements, Roy thought she had fallen back asleep. He emerged from the dark shadows of the heavy curtains and crept towards his unfinished canvas. Being careful to avoid the places that he knew would creak and moan beneath his weight, he walked softly across the hardwood floors. He wanted to take advantage of her current state so that he could paint more on the canvas. Judith heard every step he made, despite her racing heartbeat.

Roy was particularly delighted at the fact that the shackles had cut Judith's ankle during her wild attempt to flee her imprisonment. The blood from the wound had seeped into the white sheets that she lay on, and made an excellent addition to her portrait. From his paint collection on the floor he selected an aged stained bottle that had once contained button mushrooms marinated in garlic oil. Any residue of the mushrooms was long gone, and the garlicky smell had been washed away with the putrid smell of its current contents.

He shook up the contents of the bottle and gingerly unscrewed the top to make sure he wouldn't spill any of the contents. Immediately, the smell of death permeated the room, and Judith struggled hard not to gag. Having been a doctor for years, she knew the smell well; it was rotten blood and flesh. Although she was dying to know what was happening only a few feet from where she lay, she kept her eyes shut tightly and listened.

Roy brought the old mushroom bottle to his nose and sniffed its contents as if he were holding a crystal glass full of fine wine. He inhaled the rancid mixture and swirled it carefully around in circles, splashing small pieces of rotten flesh onto the inside of the glass, only to watch them fall back down and settle to the bottom. After enjoying the bouquet of his own concoction, Roy dipped his favorite paintbrush into the bottle and painted the bloody scene of Judith's wounded ankle into the painting. Horrified, Judith listened intently to each brush stroke sweep across the canvas.

Judith's hallucinations were long gone by the time Roy finished the painting. She was keenly aware that he had stopped painting, and listened to his slow and steady breath. Mesmerized by the art that he had created, Roy stood in front of the canvas, admiring his masterpiece. Realizing that Judith hadn't stirred in quite some time, Roy wondered if the drug had done some permanent damage like placing her in some sort of a coma. He knew she was still breathing because he could clearly see the rise and fall of her chest, but that had been her only movement in more than thirty minutes. Watching Judith carefully, he removed the paintbrush from between his teeth, placed it in a container of water that held the other brushes that he used, and capped the remainder of the opened paints, including the mushroom bottle. Sitting Indian style on the floor, he carefully swirled the paintbrushes in the murky water to remove most of the paint before he washed them with a cleaning solution that he kept in the kitchen. Several drops of paint had splattered on the floor, and after he finished swirling the brushes, he grabbed a towel hanging from the easel and wiped them up.

When the floor was cleaned of the paint droplets, Roy picked up each one of his paints and placed them into a canvas bag. Then, he stood up to check on Judith who still lay motionless on the bed. The sight of her breasts rising and falling with each breath stirred Roy's excitement, and he hurried out of the room towards the kitchen with his painting supplies. From the canvas bag full of paint, he withdrew the old mushroom bottle and placed it back inside the refrigerator next to the other ones that he kept. He usually cleaned his brushes immediately after finishing a painting, but he could not stand to be away from Judith for long; he deposited the brushes into the sink for the time being, and walked to his bedroom to remove his clothes that were covered with paint.

As soon as she was sure that Roy had left the room, Judith took a chance and opened her eyes. She could still smell remnants of the rotten blood flesh. At first her vision was blurred, and she focused on the nearest object to gain better visualization and perception. The easel and canvas slowly came into view. They were faced slightly in the opposite direction, so Judith could not see what had been painted. Her vision was improving by the second, and she took in her surroundings slowly, careful not to jerk her head, so as not to trigger any more hallucinations. After inspecting the room, Judith took a deep breath and confronted the warped reflection the mirror above that had caused her so much fright before. This time, she only saw a slightly distorted version of the truth; she was shackled to a bed in a room decorated with black and red designs and prints. There were heavy curtains covering what she supposed was a window, although absolutely no light came into the room. As she studied her reflection for anything that might help her escape, she noticed that her ankle was clotted with blood, and the sheets were soaked in crimson around her foot. She attempted to move her foot within the confines of her restraint, and a sharp pain shot up her leg as the metal chains rattled and clinked. Somehow, while trying to silence the chains, Judith managed with great difficulty to swallow the screams of pain that were desperately trying to come out. She froze in horror, praying that the masked man had not heard anything.

Roy did hear the chains rattle. Smiling, he slipped off his mask, shirt and pants, revealing a lean milky white body and a large shock of dark brown hair. He wore no jewelry, had no tattoos or major scars, and no piercings; he liked to refer to his own body as a clean white canvas. Crossing the room, he sat down in front of his computer and accessed the live feed from the surveillance camera inside Judith's room. Using the mouse, he clicked on several options, directing the camera to zoom in closer to Judith. After several seconds a clear picture came into view, and Roy leaned back in the chair to watch Judith observe her new surroundings. The look of pure horror in Judith's face as she searched the mirror above her was more than enough to give Roy an erection. Because the camera was hidden in the ceiling above her, it was as if at times that Judith was staring directly at him. Roy ignored his erection and pushed away from the computer. She was ready. It was finally time to meet her, and this time, he would leave the ski mask off.

Judith held her breath at the first sound of his footsteps from somewhere in the house. One by one, they became louder and louder as he neared the bedroom door. She quickly shut her eyes and pretended to sleep in the same position as she had when he was painting. After what seemed like an eternity of waiting, she heard the bedroom door slowly open, creaking slightly at the hinges. She dared not open her eyes to look. More footsteps slow and deliberate, until she could feel his dark presence beside the bed. She could now feel and smell his breath on her face as he leaned over her, and her heart beat so fast that she wondered if it would explode.

Roy leaned over her body, inspecting her, taking in every detail. He noticed that her breathing had sped up tremendously, as her chest heaved under the pressure of staying quiet and motionless. His attention turned to Judith's wounded ankle. He calmly picked up the chain that connected to the restraint and jerked it violently in mid air. The pain was so intense that Judith screamed out in agony and at last opened her eyes. Roy jumped on top of the bed and stood up at her feet.

Unable to speak, Judith stared up at the naked man in horror and shock.

He introduced himself to the shivering woman lying beneath him. "Hello, Dr. Judith Esther. My name is Roy." And somewhere in the background, she heard a cell phone ring.

Chapter Twenty Two

Melissa's heart sank when she heard the recorded message, "Your party cannot be reached at this time. Please try your call again later." With shaking hands, she punched the speaker phone off and ended the call. It was unusual for The Artist not to answer her phone call. She looked at Hank for answers as to what to do next.

Hank was seated beside her, tapping a pencil up and down on the desk. There was nothing for them to do but keep calling him and hope that he would answer. His thoughts turned to Judith, and he checked his watch again. Too much time had passed since he spoke to her last, and he started to worry. "Well, Melissa, all we can do is keep trying to get in touch with him. Speaking of trying to get in touch with him, do you not find it a bit strange that Judith hasn't returned any of my phone calls today?"

Melissa nodded. "Kind of. I know Judith, and she always calls back. She did say that she might go back to her office to reschedule everything, though. She could be there. Have you tried?"

Hank stood up and walked to the office window. "No, I didn't want to bother her there, but now I think I will call."

Melissa picked up on his worry. "Hank, c'mon. I am sure that she is fine. Why don't you go back outside, get some fresh air, and try her at her office. I am sure that's where she is. And when you come back, we can try calling him again."

"Alright, but don't try to call him while I am gone. I want to be here to listen to everything he says."

"I wouldn't dare do that! I am nervous as hell as it is. Do you honestly think I could do this by myself?"

"Ok, I will be back in a minute." Hank left the office and walked down the flight of stairs. He didn't feel like stepping out, so he stopped just inside the lobby and dialed Judith's office.

Judith's secretary, Sandra, answered. "Dr. Esther's office. How may I direct your call?"

"Hi, Sandra, it's Hank. How are you today?"

"Oh, hi Hank! I am doing pretty good. Kind of a slow day, with Judith not here. She always livens up the place. I was happy when she told me that she was coming back tomorrow, even though, I hate that her vacation time didn't go so well. She didn't go into much detail, so I didn't ask."

"Oh, so she's not there now?"

"No, she's not. She stopped by for a little while around lunch time, just to reschedule everything. We talked for a little bit, and then she went to her office. I am really not sure when she left, though. I had stepped out of the office, and when I returned, she had left a note saying that she was gone, and that she would be here first thing in the morning."

"Do you know where she was going when she left?"

"No, I don't." Sandra paused. "Hank, is everything ok? You sound worried."

"No, no, no, I'm fine. Really. I had to fly to New York for some business today. Judith dropped me off at the airport, and that's the last time I have spoken with her. I have called several times, and I can't seem to get her on the phone."

"Oh, well, I wouldn't be too worried! If she hasn't called YOU back, then that must mean she is at the hospital. Cell phone reception isn't always the best up there, as I am sure that you know already. Try the pediatrics' ward."

"No, that's ok. If she is there, I don't want to disturb her. Do, me a favor though."

"Sure, what do you need?"

"If you see her, or she calls back to the office, please tell her to call me back."

"Absolutely, Hank. Take care!"

"Thanks, Sandra." Hank ended the phone call and placed his cell phone back inside his pants pocket. Talking to Sandra had made him feel much better. Hank couldn't count how many times in the past that he had tried to call her cell phone while she was in the pediatrics' ward, but her phone never rang. And then, as soon as she stepped outside, her phone would register missed calls. He ascended back up the stairs to Melissa's office.

Melissa asked, "Well, did you get her on the phone?"

Hank shook his head. "No, but I talked to her secretary. Judith did stop by the office to reschedule for this week, and her secretary told me that she was probably at the hospital, which has notorious bad cell phone reception. I am sure that is where she is."

"See? I told you not to worry! So, do you want to try this guy again?"

Hank nodded. "I am ready when you are."

Melissa glanced down at her notes and recited everything again in her head. When she was ready, she dialed the number and put the call on speaker phone. She realized that she was holding her breath after the second ring, and exhaled slowly to keep her composure. Hank mouthed to her, "Are you ok?" She nodded back that she was fine.

The Artist answered the call on the fourth ring, and Melissa's eyes went wide. "Hello Miss Edwards."

For a split second, she didn't think she was going to be able to talk, and then she stuttered, "Uhmm, hi. Hello." She laughed nervously and glanced down at her notes.

The Artist breathed heavily into the phone. "I trust that you received my shipment?"

Melissa responded quickly, but managed to maintain herself. "Yes! I did! They are, of course, all fabulous, as usual, which leads me to why I called you." Hank motioned with his hands for her to slow down and breathe deeply, and Melissa nodded back. "Your paintings have made quite an impression on a very valued client. He has been waiting for this shipment to arrive, so when I received it, I called him first thing this morning so he could get the first look at them. I think you will be happy to hear that he purchased one of your paintings for five thousand dollars." Melissa held her breathe for his response.

"Yes, I am pleased. Which one did he purchase?"

"He purchased the smallest painting of the Manchac swamps."

Roy was surprised. "For five thousand dollars?"

In an instant, Melissa lost all nervousness, and threw herself into the marketing role that she was so good at. "Yes! Can you believe it? Five thousand! But that's not the good news. Are you ready for this?"

Roy was delighted at the sound of five thousand dollars, but he couldn't keep his attention away from the hallway that led to Judith's room. "Miss Edwards, get on with it. Spit it out. I am quite busy at the moment."

Melissa was not fazed. "Oh, I am so sorry to have bothered you. The good news is that this client has asked me to call you on behalf of himself and"

The Artist cut her off, "Miss Edwards, I have already told you that I will not paint a custom commissioned painting. Is this what this is all about?" He glanced down the hallway. "I really don't have time for this right now."

"No, I would never call you and ask you to do that. This client is asking that you paint anything you want, anything at all, of the same size or smaller as the one that he purchased this morning, and he is offering a price of ten thousand dollars for a speedy delivery."

The sound of ten thousand dollars captured his attention, and The Artist temporarily forgot about the hallway. Still naked, he sat at the dining room table and glanced up at Jillian. He wondered why the client hadn't chosen his best painting of the shipment, 'Sisters'. "I am surprised that he chose the smallest painting. It wasn't near the detail that I put into 'Sisters'."

Melissa and Hank quickly looked at each other. "Well, funny that you should mention that. He is also thinking of purchasing that painting as well, but he isn't sure where he can put it, because of the size. He is limited to smaller pieces at the moment." Melissa crossed her fingers.

"Hold on, Miss Edwards." The Artist thought about the offer while staring at Jillian on the wall. He remembered Judith shackled to the bed down the hallway. The cell phone had rung right in the middle of his introduction to her, and four minutes later had rung again; he was still irritated at the interruption. The horror on Judith's face had been priceless. Still, his ego had never been stroked at this level, and the money for his creations took priority over anything a woman could ever do for him. "How fast does he need this painting?"

Melissa glanced down at her notes. "Well, he is waiting in the lobby. Would you like to speak to him?"

The Artist quickly responded, "NO! That will not be necessary. I will speak to no one but you. Ask him for me."

"Absolutely, hold on just a minute." Hank took the time to listen to the background for anything that would help them find out where he is. He listened for cars, boat horns, trains, airplanes, television. Nothing. All he heard was the steady slow breath of The Artist. He motioned for Melissa to continue. "Sorry for the wait. I just spoke with him outside, and he said that he needed it if at all possible within the next two days, and he will pay for the overnight shipping." She crossed her fingers, closed her eyes and asked a question that she and Hank had debated on, hoping he would take the bait. "Sir, is this something that you think you can do in such short notice?"

The Artist laughed out loud. It wasn't a real laugh, because the question wasn't funny. It was a slap in his face for anyone to doubt his artistic abilities. Melissa heard the tone of the laugh and closed her eyes. She had warned Hank that it would make him angry, possibly causing him to blow the deal off. When The Artist spoke, Melissa opened her eyes wide at Hank, who smiled back with approval. The plan had worked.

"Miss Edwards, with all due respect, you are not an artist! You are simply my agent. Don't ever question my abilities again! Of course, I can paint something of that size within that time frame, and have it shipped to him that quickly! It's nothing for me! I painted 'Sisters' in one evening!" The Artist scoffed. "However, I will only agree to these terms, if, this client agrees to purchase 'Sisters' as well, for, hmmmm, let's say at the price of seven thousand."

Melissa grabbed Hank's hand. It was too good to be true! "Sir, can you hold on for one more minute while I discuss your terms with the buyer?"

The Artist smiled wickedly and crossed his legs under the dinner table. "Yes, I will hold."

Melissa and Hank silently high fived each other and waited several minutes before returning to the conversation. Melissa opened and closed her office door for realistic effect, and rustled some papers at her desk. Then finally, she sat back down and leaned into the speaker phone. "Sir, you are quite the bargainer. He has agreed to your terms.

That is a total of twenty thousand dollars for three paintings in one day! You deserve congratulations. In my experience as an art agent, I can honestly say that I have never known anyone but you to be able to pull this off. You are truly amazing!"

The Artist had temporarily forgotten all about Judith as Melissa practically worshipped him through the phone. "Thank you, Miss Edwards. I have to go now. I have work to do."

The phone call was ended, and Melissa and Hank took a moment to breathe. Their plan had worked. The Artist had fallen for it hook, line and sinker. Hank couldn't wait to tell Judith the good news, and hoped that she would call him as soon as she left the hospital. The next thing they had to do was call Chief Big D, and have Melissa's address flagged as soon as possible.

Chapter Twenty Three

Chief Big D and Marcus Donnarumma were still at the UPS store, making small talk with Jiles McGhee, the manager, while waiting for Hank's phone call. They were in the middle of a conversation about how lame it was that the Gulf Shores fishing pier had not been rebuilt yet, when Big D's cell phone rang. He flipped his phone open quickly. "Big D, here."

"Hey Chief. It's Hank. I have extremely good news."

"Talk to me! What happened?"

"He fell for it. He agreed to the whole set up, plus some. This guy is something else. Talk about ego! When Melissa mentioned that the buyer was debating on whether or not to purchase the painting 'Sisters', this Artist guy actually said that he wouldn't agree to painting another one until the buyer bought that one as well! It didn't faze him at all. I mean, if there wasn't blood all over those canvases, I would say that he probably just copied her face from a newspaper clipping. That's how calm he was."

Big D whistled into the phone and gave Marcus a thumbs up. "You have got to be kiddin' me!"

"Nope! So, maybe we will get lucky and see Jillian's face pop up in the new painting. Anyway, everything is done, so go ahead and do what you need to do at UPS. Hopefully, in the next day or two, we will find out who he is."

"We are on it! I'll call you back when we are finished."

Jiles McGhee got to work on the computer. He created a new security file, and entered the appropriate data and password to create a new warning alert that tagged Melissa's office address as linked with a criminal investigation. He gave it the highest priority rating and selected the boxes designated for incoming packages, especially mailing tubes. In the box titled additional information, he typed, according to code, the correct procedure that should be taken if some one attempted to mail a package to the flagged address. Then he typed the contact information for the Orange Beach Police Department along with Chief Big D's contact numbers. He also entered his personal information, so that the system would see where the alert had originated without having to track it. When he was finished, he offered his seat to Big D so he could approve everything before he sent it into the system.

Big D accepted the chair and sat down behind the desk. While he read, he asked questions to make sure he understood everything. "Ok, Jiles, right here, where you marked it as the highest priority, what exactly does that do?"

Jiles pointed at the screen to the box that was checked high priority. "That means that when the local officials are notified, the security will advise them that it could be a hostile situation, not a friendly one. When they get to the UPS store, they should detain him with force, if necessary."

"Ok, good. Now, what about our information here in this box?"

"That will tell security to alert you guys secondly, to let you know that the person in question has been called into local authority."

Big D nodded at the computer screen. "Well, ok! Everything looks perfect! Go ahead and send it in, and let's pray that this works. I have a really big and bad feeling about this guy."

Curious, Jiles started to ask Big D a question, but Big D stopped him before he could say anything. "Sorry Jiles, I can't tell you anything else, man. When all of this gets settled, I'll take you out for a beer and tell you everything. I really appreciate your help. In the meantime, mum's the word."

Jiles held his hand out to his friend, and to Marcus. "Not a problem, D. Whoever this guy is, I hope you find out soon."

Big D and Marcus left the UPS building and drove to the lab to check on the DNA results of the paintings. It was highly unlikely that they would know the results until the next day, but at least they could find out if the blood type found in the paintings matched Jillian Brannon's. Big D pulled the unmarked SUV into a parking space in front of the lab, and they both entered the building in search of Sherrie, the lab technician who took the DNA from Marcus early that morning. They found her sitting at a microscope behind the plated glass window of the laboratory room. Marcus knocked on the glass to get her attention and pointed to the waiting room when she looked up. Sherrie nodded, and met them several minutes later.

"Hi D! It's been a while since I've seen your face in here! Here are the blood results. The DNA test isn't finished yet." Big D nodded and smiled at Sherrie while Marcus took an envelope from her outstretched hand. "It looks like you boys have a match in blood type to the sample that you gave me from Jillian Brannon. My guess is that the DNA test will come back positive as well."

Marcus emptied the envelope and studied the test results. Confused, he pointed at a list of blood types on the sheet. "Wait a minute, Sherrie, there is more than one blood type evident on the tests."

Sherrie nodded and folded her arms. "That's right, Marcus. We found more than one blood type on those paint chips that you brought me. If it is Jillian's DNA on that painting, then she isn't the only one. Those other blood types belong to other people. As you can see in the test results, we found blood types O+, which matches Jillian's, and also A+, B+, O-, and the rarest form AB-."

Chief Big D stared at the results in shock. The investigation had just spiraled to a much different level than it had been only five minutes prior to walking into the lab. He hoped that he was not looking at the first piece of evidence that pointed to a serial killer, but in the back of his mind, he knew that he was. He looked at Sherrie who was waiting patiently to be dismissed. "Good work, Sherrie." He put his finger to his mouth. "Please, not a word about any of this to anyone. Not yet."

Sherrie nodded her head and returned to her work station at the microscope. Marcus and Big D stared at one another, waiting for the other to speak. Finally, Big D cleared his throat and handed the results back to Marcus. "Well, here we go! This is going to get very interesting, and extremely ugly. This town really doesn't need this shit right now. Not after the Morrison murders. Let's pray to God that he is not in our jurisdiction!"

Chapter Twenty Four

Sitting naked at his dining room table, Roy Fontaine toyed with several different scenes for his next creation. He wanted it to be perfect, one of his best paintings ever, especially since it sold for ten thousand dollars. Nothing outstanding came to mind, and after ten minutes, he decided that he would visit with Judith. Maybe she could help him envision his next masterpiece by getting to know his passion for art. Although his new murals were not yet finished in his house, he still had pictures of everything that he had painted in his house in New Orleans. He could also introduce her to all of the women who had inspired him and evoked his creativity throughout his adult life. Before he left the room, he caressed the pad of Jillian Brannon's ring finger with his thumb, and admired the shellac job that he had done on the wall. Then, he headed down the painted hallway toward Judith, gathering pictures from the walls as he walked. He could always show her more later, but for now, he needed to be motivated for his enthusiastic client in Manhattan.

During his absence, Judith had strained with all of the energy that she had left to listen to Roy's phone conversation; but behind the closed door, she heard nothing but his muffled voice for some time. After concentrating harder, Roy's conversation began to clear some, especially when he raised his voice. She had focused on his voice, until, suddenly, she heard the first tangible words, 'Miss Edwards'. At first, the name had meant nothing to her; then she heard the word 'painting' seconds later. Instantly, the fog surrounding her memory lifted, and the events of the previous night flooded her mind. She remembered the paintings, her friend Melissa whose last name is Edwards, Hank and the police, the Luminol. She remembered dropping Hank and Melissa off at the airport, and going to her office. She remembered so much so fast, that she felt as if her head would explode. Judith breathed deeply and slowly to stop her heart beat from accelerating. When it slowed down, she rolled her head slowly to her right, and began to silently cry in fear for her life. She had made the connection as she stared at the back of the canvas on the easel. Roy was The Artist, and he had kidnapped her. During the time he was gone, she was able to think more rationally about her situation after she had made the connection. She focused more on the events that had led up to her waking up in the nightmare she was lying in now.

The silence was now interrupted by his footsteps somewhere in the house, then again in the hallway closer to her. She also heard ripping noises that sounded like paper being torn. When her bedroom door finally opened, Judith lifted her head at the doorway. There he stood, still naked, but covered with photographs that were taped to his body. After his grand and shocking entrance, he walked to her bedside and spoke to her.

"Hi, Dr. Esther. Please forgive me for leaving you in such a hurry. You see that there is an easel and canvas to the left of your bed. If you haven't guessed by now, I am an artist."

Turning her face away from Roy, Judith refused to look at him. She did not want to see his face again, or what was in the photographs that were dangling from his body. He continued to talk. "I was hoping that we could hang out for a while, get to know each other a little bit better before, well," he paused for effect, "before I have to work. But, something has come that I have to attend to."

He stared down at the back of Judith's head, waiting for her to look at him. When she didn't, Roy grabbed her face with both hands and wrenched it towards him. Judith gasped for air as he grabbed her throat, for two reasons. One was because he was cutting off her airway, and two, because she was eye level with a taped on photograph dangling from his left nipple. It was a picture of a headless naked woman, covered in blood, mud and grass. She shut her eyes quickly and bucked her body in attempt to free her throat. Roy let her struggle for several seconds before he released her airway. Judith gasped at the air until she could draw a breath. After she settled down, he spoke again. "As you may or may not know now, I do not like to be ignored when speaking, especially in my own home. Do you or do you not understand that now?"

Judith nodded her head quickly. Her throat was burning so badly that it felt like it was on fire, and the tears trickling down her cheek were just as hot. Roy raised his fist to her face and demanded, "Say that you understand!"

Judith opened her mouth to speak and managed to utter a strained but quiet, "Yes."

Roy smiled at her and lowered his fist. "So, as I was saying before you so rudely ignored me, was that I have something pressing that I have to attend to. I hope you don't mind the inconvenience."

Fearfully, Judith shook her head.

"Good, then I would like for you to take a look at some of the pictures that I have collected over the years. Look at each one carefully. This is some of my artwork. I want you to get a true feel of my talent, and then I will show you your portrait that I painted of you while you were asleep."

Horrified, Judith did exactly what he told her to do. She looked at each picture for several seconds, and tried hard to suppress her gag reflection. The last thing she wanted to do was hurt his feelings or mock him. When she gazed upon the last one, she said a silent prayer for each one of the women captured in the photos. They were all mutilated to some degree, some more than others. There was only one headless shot, which was the one she saw first. It was actually easier to look at compared to the rest, which all showed the last expressions on the dying women's faces.

At last, Roy turned away from the bed to retrieve Judith's picture from the easel. When he returned to her bedside, he raised the portrait up so that Judith could see it. She could smell the rotten fleshy smell on the canvas, and knew that Roy had used someone's blood to help create the painting. She couldn't help it any longer and reflexively gagged. To her relief, Roy was not angered by this. Instead, it seemed to please him. She understood why. He simply enjoyed the horror.

Roy stood there proudly for several minutes in silence, observing the way that his artwork had affected Judith. Satisfied with her reaction, he slowly opened the drawer in the bedside table. Judith carefully watched his movements. From the drawer, he withdrew a small black bag and placed it on the bed beside her. When he opened it, she saw the vial, and began to plead with him. "No, no, no, no, please! Please Roy, no, not again!"

Roy laughed at her. He knew that from her medical background she would probably guess what he had drugged her with. In fact, she hadn't guessed; she knew it was a hallucinogenic, but didn't know which one. Staring at the vial, she saw Ketamine. Crying desperately, she pleaded with him again, "Please do not do this to me again!"

Casually, Roy asked, "Why not? Tell me. I want to know."

Hoping that she could somehow change his mind, she whispered through sobs and tried to point at the ceiling. "It's too much, please! The hallucinations are just too much."

Roy looked at the ceiling at his own morphed reflection in the mirror. "Oh! That IS interesting!" He filled the syringe once again, and stabbed her in the shoulder muscle while she screamed in terror; she could still hear herself scream as Roy's face vanished into complete darkness.

Chapter Twenty Five

With the constant background music of thousands of horns blaring and people shouting, the sun began to set over the bustling borough of Manhattan. The roads were deadlocked with traffic, and the sidewalks were packed with pedestrians hurrying home from work. Hank watched the lively scene unfold from the window of the office, while Melissa finished making the last copy of her files on The Artist. Directly across the street from Melissa's office was a seedy little bar that attracted an array of prostitutes and thugs. Already he had witnessed one woman being slightly roughed up by her pimp in front of the bar, and a drunk stumble blindly out into the road, almost running right into a taxi cab; the drunk had been saved by a man carrying a sign that read "The End is Near". Right after that had taken place, a group of young school girls in Catholic uniforms had walked by on their way home from school, passing a smaller group of Goth kids who had taunted them. Hank shook his head in amazement as he watched so many people from all walks of life interact on the street below him. Born and raised in Orange Beach, Alabama, it was a completely different world to him. He wished that Judith had come with him. Although she had been to New York countless times, he wished that he could have shared his first time with her. She still had not called him back, and Hank debated whether he should call the hospital or not. As the minutes ticked by with no return call from her, an unsettling feeling washed over Hank. He watched a collection of brightly clothed drag queens carrying various musical instruments enter the sleazy little bar across the street, and then turned away from the window toward Melissa. He had made up his mind.

"I think I am going to go ahead and call the hospital to check on Judith. Something just doesn't feel right. She should have called by now. It's six o'clock already."

Pushing her glasses up from the tip of her nose, Melissa looked up at Hank. She saw the worry in his expression and smiled reassuringly back at him. "Go ahead, Hank. Call her. I am sure she is fine, but I know it will make you feel better, so go ahead and call her. You haven't stopped worrying about her since we've been here." She stapled the last group of papers together and placed them in a folder on her desk.

Hank nodded. "You're right. I have been worrying all day. It's just not like her not to call back." He reached into his pocket and fished out his cell phone. "I would walk outside to call her, but I don't think I could hear my own words if I did! Don't you ever get tired of all the noise out there?"

Melissa laughed. "Yes, I do. Why do you think I wanted to come to Orange Beach?"

Hank scrolled through the saved contacts in his cell phone and pressed the number for the hospital in Foley. "Well, I can totally understand why! It's a madhouse down there, especially that nasty little bar across the street!" He listened as the phone rang. When the operator answered, Hank responded. "Pediatrics, please."

The hospital operator transferred him to the pediatrics' ward and placed him on hold. A wordless rendition of Culture Club's song 'Do You Really Want to Hurt Me' piped through the cell phone, and Hank thought of the drag queens who had just entered the bar below. Finally, after Hank found himself humming along to the song, a nurse picked up the phone. "This is Nurse Angela, can I help you?"

Hank cleared his throat. "Hey, Angela. This is Hank Jordan. I'm looking for Judith. Is she around?"

"Oh, hey, Hank! No sorry, she isn't here. She is still on vacation, but you should know that!" Nurse Angela giggled into the phone.

Immediately, Hank was alarmed. "Yes, I know she is on vacation, but there has been a change of plans. She returned to her office earlier today to reschedule her week, and I thought she would be there since I can't reach her on her cell phone."

THE ARTIST

Angela rustled through some charts. "Uhm, well, hold on a second and let me see if she signed in today." She checked all of the paperwork but found no sign of Judith being there. "No, it doesn't look like she has been here, but she might have come in to see some of her patients. Hold on and let me page her. I'll ask if anyone has seen her as well."

Hank was put back on hold. The Culture Club song had finished, and another song from the eighty's had started. This time it was a wordless rendition of Prince's 'Doves Cry'. Instantly, Hank remembered from high school the first words of the song 'paint, if you will, a picture, of you and I engaged in a kiss'. It sent chills up his spine as he thought about The Artist painting a picture of Jillian Brannon. He suffered through one more song until Nurse Angela returned to the phone.

"Sorry, Hank. It looks like Dr. Esther hasn't been here at all today. I spoke with everyone who is here, but no one has seen her. I also checked her patients' files, and Judith didn't sign any of them today. You should try her on her cell again."

Hank heart began to beat faster as he listened to Nurse Angela. "Ok, well, thank you for looking. If you see her, or talk to her, please tell her to call me. It's extremely important."

Nurse Angela heard the worry in Hank's voice. "Absolutely, Hank. I will tell her if I see her."

Hank ended the phone call and glanced at Melissa who was perched nervously at her desk. Although she couldn't hear what the nurse had said, she understood that Judith had not been at the hospital that day. He remained silent as he pressed Judith's cell phone number into the phone. When he heard the voicemail pick up, he immediately ended the call, and then called her house phone. When he heard her familiar voice on the answering machine, he bit his bottom lip in frustration and slowly replaced the phone back into his pocket. Something was very wrong. He stared out of the window into the afternoon smog, and wondered what he should do. What if she is on the beach? Or swimming? Or at the grocery store? She could be anywhere. He could send someone from the police department to check on her, but he didn't want to make her nervous with worry while he was away.

With dread, Melissa interrupted his thoughts. "Hank, I know I have been trying to calm you down, but I think maybe you should send someone to check on her, in light of everything that has happened. I agree with you. She should have called by now. I know how much you mean to her."

Hank quickly turned from the window. "I was just thinking about doing that. It's just that, well, if she is ok, and just hanging out on the beach, I don't want to make her feel paranoid by sending someone over there." Hank studied Melissa's face, and saw the worry in her eyes as well. He took a deep breath and opened his cell phone again to call Marcus Donnarumma. Ironically, as soon as he opened the phone to punch in the phone number, his cell phone rang. Hoping it was Judith, he looked at the caller id and saw that it was actually Marcus calling him. He answered immediately, "Marcus?"

"Hey, Hank. I'm back at the station with Chief Big D, and we need to talk. We just got back from the lab, and man, do we have some news for you! You aren't going to believe this!"

Still thinking of Judith, but not wanting to interrupt, Hank asked, "What? What happened?"

Marcus sucked in a long breath. "Well, for starters, the DNA isn't back yet, so we are not totally sure that it is Jillian's blood in that painting. But we did find out that one of the blood types did match hers."

Hank was confused. "Wait a minute. Did you say that one of the blood types matched hers?" He paused as it dawned on him what Marcus was saying. "Oh my God, Marcus! That means that there was more than one blood type found." His pulse quickened. "How many were found?"

Marcus sighed. "Five, including what we think is Jillian's. Hank, it looks like we may have a serial killer on our hands. We need you back here as soon as possible."

Hank's mind was reeling. A serial killer? What if this Artist guy was on to them? What if he knew that they had discovered the paintings? What if he knew that Melissa had visited Judith and brought the paintings with her? He had to find Judith! "Marcus, get in your car and drive over to Judith's house, now!"

Confused, Marcus asked, "What? Why? Hank, what's going on?"

Hank was almost breathless with fear. "I haven't been able to reach her all day long. I haven't talked to her since she dropped us off at the airport. She hasn't answered her cell phone or house phone, and no one has seen her since she was at her office at lunch!"

Marcus immediately jumped up from his office chair and ran toward the exit of the police station. With his cell phone cradled between his shoulder and his head, he put his jacket on while talking to Hank. "Ok, Hank, I am going now! Just calm down, man. I'm sure everything is ok." In the back of his mind an alarm went off too, and the hair on the back of his neck stood straight up. He ran quickly to his car.

Trying to breathe as calmly as he could under the circumstances, Hank stayed on the phone with Marcus until he reached Judith's house. "Are you there yet?"

Marcus pulled into Judith's driveway and cut the engine to his car. "Yes, I just pulled in. As much as I can see from the driveway, all the lights are off in her house."

Hank sat down on one of Melissa's office chairs and leaned onto her desk. "Is her car in the driveway?"

"Yeah. I parked right behind it." Marcus stared at the house for several seconds before he exited the car. With one hand on his gun, he quietly walked up the stairs and approached a window. "Hank, I am looking through the front window, but I don't see anything. You want me to check the beach before I knock?"

"Yeah, she might be on the deck, or the beach. Just walk around back real quick."

Marcus breathed heavily into the phone as he walked down the stairs and around to the back of Judith's house. She wasn't on the deck. He scanned the beach. No one was there except an elderly couple walking twenty yards away. He looked back at the dark house. Something didn't feel right, but he didn't dare say that to Hank who waited patiently on the phone. "Ok, man, I'm going to knock. Maybe she's asleep."

"Yeah maybe." But he couldn't make himself feel better. A cloud of dread hung over his head; he knew that she wasn't asleep. He listened intently as Marcus bounded up the back stairs and tapped on the sliding glass doors. Then he heard him slide them open and call out Judith's name. His patience had worn out. "Marcus! Do you see her? Is she there?"

"Hold on, man. I am looking through the house."

Hank's heart raced with fear. He couldn't stop from screaming into the phone. "I don't want to hold on anymore! Is she there? Tell me what you see!"

Marcus didn't know what to say. He didn't see anything but an empty dark house. Judith was no where in sight. Hank was screaming at him on the phone as he hurriedly checked the last room. His mind was spinning with trepidation; the dark house was giving him the creeps. Not even twenty four hours had passed since it had been lit up from the effects of the Luminol. Hank was still screaming at him on the phone; he walked toward the back door so that he could get some fresh air and try to calm Hank down. When he was almost to the door, he glanced one more time around the living room to make sure he hadn't missed anything. His eyes were immediately drawn to the dining room table. There lay Judith's purse and keys. He had to tell him. "Hank! Stop yelling and listen to me!"

Hank stopped immediately, but he wasn't sure if he wanted to hear what Marcus had to say. "Marcus, tell me something!"

Marcus sat down on the couch and placed his head in his hand. "Hank, her purse and car keys are on the table. But, Judith is not here. Man, I really don't know what to think…."

Marcus was still talking to him on the phone, and Melissa was pulling on his arm trying to get his attention. Hank couldn't move or breathe. In the middle of Manhattan, far away from the sugar white sands of his beloved island, his whole world came crashing down around him.

Chapter Twenty Six

Roy gathered up his paints and brushes and walked into his bedroom where a blank canvas lay ready on an easel beside his computer table. He wanted to watch Judith sleep from the surveillance video feed while he painted his next masterpiece for the new client in Manhattan. The request from Melissa had certainly come at an inopportune time, however the promise of ten thousand dollars for a new painting of his choosing and the purchase of his painting 'Sisters' was enough to put his plans for Judith on hold for a while. He steadied the stretched canvas and stared at the computer monitor as Judith lay shackled to the bed in the next room. Studying her facial features, which he already was familiar with painting, Roy had a sudden burst of creative energy followed by an extremely unique idea, one that he had never had before. He had painted plenty of the women of his past into his paintings. But never had he painted them into a picture while they were still alive; much less actually selling the painting while they were alive. It was a daring move, and Roy debated on whether he should do it or not. After staring at her in silence on the computer monitor for several minutes, Roy decided it was too good an idea to pass up. He whispered out loud to himself, "Now, this is true art!"

Closing his eyes, Roy envisioned a scene taking place in early fall in the swamps of Louisiana. In his mind he saw an old rope attached to a moss covered cypress tree that leaned out over the swamp water. The rope was a swing with an old wooden seat, set high enough to sweep out over the edge of the grassy swamp bank and over the murky dark water. Bright sun rays fought their way through the overhanging of dense moss that covered the cypress trees, turning the inky black water into a rippled mirror. He saw Judith on the old swing, flying through the air above the water, with her hair swaying behind in the autumn wind. He would have preferred to strangle her with the rope that hung from the imaginary tree, but he knew he couldn't sell that. Sighing in satisfaction at his vision, Roy finally opened his eyes and began preparations for his new masterpiece. Although he did not want to disturb her, the first thing he needed to do was extract some blood from Judith. If he was going to execute his plan perfectly, he simply could not use someone else's blood for this painting; it had to be hers.

Roy quietly walked through his macabre hallway to the bedroom where Judith lay unconscious, and pushed the door open. The black bag that held the Ketamine was still on the bed beside Judith. In addition to the drug, it also contained a tourniquet and syringe that Roy had used many times in the past to draw blood from his victims; it had always been the easiest way to collect blood for his paints. He removed the two items from the bag and cautiously approached Judith's arm. Never before had he taken blood this way from a live victim, and the thrill raced through his body at the prospect. Judith turned out to be a perfectly still patient, and Roy nodded in approval as he placed the tourniquet tightly around her arm and tapped lightly on a vein. As he steadied the syringe near her swollen vein, he was sidetracked by the vision of sticking the needle into her eyeball. In a sick and twisted but very brief fantasy, he wondered what would come out. Shaking the fantasy off so he would not waste valuable time, Roy turned his attention once again to the blue vein. Holding his breath in excitement, he pushed the needle delicately into the vein, and slowly drew out the blood that he needed for his masterpiece. Judith never even flinched as her blood was stolen from her body. She was once again lost in the drug induced coma.

After a full vial of blood had been drawn, Roy slipped the needle from her vein and quickly untied the tourniquet. Her blood was rich and beautiful as he shook it carefully in the vial; he stared in awe at the striking crimson hue. From a very young age the color of blood had always excited Roy. He remembered being completely dissatisfied with crayons when he was a young child, specifically because he could not render the color of fresh blood on his drawing papers. It wasn't until Irene, his mother, had bought him a set of paints for Christmas one year when he came close to mixing the vibrant shade of crimson. That had been so many years ago. The paint set had been cheap poster paint from a local store, but at age seven, it hadn't mattered to him. He had spent hours in the swamps and in his bedroom, painting morbid scenes of death with that poster paint. Completely unaware that she was feeding the creativity of a monster, his mother had saved as much money as she could and gradually began buying better paints for him. Since then, Roy had more than mastered the art of mixing the shade of fresh blood.

With the vial of blood in his hand, Roy allowed himself several minutes with Judith before leaving the room. He couldn't help himself as he was drawn to her shackled body. With her jeans still unbuttoned, it was easy for Roy to slip the vial of blood beneath her panty line. For several seconds, his fingers rolled the glass vial of blood across Judith's pubic hair. The feel of the course hair underneath his fingers sent a shiver of wicked desire through his body, and Roy shook uncontrollably as he craved more. He wanted to penetrate her, to hurt her in ways that most people couldn't even dream of. However, too much valuable time had passed, and Roy slowly resigned himself to a later date with his new captive. He had to paint. The brief molestation of her pubic mound with a vial of her own blood was enough to satisfy him for the time being, so he slowly slid his fingers from her panties and returned the tourniquet to the black bag beside the bed. He closed the door as quietly as he had opened it, and slipped down the hallway toward his canvas that patiently waited for him.

There was no time to thaw out Jillian Brannon's fingers. Although he enjoyed her help in mixing the paint, it would take too long and steal precious time that he needed to spend with Judith. From a cabinet in the kitchen he took an empty jar, filled it with Judith's blood and hastily returned to his bedroom.

Chapter Twenty Seven

Chief Big D was on his cell phone with the airline trying to change Hank's and Melissa's return flight back to Pensacola. After several minutes on hold, the airline operator returned to the phone and told him the bad news. "We are sorry, sir. There are no more flights this evening to Pensacola. But we can put them on the first flight out at 7:30 a.m. tomorrow morning."

"Ok. Go ahead and put them on the flight in the morning." As he closed his cell phone, Chief Big D sighed unhappily for two reasons. One was because he needed Hank immediately in light of the news that he and Marcus had received from the lab. They were now looking at a huge possibility that they had some psychopath serial killer on their island, and Hank was the best detective that they had. Secondly, he sighed in fear for Hank and Judith. Even though there was no sign of trouble or kidnapping in her house, it was highly unlikely that Judith disappeared on her own, and everyone knew it. He had received a desperate phone call from Marcus Donnarumma thirty minutes ago, and now, as he stood in Judith's kitchen again, he watched in dismay as the house bustled with a small team of officers looking for any clues to Judith's whereabouts. So far, they had found nothing but her purse, keys and cell phone full of messages from Hank. As he glanced around the house, he remembered the ghastly effects of the Luminol that had lit up the living room not even twenty fours ago. The sight had been spectacularly morbid. Dreading having to call Hank about the news with the flight, he let out a long pent up breath, and focused on the rippling water through the sliding glass door as he pressed Hank's number into the cell phone.

Hank answered the phone on the first ring. "Chief, tell me you got our flights changed."

Chief Big D sighed heavily into the phone. "Listen to me, Hank."

Before he could finish what he wanted to say, Hank interrupted him. "Damn! Chief, you gotta get me down there! Please do not tell me that there isn't another flight out tonight!"

"Hank, seriously, settle down! You knew there was going to be a big chance of that. There isn't one single flight back. I've got both of you on the next flight out at 7:30 a.m. It's the best we can do."

Hank groaned in desperation. There was nothing he could do but wait. He cleared his throat and concentrated on speaking the words that he dreaded to speak. "Chief, I have got a really bad feeling about this. You have to trust me on this one. I know Judith! I am telling you the truth when I say that she would never skip out like this!" Hank paused momentarily to slow his breath. "Chief, this Artist guy has either kidnapped her, or had someone else do it for him. Do they have the helicopters over the water yet?" Another fear of Hank's had been that Judith had gone swimming and drowned. The beach had been completely searched and showed no signs of her taking a walk.

"Yes, they are circling the area right now. Nothing's come up yet, Hank." Chief Big D cringed at the desperation in Hank's voice, and hated the fact that he had no answers to give him. All he could do was make a futile guarantee that Judith was ok. "Hank, we'll find her! I promise! Now, I need you to focus on this the best you can while you are up there. Pore over those files. Look for ANYTHING that will help us find this guy! Have you seen anything yet that jumps out at you?"

Hank shook his head and slumped down in Melissa's office chair. He stared down at the pile of papers that she had copied for him. "No, Chief, I haven't but we are trying. Please, just find her. And call me if you find out anything, immediately!" Hank lost his cool and slammed his cell phone shut. With one swift motion of his arm, he sent the stacks of paperwork on the desk flying into the air and yelled at the top of his lungs in frustration.

Melissa hurriedly bent down to the floor and began gathering up the paperwork and file folders while trying to think of something to say. Her hands were shaking uncontrollably at the thought of her best friend being kidnapped by The Artist. When the last piece of paper was taken up, she slowly replaced the stack back on the desk and put a hand on Hank's shoulder. "Hank, I am so sorry that I got you and Judith into this mess." On the brink of tears, her voice quivered. "We need to keep busy and try to see if these files contain anything useful."

Embarrassed by his outburst but unable to have prevented it, Hank buried his face in his hands while Melissa spoke. He knew she was right, but the thought of Judith being in danger was paralyzing him. When he closed his eyes, he could see her smiling. He could smell her. He could hear her voice telling him that she loved him. This wasn't supposed to happen to her; he was supposed to protect her. He opened his bloodshot eyes and looked back at Melissa. "I know. I am sorry about that. It's just that…"

Melissa tightened her grip on his shoulder. "Shhh. It's okay, Hank. You don't have to apologize. It's only paper. Now, let's dive in and see what we come up with, okay?"

Finally Hank nodded and picked up a stack of the papers. It was the only thing he could do. "Ok, I'll take this stack, and you take that one."

They divided up the paperwork and began to read. Most of the files contained dimensions and descriptions of the paintings with photocopies of them to look at. Each photo copy listed its owner or if unsold, listed the gallery in which it was hung. After almost one hour of silence and reading, Hank became restless. He put down his stack of papers and interrupted Melissa's research. "Are you responsible for the paintings in these galleries?"

Melissa nodded back. "Yes, I am, until they are sold. Why?"

Hank thought for a moment. "Well, if you are responsible for them, then that means that you can remove them if you want to, right?"

"Well, technically, yes, but I have a contract with each one of those galleries for a certain period of time. I will need a damn good reason to remove them without being in breach of contract."

"What could be your reason?"

Melissa sat in silence, pondering how she could manage to retrieve the paintings from the galleries. "Well, I could lie and say that I need them temporarily for a show. Maybe tell them that the show is just a display, and that none of the paintings will be sold, and that their gallery will be listed in case someone was interested in buying. That would probably work, even though I have never done it before."

"That sounds good, but what if the gallery owners wanted to come to the show?"

Melissa frowned at first; they didn't have time to put together a show if they were scheduled to return to Orange Beach in the morning. Then suddenly the answer occurred to her. "Well, then I would say it was for a show in Alabama and that I am leaving first thing in the morning. No one would have the time or interest in going out of town for that."

Hank began jotting down notes in his notepad. "Ok, well, then I say, let's get out of this office, and try and collect as many paintings of his that we can before we leave tomorrow. I want to nail this guy to the wall, and I want as much evidence as I can find while I am up here. Start making the phone calls. How many galleries are there?"

Melissa was already reaching for the phone. "There are six in Manhattan and one in upstate Louisiana. Shreveport."

Twenty minutes later they were en route to the first gallery. All six galleries had agreed to temporarily relinquish the paintings in hopes that their galleries would get more attention from the showcase of The Artist's works. From the five galleries in Manhattan, there were a total of twenty five paintings. The gallery in upstate Louisiana had three, but they would just have to wait in order to get those. The owner had happily agreed to mail them to an address that Melissa promised to give him in the next couple of days.

Hank rolled down the window in hopes of receiving some fresh air, but quickly rolled it back up when he got a whiff of the city's fumes. Instantly, he missed the smell of the salty air back home when he and Judith would spend hours on her deck looking over the Gulf waters. A painful stab of fear rushed through him and he tried desperately to push it from his mind as the taxi pulled up to the first gallery. Melissa left him to wait in the car at the curb and dashed into the entrance of the gallery. Minutes later she returned to the taxi with four paintings rolled carefully and bound by plastic. The second gallery proved even quicker as it was trying to close for the day. A worker was standing at the curb waiting for her with the paintings in hand. By the time they reached the last gallery, Hank was tired of sitting in the taxi and offered to go in with her. As he held the door of the gallery open for her, Melissa told him the name of the owner. "His name is Andrew Preston. Great guy! His brother Benjamin owns the gallery in Louisiana. And Benjamin at one point was The Artist's agent. That was a long time ago, but anyhow, that's how The Artist's paintings came to New York. I have only spoken to Benjamin a couple of times. We have joked back and forth about who The Artist really is and what he might look like; he has never seen him either." Melissa entered the gallery and pointed to a man walking towards them. "That's Andrew walking towards us right now."

The owner of the gallery welcomed Melissa and shook Hank's hand. "Welcome, welcome. Can I get either of you a glass of wine?"

Hank politely declined as did Melissa. Neither one of them was in the mood to hang around, but Andrew did not take the hint. Forever in a mindset to sell, he began taking them on a tour of his gallery. Everything he said went straight into Hank's ear and out the other, until, they came up on four of the Artist's paintings. The other paintings that Melissa had collected from the previous galleries had been wrapped up and Hank had no idea what they looked like. He had seen all of the photo copies but they were too small to study. These were in plain view.

Andrew pointed at the paintings. "Well, here they are. Some of his finest, in my opinion. I am quite confident that they will sell soon. Remind me, where is this showcase you are placing them in?"

Melissa cleared her throat and pretended to be studying another painting on the wall. "Oh, uhmm, it's just a small showcase in Alabama."

Andrew's face lit up. "Well, I surely cannot attend; however, my brother might be interested. Louisiana is only one state away! I am sure he will be delighted! Have you spoken with him about it yet? As you may remember, Benjamin was once The Artist's agent. He is solely responsible for bringing his beautiful work to New York."

Melissa cringed. "Yes, I have spoken with him, but I haven't told him where the showcase will take place yet."

Andrew began rolling up the paintings as he spoke. "Ah, I see. Well, make sure you invite him. You know, he takes great pride in the fact that he 'found' The Artist. He would be extremely appreciative."

Melissa smiled back sweetly. "Of course, Andrew. Thank you for lending me these paintings."

114

Hank watched the painted face of a beautiful woman disappear as Andrew rolled up the last piece of canvas; he wondered who she was. Was she dead? Had The Artist killed her? Was her face in a cold case file somewhere collecting dust and cobwebs in the basement of a police department? His thoughts were suddenly interrupted as Andrew passed the rolled up canvases to him. He took them from the man and smiled. Melissa thanked Andrew again, shook hands and promised to let Benjamin know in advance where the showcase would take place.

With the paintings safely stowed in the trunk of the taxi, they rode back to Melissa's office in silence. Hank paid for the ride when they reached the office and helped Melissa carry the paintings inside. Once they were inside, he called Chief Big D, and Melissa watched his hopeful face fade away as he received no news on Judith's disappearance. She hadn't been found walking down the beach, and her body wasn't floating in the water. She was nowhere to be found. Melissa settled Indian style on the floor of her office to begin unwrapping the paintings, but Hank stopped her. "You know what, Melissa? I think we should leave those wrapped up until we transfer them back to Orange Beach tomorrow. We will gain nothing by looking at them now, and I want to preserve them until we get them to the lab."

"Yeah, you're right. I need to call Benjamin back from the gallery in Louisiana anyway. If he hears from his brother before me about the location of the showcase, he will get his feelings hurt." Melissa picked herself up from the floor and reached for her phone. From her rolodex she found Benjamin's number and dialed. "Hi, Benjamin, it's Melissa again. I just left your brother's gallery, and you know, I didn't even tell you that I was thinking of showcasing the paintings in Alabama! While I was talking to him, it dawned on me that you might like to attend, since it is so close!" Melissa crossed her fingers and hoped for the ability to lie her way out of this.

Benjamin ruffled through some papers. "Okay, I am looking at my calendar. I would love to come, but I hope it's not next weekend. I am going to an art auction in New Jersey."

Melissa sighed in relief. "Oh, damn, Benjamin! The showcase is next weekend! I hate you will miss it!"

As Hank listened to Melissa talk to the gallery owner, a sudden thought occurred to him as he remembered something that Melissa had told him earlier. Benjamin had been an agent of The Artist a long time ago; Hank wondered if he kept files as immaculate as Melissa's. If he did, maybe they could find some useful information to help track this artist down. He waved frantically at Melissa to get her attention. Melissa interrupted Benjamin, "Uhm, Benjamin, I am so sorry. Can you excuse me for just one minute?" She quickly placed the call on hold and looked expectantly at Hank. "What is it?"

Hank pointed to the paperwork on her desk. "Did Benjamin keep files like that on The Artist when he was representing him?"

Melissa shrugged her shoulders. "I have no idea, but he should. Most art agents do."

"How can we get them from him if he did?"

"That should be easy enough. I will tell him that I am trying to put together a sort of biography of his works for the showcase."

Hank clasped his hands together in gratitude. "That is an excellent lie, Melissa. Thank you! Have him fax over what he has."

Benjamin had indeed kept detailed files on The Artist and was more than happy to send them to Melissa. She and Hank waited impatiently for the fax to arrive, hoping that it would give them some insight into this mysterious man.

Chapter Twenty Nine

Melissa and Hank sat at the office desk and ate Thai food delivered by a local restaurant. Even though Hank had absolutely no appetite, he knew he had to eat something. He had never eaten Thai food before, and Melissa had to talk him into trying it. She had ordered two side orders of Fug Tong Gang Buad, which to Hank's surprise was slices of pumpkin cooked in coconut milk, and one large order of Pla Rad Prig to share. When it had arrived, Hank looked at the food like it was from another planet. "Melissa, what in God's name is this stuff?"

Melissa had laughed at him. "Pla Rad Prig is fried fish with a spicy tamarind sauce. It's good! And don't worry; I had them put the sauce on the side in case you didn't like it."

Hank poked at his food with little interest. He was sure that it was good, and appreciated Melissa's efforts to introduce him to other cultural cuisines, but he couldn't taste a thing. The inside of his mouth felt like sand paper no matter how much bottled water he drank from Melissa's office refrigerator. At one point he considered going down to the little bar below the office and drinking a beer to settle his nerves, but watching the current patrons who stumbled in and out made him decide not to.

As if Melissa could read his mind, she waved him toward the refrigerator. "There is a six pack of Heinekens in the bottom drawer of the fridge, Hank, if you want one."

Hank put down his plate and stepped away from the window. "I would love one, thank you! I was just thinking about actually going into that bar downstairs until I saw some of the people go in and out. Changed my mind quickly."

Melissa shoved another bite of the Thai food in her mouth and nodded. "Yeah, I could see on your face that you need a drink. Help yourself."

Hank walked over to refrigerator and found a cold bottle of beer. The cold waft of air that settled over him as he closed the door felt good; he felt even better as he popped the top off and chugged the liquid down his throat. He was far from being an alcoholic, but he feared that if he had a whole bottle of scotch sitting in front of him, it would be finished before midnight. His nerves were completely shot and there was absolutely nothing he could do about it but wait for the morning to come. He finished the first beer while standing beside the refrigerator door, then opened it back up for another one. As soon as he popped the second top off, the phone rang and the fax machine came alive. He ran over to machine where Melissa sat waiting, eager to see what Benjamin the art dealer had recorded over time. Several minutes later, they had a stack of fifty two pages. Like Melissa, Benjamin had made photocopies of each painting that he sold; however, they were discolored Polaroid pictures from a long time ago, before the age of the digital camera, too small and fuzzy to get a clear view.

There was a client list dating back to the very first painting from The Artist that Benjamin ever sold. It was to a woman by the name of Emily McLane. The second painting, sold several months later, was purchased by a man by the name of Samuel Welch. Hank read the list of names, hoping that something stuck out as interesting. The next page caught his attention. Almost two decades ago in 1987, a woman by the name of Clover Fontaine purchased ten of The Artist's paintings from Benjamin. It was those sales that had initially given the agent the idea to expand his client base outside Louisiana. Hank noticed that after those sales, Benjamin had begun to sell his paintings to dealers and buyers from New York where his brother Andrew lived. He searched through the remainder of the names on the list and found Clover Fontaine's name several times. By the time Benjamin was dropped as an agent, he had sold over one hundred of The Artist's paintings, twenty two of which were purchased by Ms. Fontaine. Hank looked over at Melissa who was reading from one of the faxed papers.

"Hey, Melissa. Have you ever sold a painting to a woman by the name of Clover Fontaine?"

Melissa nodded. "Yes, I have. Why?"

Hank stared down at the paper for a moment before he spoke. "How many paintings have you sold her?"

Melissa mentally counted and responded. "I think around five, but I am not positive. I can tell you for sure." She rose from the floor and walked to her desk. "Hold on one second." Rummaging through the pile of her own paperwork, she came across several files, and opened them. "Okay, according to my records, she has purchased six of his paintings, all from Benjamin's gallery. Why?"

Hank was astonished at the number of paintings that this woman had purchased over the years. "Well, according to Benjamin's papers, Ms. Clover Fontaine purchased a total of twenty two paintings from him while he was The Artist's agent. According to you, she has purchased six from that gallery while you have been representing him. God only knows how many she has purchased while other agents have represented him. Does that strike you as odd? I mean, I do not know the world of art, and I understand there are serious collectors out there. But, this strikes me as strange. This guy wasn't even that well known back then."

Melissa frowned but didn't know why. "Yeah, I agree that is a little strange, but I don't know why it is? Where are you going with this?"

Hank pondered his interest. "Well, to be honest, I am not quite sure where I am headed with this. But it does make me think of one thing. Let's say that you, Melissa, are an aspiring artist. Before you get famous, who would be the one person who would collect your artwork?"

Melissa chewed on a piece of the Thai pumpkin and thought about his question. In mid chew, the answer suddenly came to her; her jaw went slack. "My mother." She managed to swallow the bite of pumpkin before she choked. "Oh my God, Hank. Do you think it's possible?"

Hank leaned back into the chair and stared at the ceiling. "Right now, I think anything's possible. Have you ever met this woman?"

Melissa shook her head. "No, but if she is buying from the gallery in Louisiana, I am sure that Benjamin has. I'll call him."

Hank held his hand out to stop her. "Wait, wait a minute. What are you going to say to him if he asks you why you are asking about her?"

Melissa rolled her eyes and smiled. "C'mon, that's easy! Remember? I told him I was trying to put together a little history of The Artist's paintings? What better way than to interview some of his earliest buyers and collectors?"

Hank smiled in agreement. "That's beautiful! Before you call him, let me set your phone up with a recorder so we can play the conversation back." It took only five minutes for Hank to rig Melissa's office phone. He tested it by dialing his cell phone and speaking for thirty seconds to Melissa. The playback of the recording was perfect.

Melissa sat at her desk and called Benjamin's gallery but no one answered. "Benjamin is definitely a night owl, but it's already ten pm there. I am sure he is home, and I don't have any other way to get in touch with him. We were lucky to catch him when we did."

Hank shrugged his shoulders, picked up a phone book and pointed at it. "I am sure that he is listed in a phone book down there."

Melissa had already thought of that and was punching in keys on her laptop to access the online white pages for Shreveport, Louisiana, where Benjamin's art gallery was located. There he was: Benjamin Preston. She dialed the phone number that was on the computer screen, and Benjamin picked up almost immediately. "Melissa! I was just getting ready to call you to see if you got that fax!"

Thankful that he wasn't already asleep, Melissa responded. "Oh, thank you, Benjamin. I am sorry to call you at home this late, but I had one quick question. I did receive the fax, and thank you so much for sending it. Something caught my attention."

"Okay, fire away. I am not doing anything right now but checking my email for the day. What's your question?"

"Well, I came across the name of Clover Fontaine in your papers. Now, she has purchased six of The Artist's painting while I have been representing him, and I see here that she purchased twenty two while you were his agent."

Benjamin interrupted her with a hearty laugh. "Clover? God, I have known her for almost twenty years, since the first day that she came into my gallery and purchased her first painting by The Artist. Sweet lady. Very quiet, though. Back then, The Artist's paintings weren't expensive at all, but even then I was surprised that she could afford one. She doesn't look like the type who would have any money. Clover is a rough looking woman. But looks can be deceiving. She came in here several months ago and purchased one of the paintings that you represented, and as you know, it sold for a thousand dollars."

Melissa didn't allow even the slightest pause in conversation and picked right up where he left off. "Wow! Well, in any case, I would love to interview her about her passion for The Artist's work since she has been such an avid collector for all of these years."

"Well, that certainly shouldn't be a problem. Of course, I need to speak with her first, to make sure that she doesn't want to remain an anonymous buyer. But as long as she agrees to it, I can give you her phone number and address."

Melissa knew it was too late at night for him to call her, so she didn't even ask; she didn't want to sound anxious. "That would be great Benjamin. I would really appreciate it. Can you call her in the morning? I have an early flight out of New York, and I will call you tomorrow afternoon."

"Sure thing, Melissa. We'll talk then."

Melissa hung up and looked at Hank. "Well, it looks like we have to wait. Are you staying up?"

Hank nodded absentmindedly. He was deep in thought wondering where Judith was, who The Artist was, and who Ms. Clover Fontaine would turn out to be.

Melissa walked over to the couch and grabbed a throw blanket. "Well, I am going to try to get some sleep. We have to be up and out of here in five hours for the pre-fight check." Hank was deep in thought. "Hank? Hello?"

Hank jerked his head around to face Melissa and nodded quickly. "Yes, I heard you. Go ahead. I'm going to stay up. I don't think I can sleep right now. Maybe I'll catch some on the plane."

"Suit yourself. There's coffee in the back if you want some." She laid down on the couch and closed her eyes while Hank stared off into the brightly lit Manhattan night.

Meanwhile, approximately fifteen hundred miles away in Orange Beach, Alabama, Roy Fontaine painted slowly and deliberately, taking great pains to create the perfect background scenery for his new painting. Occasionally he would take small breaks from his work to watch the monitor. Judith still lay motionless on the bed. A bead of blood had trickled down her arm and dried where Roy had neglected to staunch the bleeding after removing the needle from her vein. When he began to paint the cypress trees he noticed out of the corner of his eye something moving on the monitor. He laid down the paintbrush and watched the screen carefully. There was a dark spot growing underneath Judith's pelvis, and he knew right away what was happening. He was completely hypnotized as he watched the urine spread around her on the bed. Dashing over to computer he punched in some keys on the surveillance system in order to freeze frame the image and save it for later. It would make a beautiful painting.

Energized by the image Roy returned to the cypress trees. He worked steadily into the night until his stomach craved nourishment. Tonight was a perfect night for sardines and crackers, his favorite "painting food". When the painting of Judith swinging over the swamp water was finally finished at precisely four o'clock in the morning, Roy Fontaine laid down in his bed to catch some sleep before he mailed it to his agent.

Chapter Thirty

Hank and Melissa were up and ready to move at five a.m. He had eventually drifted off to sleep a couple of hours before while looking through the faxed files of the art dealer Benjamin, and Melissa had slept straight through on the couch until the alarm on Hank's watch sounded. Even though they were both exhausted, a rush of adrenaline kicked in and hurried them toward the airport. Melissa carefully placed the paintings in cardboard mailing tubes and gathered up all of the files that she had copied plus the ones that had been faxed from Benjamin, and packed them securely in her carry-on luggage. Once outside, Hank hailed a taxi, and they were at the airport by six a.m. Hank checked his watch as they waited to board and decided to call Chief Big D.

"Chief? We are getting ready to board. Anything new?"

Chief Big D was sitting with Marcus Donnarumma in a booth at Hazel's Breakfast Buffet. He pushed his plate of fried eggs and bacon away and leaned onto the table. "No, Hank. We've got nothing so far. Did you guys find anything in those papers?"

Hank wanted to wait until he got to the station to tell them about Clover Fontaine. It was only a stab in the dark that she had anything directly to do with The Artist, and he wanted to wait to tell him at least until Melissa had heard back from Benjamin. "No, not really. There is an art agent in Shreveport who used to represent him. Melissa is waiting on hearing back from him. But we did manage to get the remaining unsold paintings from the galleries in Manhattan. I suspect there will be another bloody Luminol show as soon as we put them under the lights."

Chief Big D stabbed at an egg in disgust. "I can't wait to get this guy, Hank! Hopefully the son of a bitch will try to mail his painting today through a UPS store, and we'll catch him." He wanted to say something about Judith, but he just couldn't bring up her name. "Have a safe flight. I will personally be there at the Pensacola airport to pick you up."

In the mad rush to get the paintings from the galleries, and dealing with Judith's sudden disappearance, Hank and Melissa had completely forgotten about the UPS plan. The Artist was supposed to mail the new panting that Melissa had requested. The flight attendant called Hank's and Melissa's row. "Chief, that's us they're calling. One thing before I hang up."

Chief Big D knew what was coming next. "Yeah, Hank. What is it?"

"I want to go to Judith's house immediately."

Chief Big D sighed into the phone. "Of course, Hank. I was planning on taking you there first thing."

Hank ended the phone call and boarded the plane with Melissa. Thankfully, the flight was far from packed so the bulky mailing tubes containing the paintings had plenty of space in the overhead luggage compartments. The four hour flight was excruciatingly long; Hank drank five cups of coffee to keep himself from dozing while Melissa munched on peanuts and stared nervously out of the window. When the plane finally touched down in Pensacola, Hank was so restless and frustrated that he was ready to jump out onto the tarmac as the plane taxied in. Melissa placed a hand on his arm to steady him. It was all she could do to help; there simply were no words to say.

Hank looked at Melissa and tried to smile at her attempt to calm him. "Thanks." He stared out the window. "I want you with me as much as possible so I can hear first hand if we can contact this Clover Fontaine woman. I haven't told Chief about it yet."

Melissa nodded. "I am not going ANYWHERE without you! I want to help find her. Anything you need me to do, I'll do it."

The plane finally stopped and the seat belt light went off. Hank quickly unloaded the mailing tubes, grabbed his luggage and practically ran towards the front of the plane. Melissa was close behind with her luggage full of paperwork. They were about fifteen minutes early, but as they walked outside, they saw that Chief Big D and Marcus Donnarumma were already waiting for them in an unmarked black SUV. Eager to get to Judith's house, Hank didn't even shake the men's hands; he loaded the mailing tubes in the back of the SUV and quickly slid into the backseat behind Marcus. The ride back to Orange Beach was eerily quiet; no one knew what to say as the blanket of fear over Judith's disappearance weighed heavily upon each person. Hank's hands shook uncontrollably in his lap. He was so preoccupied by thoughts of Judith that he didn't even try to control them. Chief Big D noticed it in the rear view mirror and feared for his detective; Hank was the best he had, but he wondered if he was too emotionally involved to deal with the case. He decided to wait to say anything until after Hank had seen her house. As he pulled into the driveway, Hank jumped out of the SUV before it came to a stop and barreled up the front steps to Judith's front door. Fumbling for his keys, he heard Chief Big D yelling at him from the driveway. "Hank, go on in! It's unlocked, and we have an officer waiting on the deck around back."

Hank pushed open the door and walked through the threshold. The house was dissonantly dark and quiet, the air sending sharp shrills up the back of his neck. Even though he trusted the Orange Beach police department with his life, he had to make sure they didn't miss anything. He slowly walked through the house, checking every room for any signs of struggle. There was nothing, and after fifteen minutes of searching, Hank slumped down on the couch to catch his breath. Chief Big D, Marcus Donnarumma, and Melissa appeared in the doorway to check on him. In silence they watched Hank struggle to swallow back his tears until Melissa finally spoke. "Hank, did you find anything?"

With a painfully hopeless look on his face, he slowly shook his head while staring at the floor. "No. I didn't expect to. I just had to see for myself." He absentmindedly grabbed the decorative pillow that was wedged beside his thigh and the end of the couch. Absentmindedly fumbling through the gold tassels on the pillow with his fingers, he stared at the wall across from the couch in silence. On the wall there was a picture of Hank and Judith fishing. The one next to it had been taken right after their engagement. It was a black and white photo of them at a party on Ono Island. Hank couldn't ignore the pain any longer, and for the first time since the Morrison murders, Hank cried. He lifted up the pillow to hide his face and pressed it to his eyes. Seconds later, the palm of his hand ran across the back of the pillow, and his crying ceased immediately. He held his breath. Turning the pillow over to see what he had felt on the other side, his heart beat accelerated; what he saw rendered him momentarily speechless. He should have noticed as soon as he walked into the room that the pillow didn't belong on the couch; it was specifically bought several months ago for the chair and Judith never touched it or used it on the couch. Chief Big D noticed the look of horror on Hank's face and came running to the couch. When he looked down in Hank's lap, he saw the crusty hardened saliva and nasal discharge that covered the backside of the pillow and Judith's blonde hair stuck in some of the gold tassels. It was the tell tale sign of someone being smothered. This changed everything. Hank was paralyzed with terror as he held in his hands Judith's last efforts to free herself from her kidnapper.

The officer who had been posted on the deck came running inside to see what the commotion was all about. Chief Big D was already grabbing his radio and yelling for back up. He was absolutely furious that the pillow had gone unnoticed until now. Red faced and fuming he towered over the stunned and shaken officer and yelled at the top of his lungs, "Get Hank out of here now!" Then he turned to Marcus. "Marcus, make sure that Hank is put back in the SUV with Melissa, and grab an evidence bag from the back and seal this pillow. I'm calling more units to go over this place again. We need to get to the lab as soon as possible to find out definitely what's on the back side of this pillow. Let's go, people. Move!" Chief Big D didn't need the lab to confirm it. He already knew. He just hoped and prayed that she hadn't been smothered to death.

Chapter Thirty One

Uncharacteristically, Roy had slept in. He didn't mean to, it just happened. He sprung quickly out of bed at noon and checked the monitor of his computer. Cursing himself, he wished that he had set the surveillance system to detect her movement when she woke up. He had wanted to see her when she came out of her drug induced sleep, but he had missed it. There she lay, shackled and gagged, with wide fearful eyes scanning her room of horror. He had also planned to get up early enough to drive into Mississippi to mail the painting, but that had failed as well. He had never once mailed a painting from the local UPS store, and he sat on the edge of the bed, wondering if he should or not. He still had time to drive into Mississippi and find a UPS store before they closed, but that would steal precious time away from what he had in store for Judith. He flipped on the television, sure that he would see the local news station covering Judith's disappearance, but was surprised when he saw nothing. Hurriedly, he dressed himself and cleaned up his painting area. The painting of Judith on the swing was breathtaking; he admired his work for several minutes while Judith twisted fruitlessly in her shackles in the next room. Making sure that it was completely dry, Roy carefully rolled up his masterpiece and slid it inside a mailing tube. Then, at the top of his lungs, he yelled down the hallway, "GOOD MORNING, DR ESTHER! I SEE YOU!"

Judith had struggled to keep her wits during her second round of hallucinations earlier that morning. It had been easier than the first time that she was drugged because she had remembered everything shortly after she woke up. The mirror had been scary, but not as bad as it had been. The worse thing had been the stench of her own urine, the dry heaves from lack of food and water, and fear of dehydration. Now, another fear took over when she heard his voice booming through the house. She cringed at the sound of his voice and waited in pure terror and agony for him to appear in the doorway. When he came into view, she immediately had another convulsion and dry heaved.

With a glass of water in his hand, Roy watched Judith twitch and gag until she was paralyzed with fear. Then he slowly crossed the room to the bed where she lay and violently lifted her head from the pillow. "Drink!"

Judith was terrified of the water. The last thing she wanted to do was dehydrate, but she feared that the water was drugged or poisoned. Either way, she knew that she had no choice in the matter. If Roy wanted her to drink the water, he would force her if he had to. She parted her dry lips and drank some of the water; it burned unmercifully down her parched throat. When she was finished with the water, Roy pulled up a stool and sat down beside the bed. "Dr. Esther, did you enjoy your sleep?"

She didn't want to answer him, but she didn't want to anger him either. She ran her tongue over her lips which had cracked and bled when she opened her mouth to drink the water. "Yes."

Roy stared down at her with unblinking eyes. "What about the mirror? Did it frighten you again?"

She tried to steady her breath and appear as calm as she could. "No, not as bad."

Roy raised a finger and shook it back and forth in her face slowly. "Well, I am sorry to hear that. I was hoping that you had one wild ride this morning." He glanced casually around the room. "I will be gone for a little while. You can make yourself at home while I am away, right?"

Judith felt a glimmer of hope. Was he telling her that she would be freed from the shackles? She nodded quickly.

"I see that you have already found your bathroom." He slid one hand over the wet urine stain on the bed sheets. "When I return, we have some serious work to do, Dr. Esther. You will be my assistant in my next painting. Would you like that?" From behind his back he drew a butcher knife. "I have big plans for you. Don't worry. You will

128

have your very own unique signature on the painting so everyone will know that you helped me. I shouldn't take all of the credit."

Judith gasped for air as she felt the blade of the butcher knife sweep lightly across her fingers, up her arm and across her breasts. Roy used the tip of the knife to lift her shirt up, and then cut it open quickly with a sharp movement of his wrist to expose her bra completely. Judith whimpered in defiance. She wanted to break his concentration somehow, but she didn't know what to say. Finally, she blurted out, "Why am I here, Roy?"

He nodded slowly in approval. "Well, Dr. Esther, I thought you would never ask! You are here simply because I want you here."

"But why do you want me here? Why me?" It worked. She watched as Roy sat back down on the stool with his butcher knife.

Roy inhaled deeply and smiled wickedly. "Well, I saw you one night at the FloraBama, and I couldn't get you out of my mind. So, I decided to kidnap you." He looked at Judith matter of factly.

Judith was confused. She was sure that he had taken her because of the paintings that Melissa had brought to her house. Surely this wasn't just coincidence. She decided quickly to try her luck again. "How did you know where I live?"

Turning it over and over, Roy looked at his own reflection in the blade of the knife and spoke with amusement in his voice. "I recognized your fiancé, Detective Hank Jordan from the all the press from the Morrison murders. Then I noticed your engagement ring. Your engagement picture in the local paper is great, by the way. Such a lovely couple."

Closing her eyes, Judith groaned. "What are you going to do to me?"

Roy laughed and put the knife down on the bedside table. He leaned in close to her face, his lips only inches away from hers. "Well, Judith, what do you think I am going to do to you? You are a smart woman. You are currently shackled to a bed, and I was attempting to expose your breasts with that blade right there. C'mon, you know what I am going to do you, eventually."

Judith shuddered and began to cry. "Please don't kill me, Roy. Please."

He laughed and stood up from the stool. "Ok, Dr. Esther, only if you insist." He turned his back to her and walked towards the door.

"Don't try anything stupid while I am gone. The room is completely soundproof, and you are under constant surveillance. Anyway, I don't think you will be going anywhere." He disappeared through the doorway, and Judith was left alone to comfort herself the only way she could. She started to pray.

Roy returned to his bedroom and picked up the mailing tube. He had made his mind up and decided to go to the UPS store in Gulf Shores just this one time. Apparently, Judith's disappearance was not yet known to the police, and besides, no one knew him. He needed as much time as he could possibly have with her before he had to get rid of her body. He slipped on a baseball hat and shades and pulled in behind the wheel of his van. As the garage door squeaked and groaned on the way up, he made a mental note to spray some WD-40 on it when he returned.

The neighborhood was silent and empty, and he pulled out of his driveway in the direction of Gulf Shores. The heat of the day was intense and humid with absolutely no wind to offer a breeze. Even though his windows were heavily tinted to help block out the brutal sun rays, the air conditioner in the van was slow to cool the interior, and Roy was dripping with sweat after only two minutes of driving. He cracked the window for a cool breeze until the air had chilled inside the van. The drive to the UPS store in Gulf Shores was only twenty minutes away going down Canal Road. He had decided not to go down Perdido Beach Boulevard because he would have had to cross through the State Park for a shortcut, and it would have still taken five minutes longer. As he drove down Canal Road, he watched with casual interest the barges that he passed float quietly through the canal while old men sat lazily on the banks under the shade of trees with idle fishing rods in their hands. Roy rolled his eyes in disgust at them; fishing had never been one of his hobbies. He had had enough of that when he was growing up in the swamps to last him a lifetime. Still, he thought, the scene would make a nice painting in the future. Finally, he reached the end of the road and turned left to access Highway 59 which led through downtown Gulf Shores. Several lights later, he pulled into the side parking lot of the UPS store and grabbed his mailing tube from the passenger seat floorboard. With his hat pulled tightly down on his head and shades on, Roy entered the store with the mailing tube. As he had always done in the past, he silently handed a piece of paper and a twenty dollar bill to the cashier, and waited for his change without saying a word. The cashier took the piece of paper and opened it to read. It listed an address in New York, and also read "overnight" underlined. The cashier entered the address into his computer, and without looking at the computer screen, moved the mailing tube to a mailing room behind a partition. Behind his dark sunglasses, Roy waited patiently for his change in the small front office. When the cashier stepped back from behind the petition and reached the computer, Roy noticed a strange look wash over his face. When the cashier didn't speak, Roy finally broke the silence. "Excuse, me, can I please have my change back?"

The cashier stuttered slightly but managed to maintain his composure enough to be able to follow the rules of his training that he had received only six weeks ago. This was the first time that he had encountered a security alert situation, and it caught him completely off guard. He pointed at the computer screen, as he was told to do in training, and swiveled the monitor around for the customer to see. "Uhm, sorry, sir, my computer is a little slow. We just have to wait a minute to catch up so I can open the cash drawer. Sorry about that. It will only take a second."

Roy looked at the computer screen and saw the frozen hour glass. He didn't suspect anything; sometimes his computer at home did the same thing. From behind his shades, he rolled his eyes at the cashier and folded his arms to wait for the computer to catch up.

The cashier tapped a pen nervously on the counter and stared at the screen. After a minute had passed, he asked the customer, "Sorry this is taking so long, sir. Would you like to speak with a manager?"

Roy impatiently glanced down at his watch and shook his head. "No, that won't be necessary." The room grew curiously quiet, so quiet that he could hear the clock ticking behind the register on the wall. Suddenly, the manager walked briskly into the main office area. He had just received the email alert from the security system on his computer screen; he was shocked that it was happening right there in his store.

"Hi there, sir. My name is Jiles McGhee. I am the store manager. My computer is down in the back office, and I see that this one is as well. Are you waiting for your change and mailing receipt?" With a polite and courteous smile, Jiles masterfully sized the man up and was extremely disappointed that he was wearing shades and a hat. The police should be pulling up any minute, and he struggled not to glance toward the parking lot.

Roy Fontaine was oblivious of everything except the clock ticking. He turned his back on the manager and paced the floor slowly with his head down. "How long do you think it will be?" he asked Jiles.

Jiles spoke carefully and nonchalantly so as not to alert the man in shades. "Oh, probably no more than five minutes at the most. You can have a seat right there if you'd like." He pointed to a chair just as Roy headed for the door.

Five minutes was too long for Roy. The ticking of the clock was driving him insane and he wanted to return home and take care of Judith. He called out to Jiles as he walked through the door, "Just keep the change."

Exactly three minutes had passed since the information had been entered into the computer. It had not been enough time for the plan to work. Jiles immediately locked the doors of the UPS store while dialing Chief Big D's number into his cell phone. He never saw Roy's van pull out of the side parking lot and onto Highway 59 North; it had been parked too far on the side for him to notice.

Chapter Thirty Two

Sherrie, the lab technician, stood over the microscope and confirmed Hank's fears about the pillow. She knew Judith quite well, and was terrified that she had come in harms way. After she finished examining the pillow, she led everyone back to a large research room down a hallway where the paintings from New York had been unwrapped and placed on research tables.

Hank had calmed down considerably since the shock that he received back at Judith's house, although his findings had taken a toll on him. With minimal amount of sleep from the night before, his face was haggard and worn by sadness and frustration. He said nothing as he followed Chief Big D into the research room, but tried to perk up when he felt the Chief's bear like hand stopping him from entering the room.

Chief Big D led Hank instead into a smaller room across the hallway so he could speak to him in private. "Hank, you probably already know what's going through my mind right now."

Looking into his eyes, Hank nodded and spoke softly. "Chief, you can't take me off of this case. You can't do that to me. I know what you are thinking, and yes, I am emotionally attached to her. You're absolutely right about that, but, Chief, I have to take this guy down. I have to find him, and I have to save Judith."

Chief Big D rolled a toothpick over his tongue and grumbled something under his breath while he made his decision. If Orange Beach was dealing with a serial killer on the loose, he could not afford to lose his best detective. On the other hand, he realized the grave danger of Hank messing things up by prioritizing the wrong things. He couldn't blame him if he tried. If it was his own wife out there missing, probably in the hands of a serial killer, he didn't know what he would do. He stared back at Hank and saw the dedication and resolve in his eyes and finally made up his mind. He spit out the toothpick and cleared his throat. "Hank, I am only going to tell you this once. If you mess up in any way, you will be pulled immediately from the case, and Hillary will take your place. Am I clear?"

Hank nodded appreciatively.

"I know you want more than anything to find Judith. God knows, we all do! But you are going to have to find a way to deal with your pain in a productive way right now. You can't work a case like this with too much frustration and grief on your shoulders. It won't help anyone. Do you think you can handle it? Honestly?"

Hank never missed a beat. "Chief, I promise you that you will be the first one to know if I can't handle it; I will personally excuse myself from the case. I want to find this bastard more than anything."

Chief nodded slowly at Hank. The only option he had was to trust him. He opened the door and pointed at the research room across the hallway. "Alright, let's get this show started."

They walked into the room and joined Marcus Donnarumma, Melissa and Sherrie at the research table. Seconds later, Hillary walked in and gave Hank a quick hug before sitting down. The paintings were all depictions of life in Louisiana. Just as Melissa was about to give a detailed description of each of the paintings, Big D's cell phone rang. He checked the id and quickly flipped it open when he saw the number of Jiles McGhee. He frantically waved at everyone in the room to stop their conversations. "Hello? Jiles?"

"Chief, I have got really bad news." Jiles took a deep breath to slow his breathing. "The guy you are looking for was just here! You didn't receive a call?"

Chief Big D's face flushed red with anger. "What? When?" Suddenly, he heard a beep on his cell phone from call waiting. "Hold on, Jiles." He jerked the phone from his ear and looked at the caller id which read Security One, UPS. "Christ! Jiles, hold on, that's them calling now."

Jiles tried to interrupt him but was put on hold before he could say anything. Several seconds later, Chief Big D returned to the phone breathless. "Jiles, are you there? Is he still there?"

"No! That's what I am trying to tell you! I couldn't keep him here long enough! I have the painting!"

Chief Big D snapped his fingers at Hank and Marcus to follow him, and they ran toward the exit of the lab, leaving Melissa and Sherrie behind to wonder what was happening. "Dammit! Ok, Jiles, we are on the way!" He snapped his cell phone shut and repeated the conversation back to Marcus and Hank while they ran toward the unmarked SUV. Hillary stayed behind with Melissa and Sherrie. By the time they arrived at the UPS store, Roy was almost home. Hank was the first to reach the UPS door, having jumped out of the SUV while Chief Big D was putting it into park. Jiles let them in immediately. Ringing his hands nervously as he darted into the back room, he returned several seconds later with the mailing tube and handed it to Hank. Hank ripped open the top of the mailing tube before Chief Big D or Marcus could stop him and the painting fell out onto the floor.

"STOP!" yelled Chief Big D, and the whole room became silent. The painting, still partially rolled up lay on the floor at their feet. Everyone stared at the tips of moss covered trees that were peaking out from the unrolled portion. Jillian Brannon's face had appeared in the painting at Judith's house, and now Judith was missing. In the back of his mind, Chief Big D feared the worst. "Hank, go outside, now."

Hank started to protest. "But, you said…"

"NOW, Hank!" Hank yanked open the door of the store in frustration and stood at the opposite side of the window.

Marcus suddenly understood and closed his eyes while the Chief got down on the floor and unrolled the painting. He opened them only after he heard the Chief's angered and helpless voice say what he had feared. He spoke quietly. "Holy mother of God, Chief."

Chief Big D quickly rolled the painting up and sat down on the floor with his head in his hands. "Marcus, take Hank away from here. Do it now. Take him back to the lab. He doesn't need to see this."

Hank heard him say it. He had walked back into the store as the painting was being rolled back up. Everyone heard his footsteps and turned to face him. With hot tears streaking down his cheeks, Hank pointed at the painting with shaking hands and gulped for air. In between desperate sobs, he yelled. "No! You let me see her. Chief, you let me see her! Show me!"

Chief Big D shook his head slowly back and forth and then finally unrolled the painting back onto the floor. He cringed in agony as he heard Hank scream at the top of his lungs as Judith's face came into view. Hank dropped to his knees at the bottom of the painting and stared helplessly down at the face of his fiancée.

Chapter Thirty Three

Melissa was unsure of what to do. Hank Jordan, Chief Big D and Marcus Donnarumma had left her in the lab with Sherrie and Hillary in such a hurry to get to the UPS store, that she didn't have time to ask what she should do. Surrounded by the paintings in the research room, she sat at the table watching Sherrie work and waited for their return in silence. Minutes ticked slowly by as she glanced down at her watch in anticipation of the Luminol tests on the paintings. Knowing that the paintings were most likely covered in blood masked by paint sent shivers up her spine, and she disgustedly pushed the edge of one of the canvas' several inches away from where she sat. She desperately wanted to call Benjamin back to find out if he had spoken with Ms. Fontaine about The Artist's paintings, but Hank had been adamant that he be present at the time she called. So, Melissa continued to sit in frustrated silence as the minutes slowly passed. Her heart sank as her thoughts quickly led to Judith. She dared not imagine what horrors her friend must be going through, but with the paintings surrounding her, she couldn't help it. Just as she began a silent prayer for her dear friend, the research room door suddenly burst open. Chief Big D, pale and sad, towered in the doorway. Behind him was Marcus Donnarumma and Hank, who hung his head out of clear view. The look on Chief Big D's face spoke volumes to Melissa, even though she still did not know what had just taken place. She bit her lip and anxiously waited for the men to speak.

Sherrie looked up from her microscope and waved them into the room, but Chief Big D remained in the doorway, as if it would support his weight in case he passed out on the floor. Finally, after what seemed like an eternity, he passed through the threshold and slowly sat down at the table. Marcus followed him in and handed him the mailing tube that UPS had taken from The Artist. Melissa hadn't seen the mailing tube at first, and when she saw the transfer, she gasped in horror and looked at Hank's face for the first time.

She whispered in morbid fear. "No, no, no, no. Please. Don't tell me what I think that is." Hillary moved quickly by her side to comfort her.

Sadly, Chief Big D nodded his head and stared at the paintings that surrounded him. "We just left the UPS in Gulf Shores. You know the plan? It didn't work." He slammed his fist down on the table in frustration. "He left before we could get there."

Melissa swallowed hard and looked at Hank's swollen red face. "And the painting?"

Unblinking, Hank focused his bloodshot eyes on Melissa and grit his teeth in agony. "It's her, Melissa. It's Judith in the painting."

Melissa quickly buried her face in her hands and began to cry. Sherrie came around the research table and huddled around her to comfort her as Chief Big D reopened the mailing tube. His big hands shook as he slid the rolled canvas from the end and placed it onto an empty spot on the research table. He glanced quickly back at Hank for confirmation that he was ready for this, and Hank nodded back in silence. With her eyes closed and her face still buried in her hands, Melissa could hear the painting being slowly unrolled, and she cringed in anguish. To the unknowing eye she knew that the painting would be lovely to look at as she remembered so many times before being enthralled with The Artist's latest work. But now, it was different. She feared that the painting would reveal the face of her best friend, dead at the hands of its creator. From what seemed far away, she heard the voice of Hank speaking to her in the background. Her head was spinning, and his voice turned into the sound of rushing water. In an effort to stop the sound and catch her breath, she opened her eyes and caught a glimpse of the painting before she collapsed in a panic attack. For a fleeting second, she saw Judith on a swing underneath a tall moss covered cypress tree, and then everything went black.

About a minute later she came to. Hillary held a brown paper bag to her face, and Melissa concentrated on breathing in and out to control her breath. Everyone in the room was silent, waiting for Melissa to calm down from the panic attack. When she finally was able to get her breathing under control, she slowly lowered the bag from her face and concentrated on the painting of Judith. Hank interrupted the silence and placed a hand on Melissa's back. "Are you okay?"

Melissa nodded. "Yeah, I think so." She shook her head sorrowfully at the painting. She had been right. The painting was indeed beautiful, perhaps The Artist's best work to date. "I am ready to do this."

Marcus and Sherrie began to work quickly, spraying Luminol on each painting that rested on the table and chairs that occupied the room. When the last painting was sprayed, Sherrie walked to the door and flipped the light switch. To no one's surprise, the entire room glowed eerily in bright blue chemiluminescence as each painting proved to contain blood infused paint. During the short time before the blue light faded away to darkness, the sight was unimaginable to all those who sat in the research room, and confirmed once again, all of their fears. The Artist was a serial killer, and he had taken Judith from them in a blink of an eye.

Sherrie flipped the light back on to reveal the chalky white expressions on each person's face. Hanks red eyes were glued to the image of Judith in the painting on the table, as if she would disappear forever if he looked away. Melissa was the first to speak. "Chief, I need to tell you something. Well, Hank and I both do."

Chief unlocked his stare at the opposite wall and focused on Melissa. "Go ahead. I'm listening."

"I spoke to Benjamin Preston, the owner of the art gallery in Shreveport, Louisiana, late last night about some old paintings that he had sold for The Artist years ago. He used to represent him way before I did. Anyway, Hank found something interesting in the paperwork that I think you need to know about. We don't know if it's important, but it might be."

Chief Big D leaned toward Melissa with growing interest and nodded. "Okay, what is it?"

"Well, there is a woman by the name of Clover Fontaine who took a very serious interest in The Artist's paintings way before he became famous. According to his records she bought what we think might be a strangely large quantity of his works over time, especially when he first appeared on the market. She has even purchased them since I have been his agent."

Hank held up his hand and interrupted Melissa, who was more than appreciative; her mouth was still dry from her panic attack. "Chief, we don't know if Ms. Fontaine is of any importance, but we think she might know who the guy is."

Confused, Chief Big D scratched his head and tried to make a correlation. "Why would you think there is a chance of that, Hank? So, a woman likes his paintings. I don't get what you are trying to say."

Hank took a deep breathe and asked him the same question he had asked Melissa the night before. "Well, it's just a hunch. But right now, it's all I have. Imagine that you are an unknown artist, trying to sell your paintings for the first time."

Chief Big D nodded. "Okay, now what?"

Hank sat down at the table and stared at Judith in the painting. "Who would be the one person in your life who would buy your paintings and support you before you made a name for yourself, before you became famous, and continue to do so over the years?"

The confusion suddenly disappeared from Chief Big D's face as it dawned on him what Hank's hunch was. "My mother, Hank. She would be the only one."

There was no excitement in Hank's voice. He was too distraught to find any pride in his hunch. He replied flatly. "Exactly."

"Well, let's get her on the phone, then!" Whatever enthusiasm Hank denied himself, Chief Big D felt it ten fold. What Hank had just asked him made perfect sense to him, even if it did turn out to be untrue and unimportant.

Melissa spoke this time. "That's why I wanted to tell you now. You see, Benjamin Preston is waiting for my phone call as we speak. He assured me that he would speak to Ms. Fontaine today and ask her if it was okay for him to give us her phone number." She quickly explained to Chief Big D her and Hank's master plan to get the paintings from the galleries by pitching them a lie of a showcase of The Artist's works. "He warned me that Ms. Fontaine may want to remain an anonymous buyer. In the art world, that is not uncommon."

Chief Big D shook his head defiantly and raked his chair away from the research table. "Well, I personally don't give a rat's ass if she wants to remain anonymous or not. If we want to talk to her, then I can assure you that we will, whether she wants to or not!"

Hank spoke. "Chief, I think it would be unwise to get in touch with her right now against her wishes. I mean, what if she is his mother? What if she knows the truth about his paintings? What if she is helping him to hide? I think we should let Melissa try to contact her first under the false pretenses of interviewing her for a biography on The Artist for the showcase like we initially planned."

Chief Big D thought about Hank's response for a few seconds and calmed down. "Yeah, you have a point." He stared at Melissa. "Ok, go ahead and call this Benjamin guy and see what she said to him."

Melissa flipped her cell phone open immediately and dialed the number to Benjamin's art gallery. He answered on the first ring. "Melissa?"

Melissa swallowed hard. "Hey Benjamin! I am calling back like I said I would last night. Did you get a chance to speak with Ms. Fontaine about The Artist?" She crossed her fingers.

"Yes, I did. Sweet lady, Clover is. But so shy!"

"Well, what did she say? Did she agree to the interview?"

"Not exactly, Melissa. She does want to remain an anonymous buyer. However, she did say that she had no problem at all with you taking a look at her collection. She told me that she even has paintings that date back before I was his agent, and I was sure that I had been the first one!" Benjamin laughed good naturedly into the phone. "I jokingly asked her if she knew him, hoping that finally, I could get a picture on this guy after so many years, but she said no, that she was just an admirer of his work."

Melissa was in luck; she gave Hank the thumbs up sign. "Okay, Benjamin, thank you for helping me. Do you have her number and address?" Melissa jotted down the information on a sheet of paper while Benjamin rattled on about The Artist and his wonderful talent. "Did you just say Bogalusa? I guess I just assumed that she lived in Shreveport."

"No, honey, she lives in Bogalusa, Louisiana. She always has since I have known her. She said that the storage unit where she keeps his paintings was completely missed by Hurricane Katrina, so you are in luck!"

"Thanks, Benjamin! I'll call you and let you know how it goes." Melissa closed her phone and smiled at Hank and repeated everything Benjamin had said. "How far is Bogalusa from here?"

Marcus replied. "About three hours."

Chief Big D sized Hank up. He needed to get him away from Orange Beach, away from Judith's house, so he could be productive to the case. "Hank, you and Melissa call this woman up and head out. Drive over to Bogalusa and meet her. I want to know who she is. I want to know everything about her. If you suspect anything, you better call me immediately. We will run her name through the system and see if anything comes up."

Hank wanted to stay in Orange Beach more than anything, but the look of grim determination in Chief Big D's face kept him from arguing, especially after he had ripped into the mailing tube at the UPS store. He had absolutely no choice if he wanted to remain on the case and help find Judith. Mustering up the strength to reply and push his feelings aside, Hank responded to his demands. "Yes, sir, Chief." He glanced down at Judith on the swing one more time, and then quickly led Melissa into the hallway and out the front door.

Chapter Thirty Four

Judith heard the garage door creak open. While Roy was gone, she had tried in vain to free herself from the shackles until her wrists had bled. To keep her sanity, she concentrated on thinking of ways to escape if Roy happened to free her when he returned. She had made her mind up to go for the little black bag that contained the Ketamine if she could get close to it, and pump him full of the nasty drug. Her heart raced as she heard a door open and shut, followed by the sinister footsteps of her kidnapper. She dared not to fake sleep for fear that he would only wake her by jerking the chains that were connected to her restraints, further injuring her ankle. She held her breath and waited for whatever would happen next. The footsteps grew louder and louder as he neared her door, until she could hear him breathing on the other side.

Roy stood quietly in the hallway studying the unfinished murals on both sides of the walls. It needed a lot of work before it was finished; perhaps he would never finish, and it would be an ongoing project like his old house in New Orleans. His initial plan for Judith had been to rape her and dispose of her body as quickly as possible, but while he had painted her into the picture, he decided that he would keep her around a little longer. Not to keep him company! Roy had always been a loner. He decided to keep her so he could use her to create more artwork, and he couldn't think of a better place to start than on the hallway murals. He placed the side of his face to the door and asked, "Dr. Esther, are you ready to work? I have big plans for you today."

He didn't need a reply, and simply returned back down the dark hallway to the kitchen to prepare his paints. Once in the kitchen, he removed Jillian Brannon's frozen skewered fingers from the freezer to thaw in the sink, then collected the paints from a selection in the pantry and set them on the kitchen counter. To this collection he added the clear glass jars of blood from the refrigerator, including the fresh blood that he had taken from Judith earlier. At once he became aroused at the thought of watching Judith mix paint with Jillian's fingers and paint with her own blood. It would be fascinating, he thought, to observe the reaction that she would have as she truly entered his world for the first time. He secured the skewered fingers in a plastic bag and placed them in a bowl of warm water to accelerate the thawing process, then walked to his bedroom to get ready for his next creations.

Judith wondered in fear where he was and what he was planning. Work? What was she supposed to do? What did this psychotic painter have in store for her? Did he want her to pose for another painting? Was he planning to drug her again? Her thoughts, coupled with the lack of food, made her dizzy, so she concentrated on her own heartbeat and breathing to calm her nerves. It was the only thing she could do to keep herself from going insane. The house was completely silent for a long time. She had no clock from which to tell, but she guessed that at least thirty minutes had passed since she first heard the garage door open. Finally, from somewhere in the background, she heard the faint sound of running water. It lasted several minutes, and then she heard more footsteps.

Roy stepped out of the shower and toweled off. He had been so hot during the drive to the UPS store that he had sweat straight through his shirt from the armpits, leaving a soured onion smell behind. He admired his clean milky white body in the full length mirror in his bathroom as he ran a comb through his thick brown hair. It had been awhile since he had cut it, and long wet uneven strands clumped together around his pasty white face and neck. He didn't mind his hair being long, but it had been a while since he had stepped out into the heat of the Gulf Coast sun. From a drawer underneath the bathroom sink, he found an electric hair clipper and plugged it in. From front to back, Roy shaved his entire head, allowing the wet clumps of dark hair to fall on the floor at his feet. Several times, he cut his head with the electric blade; he was used to it though after years of cutting his own hair, and didn't mind the pain. Tiny trickles of blood seeped from the small cuts and trickled down the back and sides of his head, making him look like he had just removed a crown of thorns. When he was finished, he marveled at his bald white head sprinkled with bright crimson and smiled at his reflection. When he was young, his mother had shaved his head during the hot summer times and would occasionally nick him with the blade in the process. He had always liked the way it looked before she would wash the blood off; he preferred it there.

Judith had noticed the humming electric sound of the clipper and panic welled up in her throat. Wild morbid thoughts of sadistic electrocution ran through her mind as she envisioned Roy placing her into a cold bath tub and throwing something into the water to kill her. Then, the buzzing had stopped, and she was able to breathe again. Shackled to a bed and waiting helplessly for the unknown was slowly stealing her sanity. She tried desperately to shake off the constant fear that would grow inside of her with each distant sound that Roy made. The next thing she heard almost sent her over the edge, and she whimpered in horror. It was a scraping sound on the walls, that started down the hall way and grew closer and closer to her with every footstep that Roy made.

Roy reached the door to Judith's room and slowly turned the doorknob. The unlit hallway cast a shadow on his body so when he appeared in the doorway, all Judith could see was the dark outline of a man holding something strange in both of his hands. Then to her immediate horror, Roy Fontaine emerged from the dark shadow and into the bedroom light. What Judith saw rendered her completely speechless as she stared into the face of complete and total evil. His naked body appeared whiter than before, as it was contrasted sharply by the glazed crimson blood that had partially dried on his bald head and neck. In his hands he held tightly between each finger, the skewered fingers of Jillian Brannon, so that they appeared like extensions of his own.

Roy snaked his way toward the bed, scraping the fingers along the footboard of the bed and up the comforter to where Judith lay squirming in vain to try to get away. Sobbing with tears, she shut her eyes and held her face away as far as her restraints would allow her to until she felt the bloody fingers touch her skin. Then she screamed louder than she had ever screamed in her life. It surpassed any scream of any woman that Roy had ever murdered, and it left him impressed and in awe. He had known in his wicked heart that Judith would turn out to be something special, and closed his eyes as he listened to her scream; for him, it was like music from a symphony. The more he touched her with the fingers, the louder and more desperate her cries became. With the excitement of a child with a brand new toy, he poked her with the fingernails over and over again until Judith completely lost her voice and her will to survive.

Judith was completely void of energy; she was so weak that she could no longer lift her head from the bed. She panted hotly like a beast before slaughter and stared with empty eyes at the wall across the room. Roy disappeared for several minutes, returning quickly to her bedside with a plate of sardines and crackers and a glass of water. He had seen the same look as Judith had in her eyes in many women before, and he was not about to allow Judith to give up so easily. There was absolutely no fun in that for him if she did. It would be like killing something that had already died. He needed her to remain scared and willing to beg him for her life if he was going to execute his plans the way he wanted to.

He unlocked one of her ankle restraints with a key from the bedside table, but she didn't move. Careful to avoid her kicking him in the head with a sudden burst of adrenaline, he yanked on the other restraint that held her injured ankle. The pain ripped through Judith's body and brought her back to reality. At first she didn't realize that one of her ankles had been freed, but it slowly dawned on her as her vision became clearer as the fiery pain subsided into a dull throb. She looked at Roy Fontaine who was perched beside her on the bed and wiggled her leg for the first time since she had been kidnapped.

Roy thrust the plate of food toward her face. "You haven't eaten anything since you arrived." He ran a knife over the tiny fish on the plate, moving them around in their slimy bed of fish oil. "I am going to unlock your restraints so you can sit up and eat. If you try anything, I promise you, Dr. Esther, that I will slit your throat so fast with the blade of this knife that you will still be blinking in confusion as your head hits the floor. Do you understand?"

Judith weakly whispered, "Yes."

146

With the blade of the knife between his teeth, Roy placed the plate back down on the bedside table, and worked his key into each one of the restraints. At first Judith didn't move for fear that it was some kind of mind trick, that he would kill her in an instant if she did; she didn't trust him. Delighted that he was still able to instill fear into his captive, Roy flashed a fiendish toothy grin through thin pale lips as he observed her uncertainty. He pushed the plate onto the bed. "Sit up and eat. Now."

Judith weakly rolled over to one side and tried to support herself on one arm, but it gave away fast as she fell back onto the bed. Taking a deep breath she wiggled her arms by her side to encourage blood flow and tried again; this time she was successful, although she felt a wave of nausea as soon as she was upright. She gagged reflexively and fought it until the feeling passed. From the sitting position she was able to see her surroundings from a better view point, and she concentrated on the floor as she breathed deeply in and out to steady herself. The floor was littered with dried paint that morphed across the room like some ill planned graffiti of a three year old child. After she got her bearings and was able to breathe normally, she took the plate of fish and soggy crackers without looking at Roy, and placed it on her lap. She had grown used to the smell of dried urine that she had laid in for so long, but now the smell hit her strongly in her nostrils as she shifted her weight on the bed for a better position. It reminded her of the time when she was in high school and volunteered at the local nursing home. She pushed the thought from her mind and concentrated on her food. If she had any chance to get out of this house alive, she had to eat and get her strength back. In the condition that she was currently in, she wouldn't even be able to make it off the bed, much less to the doorway. Using her fingers she picked up the slimy little fish and forced them into her mouth, quickly following each bite with a cracker and a sip of water. Although she was hungrier than she ever remembered being before, she ate slowly and purposefully, scanning the room for anything that she could use to escape. Stealing a cracker from Judith's plate, Roy watched her eyes in silent amusement.

Chapter Thirty Five

Pulling onto Interstate 10 West, Hank floored his pick up truck until he was passing vehicles at close to eighty miles an hour, and then slacked off the gas pedal in fear of being pulled over by the State police. He didn't want to have to explain the details of the case to anyone outside of the few people who already knew about it. Chief Big D wanted to keep Judith's disappearance quiet for as long as they could, so they could have a chance to get a decent lead on The Artist before the press started covering it. The plan at the UPS store had failed miserably; Jiles hadn't even gotten a look at The Artist's vehicle. They had nothing to go on except a surveillance video showing a man with dark brown hair in a hat and sunglasses, and Hank prayed that this Fontaine woman would help lead them to him. Melissa had wanted to contact her immediately, but Hank had talked her into waiting until they got closer to Bogalusa, so the woman would be less apt to change her mind since they were already there. Hank saw Judith's face everywhere he looked, in the rearview mirror, in the dashboard; he couldn't stop himself from imagining what was happening to her now or if she was already dead. Lost in his own world of horror and fear, he didn't notice that his speed had crept back up to eighty five miles an hour. He called Chief Big D on his cell phone to let him know that they were getting closer. He also wanted to find out if they had learned anything about Clover Fontaine when they ran her name through the system. Chief Big D answered in a frustrated voice. "Hank, where are you?"

148

"Hey, Chief. We just pulled onto Interstate 10. Did you run Clover's name?"

"Yeah, we got nothing, Hank."

Hank sighed wearily into the phone. "Ok, Chief. I'll call you as soon as we finish talking to her." He hung up the phone and drove in hurried silence.

Melissa finally put her hand on his arm to get his attention and spoke softly to the man in agony. "Hank, please slow down."

He glanced down at the speedometer and eased his foot off the gas pedal again. "Sorry, Melissa. I guess I just can't wait to get there. I have a feeling about this woman. I don't know exactly what it is, but I believe she is going to be able to help us somehow."

Melissa glanced down at her watch. "When do you think I should call her?"

"We are probably an hour and a half away." Hank thought for a moment. "I'd say call her in about thirty minutes. When you get her on the phone, remember what we talked about before. Make sure to tell her that you have driven several hours to meet her and that you are right outside of Bogalusa, just in case she is thinking of postponing it."

Melissa nodded her head. "Okay." She watched the passenger window as the first drops of an approaching afternoon thunderstorm fell and raced across the glass in the wind. Lighting struck ahead in the distance and thunder rumbled across the southern Mississippi skies. "I really hope you are right about this woman, Hank." She wiped a tear away quickly before it fell down her check, careful to hide it from Hank. He was dealing with enough stress already, and the last thing she wanted to do was add to it, especially since he was behind the wheel driving directly into a thunderstorm.

Suddenly, the rain came pouring down, and Hank quickly switched the windshield wipers on high to help him see the road ahead. It was a blinding rain that forced several cars to pull over on the side of the interstate. Nervously, Hank slowed down to fifty miles an hour to keep from wrecking and sailed past the slower cars in the right hand lane. After a while, the storm subsided enough to lower the speed of the windshield wipers, and Hank pressed the gas pedal to regain his speed once again. Melissa realized that she had been gripping the door tightly throughout the worst of the storm and eased her grip as Hank sped up.

The interstate sign for Highway 49 North came into view and Hank crossed over to make the exit. Thankfully, they were heading away from the storm for good. "Go ahead and call Ms. Fontaine."

Melissa fished through her purse for her cell phone and paper that listed Clover Fontaine's phone number and address. "Are you sure?"

"Yes, I am sure. We are probably less than an hour away."

Melissa punched in the number and waited for the woman to pick up, but there was no answer. An automated voicemail picked up, but Melissa didn't leave a message. She would try again in a few minutes. "No answer, Hank. What if she isn't home? What if she went somewhere and doesn't return until later?"

Hank sighed. He knew there was a chance of this happening. "Well, then I guess we will wait in her driveway until she returns. Just keep trying to call her until we get there." He reached over to the dashboard where his GPS system was located and turned it on. "When the screen is ready, type in Ms. Fontaine's address and hit enter. We will drive straight to her house."

Melissa positioned herself toward the GPS and waited for the screen to appear. She was typing the address when her cell phone began to ring. She read on the screen that it was Clover Fontaine's number so she hurriedly opened the phone. "Hello?"

A frail and quiet voice of a woman spoke softly back. "Hello. Did someone just call me from this number?"

"Yes, Ms. Fontaine? Hi, this is Melissa Edwards. I am calling you about your extensive collection of The Artist's paintings. Benjamin Preston in Shreveport gave me your number. How are you today?" She held her breath for an answer and strained her ears to hear the quiet voice.

Cover Fontaine cleared her throat and responded with concern in her voice. "Yes, Ms. Edwards. Benjamin told me you would be calling. Uhm, when did you want to meet me?"

This was what Melissa had been waiting for, and she slowly exhaled her pent up breathe. "Well, I was hoping that we could meet now, well, not literally now, but in, oh, the next thirty minutes or so."

As politely as she could, Clover declined at once. She wasn't prepared for this yet. From her conversation with Benjamin the previous night, she had been under the impression that a date would be made, so she could have time to get everything ready. "No, Ms.

Edwards, it's too short of a notice. We need to schedule it for a different time, perhaps. How about tomorrow, or the next day?"

Melissa grimaced at Hank as she heard the words that he had feared she would say. "Are you sure Ms. Fontaine? I mean, I apologize profusely for such short notice. But with the show coming up in the next few days, I only had a little time to spare to put together a biography on The Artist. You own more of his paintings than anyone else, to my knowledge, and it would be a shame not to be able to include your thoughts and information in this biography. I have been on the road for several hours in a huge thunderstorm already to get to you. Are you sure we can't meet?" The elderly woman on the other line sounded so sweet, and guilt spread over Melissa's conscious.

Clover quickly assessed the situation. Everything she had purchased by The Artist was in a climate controlled storage unit across town. If she left her house right now, she might be able to pull off what she needed to do to prepare her collection, but it would be close. "You say you are thirty minutes away?"

Melissa crossed her fingers. "Yes ma'am."

Clover sighed heavily into the phone to let Melissa know that she was a bit irritated. "Okay, then, but you have to give me more time. The storage unit is all the way across town. And another thunderstorm is coming this way."

"How much time do you need, Ms. Fontaine? I would be more than happy to wait for you to call me back. Maybe I could drive into Bogalusa for some quick sight seeing while I wait."

Clover sighed in relief. That worked out much better. She could drive over to the storage unit, clean up a bit, and meet Melissa back at her house. "Wonderful, dear. I will call you shortly."

Melissa repeated the conversation to Hank as he turned onto Highway 26. The rain had completely stopped for the time being, and the sun's rays broke though the clouds ahead. Hot steam billowed up from the pavement as Hank raced toward Bogalusa. He checked his GPS. "Only forty more miles to go."

Chapter Thirty Six

The sun over Bogalusa disappeared quickly behind thick dark clouds as the afternoon thunderstorms finally arrived. Irene Clover Fontaine looked up through the blinds and grabbed an umbrella from the stand beside her front door. Her eyes moved to a picture frame on a table beside the couch, and she softly whispered to the man behind its glass. Her husband, the man who had saved her from a life of self destruction had passed only a year ago, and Irene missed him desperately.

Right around the time when her son had turned seventeen, her addiction to methamphetamines and the fear of her own son had completely taken over her life. Her son was a terribly demented person and Irene had always known it. She had always blamed herself for not helping him while he had been young. From as early as she could remember, her son had shown all the signs of being a psychopath. He completely lacked remorse for anything or anyone in his life; he was manipulative and conning in nature, completely antisocial, and executed strange and bizarre behavior that had often scared Irene. The night of his thirteenth birthday had solidified Irene's fears about her son when he gave her a bloody gift that he had wrapped in her nightgown; it had been the cut out eyes of a neighbor's dog, which was later found mutilated, tortured and dumped on the side of a road close to her house. From that night on, Irene had stayed as far away from her son as she possibly could, drowning herself in whatever she could find to escape reality until she couldn't bear to live with him anymore. All

152

those years ago, she had finally packed some bags and left him behind, moving in and out of trailers and drug dens until she ended up on the dirty streets of New Orleans, broke and homeless. Her only possessions had been a few dirty garments and a suitcase of her son's artwork that she had managed to steal from his bedroom the night she vanished. For months she had struggled to survive, sleeping in parks under bushes and on the dirty banks of Lake Ponchatrain in makeshift homeless camps. Occasionally she would have the strength to stumble into various homeless shelters for a few nights for some free food and a cot to sleep on. There she would meet other addicts, form a quick friendship for access to drugs, and fall back into the harsh clutches of the streets. She had done just about everything to kill herself in those days; meth, crack, prostitution and various other forms of self destruction and poison. She had hated herself to the point where she didn't care anymore if she lived or died.

Finally, late one afternoon, much like this one, Irene had staggered through the doors of a small church to escape an approaching thunderstorm. The church was not known as a homeless shelter, but it had been the closest building around. Dragging her only possessions in ripped faded bags, Irene had found a bathroom inside the church, curled up in a corner stall, and passed out. Sometime during the night, a church janitor had found her while cleaning the bathroom. He had tried to wake her, but Irene was lost in a drug induced sleep that would take hours to wear off. Frightened that the woman was dead, the janitor had phoned the priest of the church and informed him of the situation. By the time that the priest had arrived, the janitor had picked Irene up from the floor and carried her to a church pew. Throughout the entire night, that priest and janitor sat with Irene and prayed for her soul, until she woke in the early morning hours. She had been scared and confused at first, thinking that the men were there to rape her and steal her possessions. She had kicked and screamed until she had no more energy, and finally gave up her defense as the men held her down on the pew. When she had realized that the men were not going to hurt her, Irene opened her eyes to her surroundings and noticed for the first time that she was inside a church. A beautiful statue of the Virgin Mary had stared down at her with loving eyes, and a nun appeared by her side.

For the next few weeks, the janitor, priest and several nuns had worked hard to nurse Irene back to health until she was detoxified from the poisonous drugs that had run through her veins for so long. Slowly, over time, Irene had gained energy and weight to fill in her sunken cheeks and thin frail body. The church gave her odd jobs here and there, which over time helped Irene gain the self confidence that she needed to stay sober and face reality after years of running from it. During her recovery, the janitor had fallen in love with Irene, and she with him. He was the first man in her life that had truly loved and protected her. He had been there with her every step of the way, from feeding her soup, to supporting her when walking, to walking beside her in the park after she became healthy again. Eight months after he had found her curled up on the floor beside the toilet in the church bathroom, he had asked Irene to marry him to which she said yes. They had a small private ceremony in the church that had helped give her life back to her and eventually moved to Bogalusa where they opened up their own janitorial business. It had been extremely successful, and Irene, for the first time in her life, had been happy and content; however her son, whom she had left behind, still haunted her mind. She never told her husband or anyone else the truth about him or the paintings that were found by the nuns in her bags. Instead, she had told them that they were the paintings of a friend's child who had tragically died. She always suspected that her husband never believed her. Out of love and respect for her painful past, he never questioned her, not even when she began buying paintings that were signed the same way as the ones from her past: The Artist.

It had been a pure coincidence when Irene Fontaine had stumbled onto her son's artwork in a small art gallery on Bourbon Street. Unlike the demented and twisted imagination of his youth, the paintings had been beautiful renderings of life in the swamps of Louisiana. She had immediately known it was her son's artwork, not only from his signature, but she also recognized his familiar style, after watching him as a child paint for so many years. The beautiful paintings had given Irene hope that day that her son had turned out to be normal and productive. Even when she had asked the gallery manager about The Artist, and learned that he was an anonymous painter, she lied to herself like she did when he had been a child: that he was a loner, and that's just the way that he was. That had been the first day that Irene bought her son's paintings. Over the years she followed his work from gallery to gallery, never once trying to contact him; one reason was because she harbored a huge amount of guilt for leaving him behind. The other reason was one that she would never allow herself to face, and that lingered in the back of her mind at all times; she feared that her son was still and always would be a monster.

Now, as she prepared for the first time in her life to share her collection of her son's artwork with someone other than her husband, she stared down at the face in the picture frame and whispered to him softly, "I love you." The only paintings that she would not share were the ones from his youth. Tattered and faded from years of being drug around the dirty streets of New Orleans, the morbid disturbing scenes were still in fairly good condition; good enough to make anyone wonder about the sanity of their creator. She needed to get to the storage unit and hide them from the art agent. After so many years of hating what he had become, she still loved her son, and did not want to do anything that would taint his reputation as such a wonderful inspiring artist. She opened up her umbrella and stepped out into the rain.

Chapter Thirty Seven

Judith stared helplessly down at the empty plate. She had eaten as slowly as she could to buy time before whatever Roy had in store for her next, but the food was now gone, and she had to face him. Sitting naked with blood streaks still dried on his newly shaven head, he had watched her eat in complete silence from a stool next to the bed. On several occasions he laughed at her, and Judith could only imagine what was going through his psychotic mind. For now she was just thankful that the skewered fingers of a dead woman were not in sight. Unable to stall him any longer, she drank the last sip of water from her glass and placed it on the bedside table. The food rumbled in her stomach as it went straight through her system, and she shifted slightly on the bed as a harsh wave of diarrhea swept over her body. She wondered if he had poisoned her and instinctively rubbed her stomach.

"Did you enjoy your dinner, Dr. Esther?"

A violent cramp struck hard in her intestines, and she weakly replied. "Yes. Thank you." Slumped over, she stared down at her legs while wrapping her arms around her midsection to help relieve the cramps. "I need to go to the bathroom, please." She hated to beg this monster of a man for anything, but if she didn't get to a bathroom soon, she would be sitting in more than just urine.

Roy didn't mind urine, but he detested feces. "Of, course you can go to the bathroom. I will personally escort you." Roy rose from the stool and held his arm out toward the doorway. "Get up and walk."

Judith unwrapped her arms and stared at the dark doorway, wondering what new hell waited to greet her outside the room. She weakly swung her legs out of bed and tested her strength with one foot before she stood up. She wasn't completely sure that her ankle wasn't broken. Nausea hit her in the gut like she had been punched, and for a split second, she felt as if she was levitating from the bed. The feeling quickly subsided as she acclimated to being completely upright, and she carefully pressed both feet to the cold hardwood floors beneath her. Gripping the edge of the bed for support she took several slow steps toward the door, taking advantage of each second to scan the room from a different view point. From wild imagination she found herself searching for claw marks on the floor and walls, or any other sign that someone else had been held captive inside the room before her; she found nothing but dried paint on the floor. Not paying attention to where she stepped, she suddenly tripped and banged her injured ankle hard into the side of the bed frame. The searing pain immediately brought her to her knees, and she held on tightly to the bed sheet as she gasped for breath. The wound on her ankle reopened and blood trickled slowly to the floor as she tried to pick herself up. Roy stood behind her laughing and kicked her backside to encourage her to keep going. Fearing that she would not get to the bathroom in time to relieve herself and wincing in pain, Judith finally managed to stand up again and limp toward the dark doorway. As she walked through the threshold and into the darkness, it took several seconds to get use to the unlit hallway. When she was able to see, she wished that she couldn't. She wanted to run as fast as she could past the horror of what stared back at her from both walls of the hallway. Death surrounded her as unfinished murdered and desecrated bodies morphed and bled into each other like swirling scenes of hell just waiting to suck her up into the paint and capture her forever. Roy had returned some of the pictures that he had shown her earlier to the walls, and the misery and torment on the dead women's faces seem to scream at her in agony as she limped slowly by. She passed a Polaroid picture that he had not shown her earlier, and the image of the dead woman lying in the sand made her pause with fear. Judith immediately looked away before alerting Roy that she had recognized the woman. She closed her eyes briefly as she remembered the severed fingers that Roy had poked her with while she had been shackled to the bed; she knew now that they belonged to Jillian Brannon, the girl who was found dead in the dunes behind Pelican Perch Condominiums.

Roy snuck quietly behind her in the dark like a panther waiting to pounce on her back. As she neared the end of the hallway, he came up so close behind her, that she could feel his hot breathe on the back of her neck. She dared not turn to face him, and painfully kept walking until he grabbed her around the waist with both arms and picked her up from the floor. Judith panicked and froze in fear. He hugged her brutally to his naked body and licked the back of her ear before he spoke. "You are walking too fucking slow."

He carried her kicking and screaming to the end of the hallway, rounded the corner to the bathroom and threw her onto the cold tile floor. Her hip hit the side of the bathtub, and Judith scrambled desperately on the floor to stand back up again. Somewhat blinded by the pain, she raked her hands through fist fulls of wet soggy hair that Roy had left on the bathroom floor before she realized what it was. Horrified, she shook her hands violently to get rid of the hair that stuck to her, as if it were thousands of snakes full of venom slithering up her arms. The more she shook, the more the clumps separated and multiplied. Roy leapt into the bathroom and turned on the bathtub full force until there was enough water to hold Judith's face under. While she was still ringing her hands and screaming, he picked her up and dunked her head in the rushing water for several seconds before bringing her up for air. He repeated this several times before Judith was able to beg him to stop. Finally he did, and she slumped down on the floor in silence. The water had brought her back to reality. There were no snakes in the bathroom, only hair that Roy had shaven from his head. Judith stood up and stared at the toilet, and then back at Roy who stood once again in the doorway. She knew that he was going to stand there the entire time, so she didn't even bother to ask for privacy. Humiliated and disgusted, she quickly pulled her pants down, careful not to expose her private areas to him, and sat on the toilet before she ran out of time. When she was finished, she pulled her pants back up with shame and degradation and flushed the toilet. The water in the bathtub had actually helped to clear her mind a little, and she glanced around the bathroom. Suddenly, she caught a glimpse of herself in the mirror. She stared back at herself, almost denying to herself that her reflection was real. There were dark swollen circles under her eyes, and her cheeks were puffy and red from crying. Her lips were cracked and dry, and she watched herself lick them to moisten the skin. From behind her, Roy appeared in the mirror. She watched as he held a knife up to her throat. The blade felt cold and menacing as he swept it across her skin, and she dared not move for fear that it would slice her throat open. She closed her eyes and listened.

"Dr. Esther, I am quite surprised that your face isn't all over the local news. Tell me. Why isn't your fiancé looking for you?"

Judith gulped hard against the blade as she searched her mind for the best answer. She knew in her heart that the Orange Beach police department would know by now that she was missing, and that Hank was probably desperately searching for her. She could only hope that they would find out who The Artist was in time to save her. Suddenly, she realized that she was supposed to be on vacation with Melissa. She spoke softly and carefully. "I am supposed to be on vacation right now. But he will realize that I am missing soon, and he will come looking for me."

Roy laughed as he swept the blade slowly across her neck and face. "Come looking for you where?"

Thinking of how Hank must feel, Judith cringed and tried to hold back her tears. She had no response for his question; she wasn't even sure that she was still in Orange Beach. For all she knew, she could be in another state. She needed time. Time to think. "Please, can I shower?"

Roy exhaled slowly and pondered her question. He didn't want to give her too much freedom; he needed to remain in control at all times. However, after her accident in the bed coupled with the stench of raw fear and sweat, her body odor had deteriorated and was certainly less than appealing. He would prefer her cleaner for what he had planned for her. Roy stared hard into Judith's eyes and searched for any signs that would keep him from allowing her to bathe. He took the sharp point of the knife and pressed it into her left cheek, just shy from piercing her skin, and quickly surveyed the bathroom for anything that she could use as a weapon. He had been in this situation plenty of times in his old house in New Orleans, but never here. The bathroom had not been properly set up for what Roy considered a "houseguest". He finally lowered the knife from her cheek and pointed to the bath tub. "Get in and lie down on your stomach."

With a flicker of hope, Judith immediately obeyed. She crossed the tile floor, pushed back the shower curtain and entered the bath tub. When she was finally positioned as best she could on her stomach, Roy quickly raided the bathroom, removing anything that he thought could be used against him. There wasn't much, but he didn't want to take any chances.

Chapter Thirty Eight

Irene Clover Fontaine pulled her car into the designated parking spot for her storage unit. The afternoon thunderstorm had worsened on the way over, and the rain pelted down hard on her windshield. Grabbing her umbrella from the passenger seat she opened the door quickly and bolted across the parking lot toward the metal door of the storage unit. It had been several months since she had last visited. When her husband had been alive, she would visit often, to dust and clean the paintings and be with her son the only way she knew how. It had always been comforting for her to walk through the maze of his beautiful creations, and lie to herself about his true nature. Denial had become the foundation for her past; she had been able to kick the drugs and live a normal life, but she had never been able to face the truth about the child that she had brought into this world. As soon as her husband died, the storage unit was no longer a source of comfort for her. It had become a mirror that offered reflections of the life that she had ran from years ago. Now, when she walked past the paintings of lovely women and scenes from the swamps of her past, she only wondered who the women were, and why her son had painted them. Each face was completely different, and no matter how beautiful the scenery was in each painting, something seemed sorrowful in the expressions of the women that her son had exquisitely painted. She had always recognized it, but had never been strong enough to question it. Once, long ago, she had picked up a newspaper from New Orleans and read about several missing prostitutes. One of the missing prostitutes was named Trina, a name and face that Irene could never erase from her mind. As soon as Irene had recognized the prostitute's face as being one of the women in several of Roy's paintings, she had quickly disposed the newspaper in a trash can on the streets of New Orleans and vowed never to read one again. She had stood there beside the trash can and forced herself to reject the idea that there was any correlation between her son's paintings and the missing woman and finally walked away in complete denial. Until this day, Irene had still not picked up another newspaper from New Orleans, for fear that she would see another familiar face.

With her umbrella held tightly between her arm and side, Irene stood in the rain fumbling with the lock to the storage unit. Finally, she got the key into the hole and turned it. The locked popped open and she lifted the metal door upwards to get inside. The room was dark and pounding as the rain poured down on the metal roof above her. To Irene it sounded like a thousand heartbeats pulsing together. Manipulated by the rain and wind howling outside, the shadows of the draped and covered paintings hovered on the dark concrete floor like fluttering ghosts. She shuddered as she flipped the light switch and closed the door behind her. The first order of business was to clean and dust the paintings and frames. It would take longer than usual since it had been a while since the last time she came. She lifted a white sheet from one group of paintings and swiped a finger across one of the wooden frames. It wasn't nearly as bad as she thought it would be. She closed her umbrella and crossed the room to a plastic storage bin on the left wall where she kept her cleaning supplies. With a dust rag in one hand and wood cleaner in the other, she began working up and down the maze of paintings, taking great pains not to stare into the women's eyes. Whenever she came upon a likeness of Trina, the missing prostitute from New Orleans, she would concentrate too hard on the frame, unconsciously rubbing the finish off the wood more and more each time, while ignoring the painting completely. Fifteen minutes later, each painting was shiny and clean and ready for the agent to view.

While she had worked, she debated on what to do with the real reason she had initially denied Melissa access to the storage unit on such late notice. In the back of the storage unit, was something that resembled a morbid shrine to The Artist. When she had been homeless on the streets of New Orleans, Irene had kept the demented paintings of her son's youth hidden and protected in bags that she carried with her at all times. After she met her husband, Irene had kept the paintings under lock and key in a wooden crate in the back of the storage unit. The week after her husband had died, Irene had removed the paintings from the crate and spread them all over the back of the storage unit so that she could for the first time in so many years, look once again at the only things she had saved from her past. It had been an extremely painful moment for her that day, and until now, Irene had not found the courage or strength to place the paintings back into the crate. She felt that if she did, she would be closing the door to that part of her life forever, and now that her husband was gone, it was the only family that she had left.

She walked past the cleaned paintings, picking up the drapes and sheets from the floor as she walked, until she reached the back of the storage unit. For a long time, Irene stared at what was left of her son. The bloody images of her son's mind called out to her from the floor and walls. Her sorrowful eyes fell onto a faded scene of a gutted dog and a grinning boy with a knife in his hand. Then she glanced above it to see what she had always known in her heart to be a portrait of herself that her son had painted shortly before she left. The woman in the painting had big blue eyes bulging from the taunt rope that wound around her neck. A knife was stuck in her side and blood spilled out of the wound into mid air. Her feet and hands had been cut off and lie on the floor around her. Another painting caught her attention as Irene began to cry in silence. It was a picture of a smiling boy swimming in a swamp of bloody water, with a dead woman hanging from the limb of a cypress tree above him.

Irene became slightly dizzy and knelt on the floor to catch her breath and calm her nerves. She didn't want to touch the paintings. She couldn't move them. No matter how many times she looked at them, it became increasingly difficult for her to handle them with her bare hands. Carrying them around in bags and boxes was easy, but touching them with her fingers had always been a nauseating experience that grew worse as she got older. She checked her watch and breathed deeply in and out. It was time to call Melissa back. She unfolded one of the white sheets and carefully spread it out over the paintings on the floor. It took three sheets to cover them all. If the agent asked, she would simply tell them that she hadn't had time to fold them before they came. She glanced one more time at her morbid portrait, and then quickly covered it with the edge of the sheet.

Chapter Thirty Nine

Forcing himself to believe that every mile that he drove brought him closer to Judith, Hank entered into Washington Parrish and drove to Bogalusa. It was all he could do to save her. He passed a sign that read "The Magic City" as he entered the city limits. The rain had picked back up again, and he turned on his windshield wipers to clear his view of the city. The mechanical voice of the GPS system directed him through downtown and onto several streets toward their destination, and Hank had to physically restrain himself from going over the painfully slow speed limit of thirty five miles an hour. According to the GPS, Clover Fontaine's address was only five minutes away. The drive through the small streets was silent except for the rain on the windshield, the puddles of water on the side of the street splashing up on the right side of the truck and the monotonous voice of the GPS.

Suddenly Melissa's cell phone rang, and they both jumped nervously at the sound. Seeing Clover Fontaine's number on the screen, Melissa quickly opened the phone. "Hello? Ms. Fontaine?"

"Hi, Melissa. Yes, this is Clover. Are you in town yet?"

"Yes, ma'am. We just got here."

There was a slight pause on the line. "Who is we? I thought you were coming alone?"

Melissa quickly replied. "Oh, I am sorry, I didn't tell you. I brought my assistant with me." She wondered why this would even matter to

Ms. Fontaine and shot an inquisitive glance toward Hank. "Is that okay?"

Clover stood in the storage unit and glanced around at the paintings. This was the most private part of her life, and for the first time she was sharing it with someone other than her husband. "Yes, that would be fine. I am at the storage unit right now. I know I said I would meet you at the house, but you might as well come here." She gave the address to Melissa.

Melissa gave Hank the thumbs up. "Thank you, Ms. Fontaine. We will be happy to meet you there, whatever is convenient for you." She typed the address into the GPS keypad as Clover spoke. "Ok, Ms. Fontaine, we are on our way."

Hank made a u-turn in the middle of the street and headed back toward downtown. This time, he couldn't stop himself from speeding and prayed that he wouldn't get pulled over. Ten minutes later, he thanked God as he pulled into the parking lot of the storage unit. The rain had eased up to a light and erratic sprinkle as if the clouds above were wringing themselves out like dish rags. He looked through the windshield at the only open unit and saw a woman waving back at them.

Melissa waved back and spoke to Hank. "Okay, here we go. Act like my assistant. No cop face. We have to find out if she knows The Artist without alerting her."

Slightly irritated at Melissa telling him what to do, Hank nodded and tried to put a smile on his face as he followed Melissa toward the woman in the storage unit. The rain mist felt icy on his pale and drawn face, and he wiped it from his forehead quickly, as if to stop it from weaving an evil web over his eyes. He had to remain calm and alert for any signs that would lead him closer to Judith. Glancing quickly behind the woman at the paintings in the room, he smiled as Melissa introduced him and herself to Ms. Fontaine. He took Clover's hand and shook it with little interest as the faces of so many women stared back at him from the canvases inside. He thought about the painting of Judith being unrolled onto the floor of the UPS store and shuddered slightly.

Melissa noticed the tension in his face and quickly caught the older woman's attention by walking inside to the paintings. She reached out to touch the first one that she came to, a scene of fishing boats tied to the dock of a small bait store.

Irene quickly ran between Melissa and the painting and put her hands up to stop her. "Please!" She inhaled slowly and offered a small laugh to cover up the intensity of her voice. "Sorry, but, Miss Edwards, I have to ask that the paintings not be touched. Please, thank you." Irene glanced away momentarily to overcome the awkwardness of the situation.

Melissa quickly brought her hand back to her side and gave an understanding smile to Ms. Fontaine. The last thing she wanted was for the woman to feel uncomfortable. "Oh, no need to apologize, Ms. Fontaine. I completely understand."

Irene nodded quickly and smiled back in relief. "Thank, you, Miss Edwards." She turned her back to them and faced the paintings.

Melissa opened a pad of paper and grabbed a pen from her purse. "Please, call me Melissa."

"Ok, Melissa. You can call me Irene, I mean, Clover." Puzzled that she would have introduced herself by the name that she had for so long not used, Irene Clover stood with her back still turned to her guests in silence. "You can call me Clover, Melissa." After she had met her husband the morning that she had woken up inside the church years ago, she had promised herself that she would turn over a new leaf and never use that name again. And she hadn't, not one time, until now. Even as she mistakenly spoke her own name, her skin crawled and she felt dirty, like she had for so many years before being saved. Irene's days belonged to drugs and filth and arrests. Clover's days belonged to love, hope and a new beginning.

Hank almost tripped over the edge of one of the frames propped up on the floor as he heard Clover speak of a different name. He studied the back of the woman, her rigid and uncomfortable posture, and lack of words. There was something bad about the name Irene, and he knew it. He said nothing, allowing her to believe that neither he nor Melissa had caught it.

Melissa caught it as well, and gave Hank a quick look before she ended the silence. "Well, Clover, where would you like to start?"

Composing herself as best she could, Clover turned to face her guests. "Wherever you like, dear. What do you want to know?" She spread her arm out over the room covered with paintings.

166

Melissa needed to get her talking and pump her for information under the pretense of creating a biography on The Artist's paintings. "Well, let's see." Melissa scanned the room quickly. "Let's start on the far left and work our way across the room. I will take a picture of each one while you give a description of the painting and when and where you purchased it. Anything else you would like to add on your own will be greatly appreciated. As you well know, The Artist is extremely admired, and I would love the chance to bring the full attention that he deserves for his life's work and tremendous contribution to the art world."

Clover completely forgot about uttering her first name, and fell into the familiar pit of denial; she smiled and beamed with false pride as Melissa spoke so highly of her son. Even though she knew in the back of her mind that it wasn't real, it felt so good to hear praise for her son and his talent. She happily crossed the room to the far left and immediately began reciting facts about the paintings and where she had purchased them. As she spoke, she grew more and more comfortable with Melissa and Hank, and began sharing her personal thoughts about each painting and what she thought The Artist might have felt and thought at the time of its creation. Her descriptions grew more and more detailed as she played out the fantasy of what she had always dreamed of; to speak highly of her son to anyone. She was careful though, not to disclose the fact that he was her son. Very careful. She only referred to him as she had trained herself to do a long time ago, The Artist.

As she spoke, Hank quickly took pictures of each one of the paintings from different views with Melissa's digital camera and pretended to be enthralled with what Clover Fontaine was saying. He listened intently for any clues as he snapped away at the camera and smiled back at the now delighted woman. She seemed completely mesmerized by the paintings around her. Hank wondered what her reaction would be if she knew that she was literally standing in a maze of canvases that were probably covered with remnants of blood from The Artist's victims, whose faces he painted into the scenery like one last punishment for crossing his path. The more pictures he took, the more restless Hank became. The faces of too many women swirled around him like the faces of dolls coming to life, and he could see Judith in each one of them. He wanted to pin the chatty woman down and demand to know if she knew who The Artist was. He felt like time was running out, and that he would never find Judith. Finally, when he could take no more of the descriptions that became increasingly longer and useless, he walked across the room to where Clover and Melissa were standing. Melissa realized too late that Hank was going to interrupt her. Hank smiled in determination and placed a hand on Clover's shoulder. She stopped abruptly in the middle of a sentence about how serene the swamps appeared in a painting and turned around to face Hank. She smiled, still caught up in the pleasure of speaking about her son. "Yes?"

Melissa tried again to stop what was getting ready to happen by also touching Clover's arm and giving Hank a pleading but stern look. He ignored her and focused intently on Clover. "Ma'am. I can't help but notice that you speak so fondly of The Artist. For years people have tried to figure out who this mysterious man is. Do you, by chance, know who he is, Clover?"

The smile on her face vanished in an instant; it was immediately replaced with fear faintly masked by fake bewilderment. Hank saw right through it. He knew that she knew him before she denied it. Clover cleared her throat and laughed nervously. "Of course not! No one does!" She uneasily pretended to wipe dust off the corner of a frame to hide her anxiety, and resumed her description of the painting.

Hank ignored Melissa and slipped out of the entrance to call Chief Big D while Clover had her back to him. The gravel parking lot was steamy after the rain, and the humidity almost choked Hank as he pulled the collar of his t-shirt away from his clammy neck. His fingers shook as he punched Chief Big D's number into the phone. He whispered as loudly as he could when Big D answered the phone. "Chief? Hurry, run Irene Clover Fontaine, Clover Irene Fontaine, and Irene Fontaine, all in Louisiana. I will call you back in a minute."

Chief Big D, excited by the urgent tone in Hank's voice quickly agreed. "You got it, Hank! We're on it."

Hank quietly snapped the phone shut and walked back into the storage unit. To cover his absence, he quickly finished taking pictures and caught up again with Irene and Melissa, who gave him a questioning look. "Well, looks like I have taken all the pictures we need for the show. Too bad we can't find out who The Artist is. We sure would love to put a face with a name. Thanks for your time, Ms.

Fontaine, but we really need to get back." He turned to Melissa and smiled. "Melissa, do we have everything we need?"

Melissa stammered. She wasn't expecting Hank to give up that easily. Something must have spooked him, she thought. "Uhm, well, I guess so." She scanned the room one last time. "Clover, it was really nice to meet you. Thank you so much for you time and help. The show should be a huge success, thanks to you." She reached out to shake Clover's hand as Hank patted her back, signaling that he was more than ready to leave.

Clover was completely clueless. She smiled and shook Melissa's hand. "I can walk you both out."

Hank held a hand up and smiled. "That won't be necessary, Clover. You have done enough to help us. We need to get back on the road; it's getting pretty late, and we have quite a drive ahead. Would you like for me to close the door behind us when we leave? It's awfully steamy out there, and I would hate the air to affect the paintings." He hoped to trap Clover in the storage unit until he could call the Chief back.

Everything was happening so fast, and Clover wasn't ready to leave yet. The paintings had to be recovered with the sheets, and she still had the task of placing her son's old paintings back into the crate. She shrugged her shoulders questioningly at their sudden haste to leave. "Uh, sure. I have to clean up here and recover the paintings. Go ahead and pull the door down behind you." She didn't quite think they were being rude, but something about their behavior wasn't normal. While she wondered, Hank and Melissa were calling out goodbyes as they disappeared behind the closing metal door. She jumped as the bottom of the door hit concrete and sealed her inside, leaving her alone with her son's artwork.

Once the door was closed Hank rushed to the truck to call Chief Big D back; Melissa ran to keep up with him. The hot Louisiana sun beat down ferociously as they crossed the steaming wet gravel. As she ran, the heel of one of her shoes found sticky mud beneath the loose gravel and became stuck as she ran right out of it. She quickly turned around, grabbed the shoe and hopped to the truck in time to witness Hank's phone call. Breathless and ignored, she waited as patiently as she could.

"Chief, did you find anything out?" Hank breathed hard into the phone.

"Hank, if I had to wait another minute, I was going to call you back. I've got a rap sheet a mile long on an Irene Clover Fontaine. She got into a lot of trouble with drugs and some prostitution years ago, mostly in New Orleans. We crossed her name with birth records from Louisiana, and found that she gave birth to a son whose name is Roy Fontaine, no middle name or initial. We ran Roy's name, and found nothing."

In Hank's mind flashed vivid imagery of a faceless man named Roy holding down Judith on her couch before kidnapping her. He shook his head violently and closed his eyes. He pinched the bridge of his nose between his thumb and pointer finger and listened to Chief Big D read from Irene's arrest records. When Big D was finished, Hank spoke. "She is in the storage unit now, Chief. We have seen all of the paintings, taken pictures and notes, and I just left her in there. She thinks we are gone. I am going back in right now. I will call you as soon as I have spoken with her."

Fumbling for his badge in the folded visor of his truck, Hank quickly snapped the phone shut and placed his pistol and holster on his belt. He repeated everything to Melissa as he slid out of the driver's seat. "Stay here, Melissa. If I am not back in five minutes, call the Chief."

Hank snuck back up to the storage unit and pressed his ear to the door. From somewhere in the back of the unit, he thought he heard the sobs of a woman crying. Slowly, he lifted the metal door and walked back inside the storage unit. He followed the sobs through the maze of painted women and swamps until he found Clover crumpled on the floor in front of her son's paintings of death. Not sure if she was even aware of his presence, Hank unsnapped his holster and steadied one hand on his pistol as he called out to her. "Irene Clover Fontaine."

Clover never flinched. Her shoulders sagged pitifully under the great emotional weight that she had carried for so long, and she sobbed to herself as it was finally coming an end. "He is my son. Roy Fontaine, The Artist, is my son."

Hank kept his hand on his gun as he knelt down beside the hunched over frame of Clover. "My name is Detective Hank Jordan, Clover, and I desperately need to find your son."

170

Clover didn't speak immediately. She sucked in a long tattered breath of air between sobs and shook her head in despair. She could no longer hide from the truth of what her son really was; it was finally time to face it. "He killed those women in the paintings, didn't he?"

Hank bit his bottom lip to keep from crying. "Yes, he did, in ways that you can't even imagine. And now he has my fiancée."

The words he spoke nearly crushed the life out of Clover as her eyes grew wide with horror. She looked out over the sea of faces of the beautiful women surrounding her as the truth came barreling towards her like a ton of bricks. She was surrounded by death at the hands of her own son. Irene Clover Fontaine, the mother of an artistic serial killer, finally found the resolve to look into Hank's pleading eyes. "I will do whatever you need me to do."

Chapter Forty

Detective Hank Jordan led Clover Fontaine through the maze of her son's paintings toward the exit of the storage unit and appeared in the doorway just in time before Melissa called Chief Big D on the phone. She watched as Hank supported the frail woman's frame and gingerly walked her across the steaming gravel to the truck. The look of overwhelming delight in Clover's face had faded into complete misery, wrecked by sorrowful tears and gasping breaths as she hobbled along and leaned on Hank for support. Stepping slowly from the passenger seat, Melissa placed a hand over her mouth and nervously sucked in humid hot air through her fingers as she realized that she was looking into the face of The Artist's mother. As the two approached the truck, Melissa held the door open for Clover to get in as Hank helped her into the seat.

Hank did not allow the uncomfortable silence to linger. Bound and driven by uncontrollable fear that he would not be able to save Judith in time, his hands shook wildly as he called Chief Big D back to tell him the news. Melissa bit her lip in silence as the call connected; the five seconds ticked by incredibly slow.

"Hank?" Chief Big D asked excitedly. "Is it her?"

"Yes sir, it's her. Her son, The Artist, is Roy Fontaine. She is in the truck, and willing to cooperate anyway that she can." Hank choked up slightly at what he was about to say next. "Chief, I have to find Judith, man."

Chief Big D and the rest of them had sat around the lab for four hours while Hank and Melissa had been gone, debating on the best way to handle the situation. If they announced Judith's disappearance, it might cause The Artist to disappear, or worse, if he hadn't already done it, kill Judith. None of them had been able to come up with the perfect solution. Chief Big D listened as Hank tried desperately to cover his emotions. "I know, Hank. I know. Now that we have her in our custody, we can move forward to try and find this guy. Do you have any ideas?"

Hank thought for a minute as he gazed through the windshield of his truck at the storage unit, and suddenly an idea popped into his head. He slapped the wheel with his palm, causing Melissa and Clover to jump. "That's it! We draw him out! It's perfect!"

"Whoa, Hank. Slow down. What are you talking about?"

"The show! The one Melissa has been lying about to everyone to get his paintings for samples for the lab! We can actually have a show. We can pull it off quickly; God knows we have plenty of paintings now to showcase!" Hank motioned excitedly to Melissa who had already caught onto his plan. "Chief, you know how he reacted to the phone call that Melissa made to him about the fake buyer and how much money he was willing to pay him for another painting. He was so pompous and prideful! Just think about how he will react if Melissa calls him to tell him about the show. If it's local, he might show up! "

"Hank, you may have stumbled on something. Okay, get back here as soon as possible. We'll all be waiting for you at the lab."

"Got it!" Hank scrambled to close the phone and step out of the truck. Within seconds he dashed back across the gravel and flung the metal door of the storage unit up. Driving Hank's pickup, Melissa followed close behind while Clover sat limply in the passenger seat. Between the two of them, they loaded as many of the paintings into the truck that the bed would hold, including the old tattered ones from Roy's youth,.

Clover, finally able to catch her breath, offered some help as they placed the last painting into the bed of the truck. In a feeble voice, she called out to Hank through the passenger window. "Detective, look in the bin that I keep on the far left wall. There should be a tarp. I use it when I transport paintings that I buy."

Hank hurried to the wall and lifted the cleaning bin open. Nestled under several bottles of cleaning solution was a folded blue tarp and bungee cords. It took several minutes to secure the paintings before Hank had the chance to thank Clover for her help. As he put the truck into reverse, he placed a hand on her shoulder and spoke softly to her. "Thank you, Mrs. Fontaine. I know this won't be easy for you, but I have to find your son before it's too late."

Clover responded with a silent nod, and then trained her eyes on something that didn't exist, far away into nothing. As the truck bolted out of the parking lot, pieces of gravel flew everywhere. Pinned between Hank and Clover, Melissa sat in the middle, holding onto the seat between her legs as Hank maneuvered the truck onto the road and headed out of town. Her mind was reeling with ideas for the show that they would have to put on at the last minute, and she wondered if they would be able to pull it off without Roy Fontaine getting suspicious. It would be solely up to her to contact Roy about the show. Judith entered her thoughts, and Melissa pressed her lips in determination to help find her friend. She would do and say anything to make it happen. She interrupted Hank's silence. "So, how are we going to do this?"

Hank shook his head. "I honestly don't have a clue on where to begin. I was just thinking about it right now. What are you thinking?"

Melissa realized that she was still clamping her hands around the bottom of her seat, let go and sat straight up. She brushed her damp hair from her face and concentrated on everything that had taken place. "Well, for starters, we have to find a place to have it. I don't know the area that well, and I have no contacts there. We need an art gallery, or maybe even better, a small banquet room at a hotel."

Hank nodded in thought. "Wherever it is, it's going to have to be small, but not too small to raise suspicion. The only person that knows what this guy looks like is Clover." Hank realized that he hadn't even asked her what Roy looked like and leaned over the steering wheel to glance at her. "Clover, do you have a picture of Roy?"

Irene shook her head sadly. All that she possessed since she left him so long ago were memories of his face. "No, I don't. All I took with me when I left were some of his paintings. I can tell you what he looked like when he was seventeen."

Hank sighed in frustration. "Ok, we can have you sit down with a sketch artist when we reach Orange Beach." He turned his attention back to Melissa. "I am thinking that the best place to have it would be at the Perdido Pass Lodge. They have a small banquet room at the end of a corridor that would be perfect for something like this. I guess we are going to have to run the risk of this leaking out to the press, but I have to believe that he will show up! Chief Big D will put the fear of God into the hotel manager not to let his employees know what is going on, and we will just have to trust that he won't say a word to the press or anyone else."

Melissa nodded and reached for a pad and pen from her purse to take notes. "Ok, what about people attending the show? Do you know enough people trustworthy enough to keep their mouths shut and pretend to walk around the show and admire his paintings? If we are going to be able to pull this off, we basically have to have 'actors' to a certain degree. It's not an uncommon practice. A lot of gallery owners use people to walk around shows. More people means more money. It attracts others who think something is a big deal if they see a lot of people there."

That was something Hank had already thought of. "I think that between the Orange Beach Police and Gulf Shores Police, we could probably have as many as fifty people there, some in on the secret, some not. Again, we will just have to rely on Chief Big D's persuasion. I don't know of a single person who doesn't respect the hell out of that man, and this is such a tight close knit community; I really believe we will be able to pull this thing off."

Melissa jotted down notes as Hank talked. "What about a banner or a sign? We have to have some things that give it legitimacy. Flower arrangements? We must have decorations of some kind. It has to look appealing and professional."

Hank turned quickly onto the interstate. "Write this down. We can definitely rely on Jiles McGhee at the UPS store for signs and banners. He already knows some of what is going on, and Chief and him go way back. As for the flower decorations, Hillary, my partner, would be able to help with that. Her sister Caitlin owns a local florist. I think that pretty much covers it. What else?"

Melissa hated to ruin the plan, but she had one fear about something that would cause Roy Fontaine to stay clear of the show. She also hated to bring up the painting of Judith. "Hank, you know that Roy went to the UPS store in Gulf Shores to mail that painting. Remember that he takes great pride in being anonymous. Do you think that having it Orange Beach would be too close for his comfort? I mean, if he does live in the area, wouldn't that be a little too coincidental, especially after he killed Jillian Brannon and kidnapped Judith?"

Hank drove in silence for the next five minutes. It had entered his mind as well, and he wasn't entirely sure that his idea was the best, but it was all that he had. The last thing in the world that he wanted to do was spook Roy Fontaine and run the risk of never finding Judith alive. He had to exhaust all other options before turning to the public for help by announcing that Dr. Judith Esther had been kidnapped, and that they finally had a lead on Jillian Brannon's killer. He looked at Melissa who was patiently waiting for his response. "I don't know what to say, Melissa. I don't have any other ideas than this one."

At that point, Clover interrupted. "You should use Benjamin Preston to assist you. He was one of Roy's very first agents. I am sure that he would help."

Melissa was interested in the concept. It would certainly add validity to her announcement when she called Roy; after all, Shreveport was not far from Orange Beach. "Clover, how well do you know Benjamin?"

"Well enough to know that he is an honorable and trustworthy man. I know he would help." As much as it pained her to know that her son was the monster whom she had always feared, it still hurt deeply to know that she would be helping to trap him. They would probably give him the death penalty, and she cringed at the thought of her son dying. Still, the knowledge that he had more than likely killed all of the women that he painted into his paintings, coupled with the fact that he had kidnapped the Detective's fiancée, fueled the overwhelming desire inside her to help others as well as her son. His capture would literally be his only hope of salvation.

Melissa sketched out a plan on her notebook and made a side note that contacting Benjamin Preston for help was definitely an option. "Hank, what do you think?"

Hank chewed his bottom lip and glanced in the rear view mirror as he passed an eighteen wheeler. "I think we need to come up with as many ideas that we can until we get back to the lab. I want to put as many options on the table that I can so that we can come up with a definite plan and execute it before night fall. Obviously it will too late to do it tonight, but we can damn sure make it happen tomorrow." He punched the gas and sped down the interstate toward Alabama.

176

Chapter Forty One

Roy Fontaine had completely stripped the bathroom of anything that Judith could use as a weapon against him. He had even removed the shower head from the metal pipe that protruded from the wall in the shower stall, and cut off the hot water. Judith stood naked and shivering, trying to crouch under the small stream of icy cold water that cascaded down from the pipe. The bar of soap he had given her was covered with strands of his hair, and unable to remove them all, she recoiled each time she used it on her body. Although she tried her best to keep her swollen foot propped up on the side of the shower wall, the cold water abused her injured ankle to the point that she felt like she would vomit each time a drop of water hit it. Her misery did not end there. Seated upon the toilet was Roy Fontaine himself with the menacing knife still in his hands, watching every move that she made in complete silence. At times he appeared bored with the whole thing, and other times his sinister eyes were glued to her naked body as if he were ready to slash her throat at any given second. She kept her eyes closed for the most part so that she could pray to God for some kind of intervention, and also so she wouldn't have to see the evil look on his face when he stared at her.

With her eyes closed, Judith wondered where Hank could be. She wondered where she could be. She guessed by the length of time that she had been unconscious when he first kidnapped her that she could literally be anywhere from Alabama, Mississippi, Louisiana, Georgia or Florida. She desperately hoped that since Jillian Brannon was found dead in Orange Beach, this was where she still was. Then, she suddenly recalled what Roy had asked her earlier about why her disappearance had not made the news yet. That meant that he was watching local news, either by television or via the internet. She hoped so much that it was the former; that would mean that she is either in Orange Beach or close to it, and close to Hank. Although she didn't believe in telepathy, as a last resort to communicate to the outside world, Judith closed her eyes tightly and talked to Hank with her mind. She repeated the words in her head over and over again. "Hank, save me. His name is Roy Fontaine."

She was so lost in the repetition that she didn't realize that her lips were silently moving or that she had stopped shivering or crouching under the icy cold stream of water. Roy noticed her strange behavior and after watching her with slight amusement, he finally interrupted her by turning the water off. That immediately brought Judith back to reality, and she cursed herself for being so unaware. She was not ready to face what was next, and here it was, staring her in the face; the shower was over.

Roy shoved a dirty yellow bikini towards her on the tip of the knife's blade, stabbing at her in mid air while smirking. Judith dodged the blade several times before she took the hint and grabbed at the strings dangling down from the knife. In her hands she held what she knew was the bikini of Jillian Brannon, perhaps Roy's latest victim before herself. It was splattered with dried blood from the stab wounds that Roy had inflicted upon her before her death, and one of the strings was separated from the bottoms from where he had ripped it from her body as she lay in the sand dunes behind Pelican Perch Condominiums.

Roy sat back down on the toilet to watch her dress. "I have cut a hole in the side of the bottoms so you can tie the string back on. I do hope it fits you, Dr. Esther. If I recall correctly, the woman it belonged to was not so far from your measurements, well, maybe a little bustier." Roy sucked on his teeth as he reminisced about Jillian Brannon.

Still standing in the shower, Judith fumbled with the hole until she was able to thread the string through and tie a knot. Then she quickly slipped the bottoms on first and then the triangle top, as she could not bear one more second of being naked in front of him. Her eyes, covered with wet strands of hair, were wild with fear as she awaited the next step of her torture at the hands of the madman seated before her. What she saw next was truly terrorizing. From the floor beside the toilet, Roy retrieved a black leather collar studded with silver spikes and a stainless steel hoop dangling from the middle. Attached to the hoop was a long black leather braided leash with a cuff at the bottom through which Roy slipped his own wrist. He held the collar out to Judith. "I also brought you some accessories."

Judith stared hopelessly at the collar as she took it from him. On the inside of the collar were two small stainless steel prongs, that when placed around her neck, would press against her throat on either side. She knew far too well why they were there, and choked back tears before she pled with him. "Please do not shock me, Roy. I don't have to wear this. I promise, I will obey you."

Roy crossed his legs and leaned forward. "Well, if you are going to obey me, then put the collar on! Use the mirror so you can attach it properly." He motioned for her to get out of the shower and stand in front of the mirror above the sink.

Unable to refuse him for fear of death, Judith stepped out of the shower and stood in front of the mirror. She put the collar on backwards so she could buckle it in the front.

"Tighter!"

Judith jumped, ever ready for the shock. She nervously pulled it tighter around her neck, threaded the ends through the silver buckles, and pulled the front side around from the back so the buckles were on the back of her neck. From the mirror she watched as Roy quickly slipped a small luggage lock on the buckle and clamped it shut. With one hand, Roy dangled the key to the lock in front of her face and pulled hard down on the leash with the other hand. Watching the key dangle, she wasn't ready for the sudden jerk, and a split second before her chin came crashing down on the edge of the porcelain sink, Roy jerked the leash violently upward again. The sudden movements caused her vision to go blank for several seconds and she stumbled backward into him against the wall. Then she felt her first shock. It launched her forward again toward the sink with the help of a push in her back, and her stomach slammed into the edge of the sink. She wasn't sure if it was the electric shock from the collar or the brutal collision with the sink that knocked the wind out of her, but either way, she grabbed both sides of the sink with shaking hands and fiercely gasped for air. Between gasps she saw the knife resting on the back of the toilet, and wished she could grab it and stab him, but it was no use. He would shock her again before she even came close to reaching it.

Roy laughed as he watched Judith try to regain her balance after the shock. He also noticed her staring at the knife on the back of the toilet; he left it there within her immediate reach just for sheer amusement. After the fun had subsided, he leaned his face close to hers and peered at her in the mirror. "Dr. Esther, I believe it is time for you to meet my other ladies, my 'beauties', if you will." He held his arm out to usher her toward the bathroom door. "Walk straight out and turn left. Pass the hallway entrance and keep walking until you reach the dining room." Roy gave the leash a small tug. "And remember the shock along the way."

Judith took a deep breath and quickly glanced in the mirror, not knowing if it would be the last time she saw herself. She turned toward the door and slowly limped. By now the searing pain in her ankle was not the only reason that Judith worried about her injury. Looking down along the way, she noticed an angry red circle spreading all around the cut, and she feared infection. As she passed through the doorway, she did exactly as she was told and took a left turn. She passed the dreaded hallway with relief but also with great anxiety of what she was about to encounter. He had just spoken of his beauties. She wondered in horror if there could be other women in this house besides herself; she wondered if she was, in fact, in some sort of torture chamber that he kept for his victims before he killed them. Shuddering at the possibility, Judith kept limping until she arrived at the entrance to the dining room. She could only see half of the room from where she stood, but she saw enough to know that there were no other women waiting to meet her. Instead, she saw more pictures decorating the walls around a dining room table. Some were small, and others had been enlarged and strategically placed around the room. She felt the leash pull taunt as Roy passed her to take the lead, and she had no choice but to follow him into the strange room. Unlike the hallway, this room told no tales of bloody crime scenes or beheaded victims. These pictures were, in fact, paintings of women's faces. She followed Roy's lead through the threshold of the doorway and entered the room.

Scanning the room slowly to take in every detail, her eyes fell on the only two fully painted murals that were not pictures. Captured in painted ornate frames, both women had been exquisitely painted on the wall. The woman in the gilded golden frame to the left was unknown to Judith; however, the woman posed in the silver frame to the right was none other than Jillian Brannon. Judith stared sadly at the smiling woman's face surrounded by colorful hibiscus flowers as Roy led her closer for a better view.

"Dr. Esther, meet my two beauties, Jillian and Sharon." Roy waited for her response.

Judith nodded her head and stared at the beautiful women on the wall. "I already know who Jillian is. She's the woman found dead in the sand dunes. Did you kill her?"

Roy smiled with delight. "Yes, I did. It was lovely, but too quick. I so would have enjoyed her company a little while longer, as I have had with you, Dr. Esther. You see, I really don't get out much. I am a very busy man." Roy played with the leash like it was a jump rope, causing Judith's head to bob up and down, while he stared up at his masterpieces. "Would you like to be added to this wall? I have asked many before you, and no one has said yes yet." Roy snickered at his own attempt at humor.

Judith tried to look away from the wall, but a small tug at the leash was all it took for her to look back. As Roy had anticipated, she did not answer him. Instead she asked him a question, just to keep the conversation going. "Who is the woman beside her? You said her name is Sharon?"

Roy let the leash go slack in his hand as he whistled up at Sharon. "Sharon, Sharon, Sharon. She was my first. It was a long time ago."

Judith noticed the way he was looking at Sharon on the wall and mistook it for a look of tenderness, something that she was sure that he wasn't capable of. "Was she your girlfriend?" She grasped at anything to keep him talking.

Roy laughed at the question. "Hmmm. I never really thought about it that way, Dr. Esther. Tell me. Are you my girl friend now?" Roy slipped one arm around Judith's waist and grabbed her right hand. He raised it slowly to the painting of Jillian and pressed her finger to the outstretched hand on the wall. "Close your eyes."

Closing her eyes was the last thing that Judith wanted to do, but she had no choice. She held her breath and allowed Roy to rub her finger over the painting until she felt something rigid under one finger. Roy stopped at this spot. "Do you feel that?"

Judith nodded and clenched her eyes tightly shut; something told her that she didn't want to see what she was feeling.

"Open your eyes, Dr. Esther." Roy moved her finger slightly to the side and so that Judith could see what she had just felt.

Judith opened her eyes slowly and concentrated on the wall next to her finger. At first, it appeared to be only the painted open palm of Jillian. Then, as Judith brushed her finger back slightly to the left to find the rigid spot again, she gasped for air as she pulled her hand quickly away from the wall. She had been touching the sliced off pad that had been missing from Jillian's ring finger when she had been found in the sand dunes behind Pelican Perch. In horror, Judith wrung her hand wildly in the air as if she had touched the Devil himself.

"Quite creative, if I do say so myself." Roy studied Judith for several moments in silence. "So, I guess what I am trying to tell you is that you will either be here, with my beauties." He swept an arm over the room. "Or, I will place you in the hallway." He let his arm fall down by his side and shrugged. "Either way, I haven't yet decided. But, for now, we have work to do. I guess you know by now that I do what I do for art, Dr. Esther. And tonight, you will help me get my new house in order. It's time to paint."

Judith hadn't the foggiest clue what he had just said. She stared openmouthed at the sliced finger pad that had been shellacked to the wall as Roy led her out of the dining room and back to the hallway of death.

Chapter Forty Two

Chief Big D, Marcus Donnarumma, and Hillary eagerly waited for Hank and Melissa to return to the lab. They had gone over Hank's proposal and talked at length with him during his drive back to Alabama, and things were already being put into motion. With a little luck and strong determination the small task force that had been assembled would be able to pull off the show with no hitches.

Hillary ended her phone conversation and returned to the table where everyone was seated. "Chief, that was Caitlin. She is more than happy to help. I ordered ten arrangements, and she said that she could be billed later, so that part is taken care of. What next?"

Chief Big D jotted down some notes. "I am waiting for the hotel manager from the Perdido Pass Lodge to call me back, and Marcus is talking to Jiles from the UPS store right now about the posters. All we can do now is wait for Hank and Melissa to return." Chief Big D glanced down at his watch.

As if on cue, Hank, Melissa and Clover Fontaine stumbled into the lab room. Everyone in the room stood up and gawked at the frail woman who was the mother of the monster they were searching for. She looked nothing like any of them had imagined, not that anyone had a clear definite visual of what a serial killer's mother was supposed to look like. Still, the elderly woman looked far too sweet and innocent to be the same woman on the rap sheet that they had been studying since Hank called with the news. Clover Fontaine, formerly known as Irene Fontaine was definitely not the same woman that she used to be.

Chief Big D crossed the room and shook hands with Hank first before he turned his attention to Clover. "Mrs. Fontaine, please, let me escort you down the hallway to a different room. There is a sketch artist waiting for you there. Do you need anything? Water? Something to eat?" He noticed Clover shivering. "Are you cold?" Sherrie quickly passed a light sweater over to Clover that she used sometimes in the lab when she got chilly.

With shaky hands Clover took the sweater and placed it around her shoulders. "No, thank you. I am fine."

Chief Big D nodded and led her down the hallway. When he returned, the room was bustling with busy voices on the phone. The only person not talking was Hank who sat silently at the opposite end of the table. His face was drawn and pale, his eyes flickering back and forth to a pencil that he absentmindedly bounced on the table. Big D's cell phone rang, and the room quickly hushed. It was the manager of the hotel.

"This is Chief Big D with the Orange Beach Police Department."

"Uh, yes, Chief. This is Ricardo, the hotel manager for the Perdido Pass Lodge. I just got your message that you called. Is everything okay?"

Chief Big D sat down at the table in front of his notes while everyone listened in silence. "Yeah, everything is okay. But, I do need your help. I know it's getting late, but I need to come over and discuss something with you that's extremely important. Mind if I drop by in a couple of minutes?"

"Well, no, I don't mind at all. It's pretty quiet around here. Come on over."

"That's great. Uh, one quick question before I do though. Is the small banquet room available tomorrow for an event during the day? We will probably need it from early morning until late afternoon." Big D heard papers rustling through the phone.

"Let me see here. Just one minute." Ricardo leafed through the schedule for the following day. "Yep, looks like it's available. How many people and what kind of event are we talking about? Need it catered? We have a great restaurant in the hotel that…"

Chief Big D cut him off. "Well, Ricardo, that's what I need to come talk to you about in private. I will be there in about ten minutes." He snapped the phone shut before Ricardo could say anything else and turned his attention to his crew. "We got ourselves a place, guys! Let's get this thing started." Everyone grabbed their cell phones again and began calling others on the force with the plan. "Hank and Melissa, you two come with me. Hillary, stay here with Marcus and look in on Mrs. Fontaine while I am gone. Everybody? Keep your mouths shut about the details of this guy and what's going on unless they are on the approved list of people who I have spoken to already."

Hank and Melissa followed Chief Big D to his unmarked SUV parked in front of the lab. The hotel was just a couple of miles down the road on the beach, and they were walking through the front entrance in no time at all. Ricardo was at the desk waiting for them and ushered them over to a piano room to the side of the lobby. He offered his hand to Chief Big D, then to Hank and Melissa who introduced themselves.

"I'm Ricardo Bowman. It's a pleasure to meet you. How can I help you?" He offered them a seat on the couch beside the piano.

Chief Big D towered over the manager and politely declined to sit for more than one reason. First, he did not want to sit. Second, he knew his large frame could be quite intimidating at times, and that was exactly what he wanted to do to Ricardo. At all costs, the manager would have to keep his mouth shut, and not being from Orange Beach, Chief Big D did not know if he could trust him. So, he politely declined and stood his ground. "Ricardo, we have a problem on our hands that we need your help with. It's top secret." For dramatic effect that Big D hoped would help instill fear into the hotel manager, he quickly passed him a file folder.

Questioningly, Ricardo looked back and forth from Chief Big D to Hank to Melissa as he took the file folder. He quickly shut the folder as soon as he saw what it contained, and pressed his lips together in shock.

"Now, Ricardo, I know that picture is somewhat of a shock to look at, at first glance, but we've been dealing with looking at it for quite sometime. Do you know who that is?"

Ricardo passed the folder back to Big D. and regained his composure. "Yes, sir. That's the girl whom they found down the beach a while back. I believe, if my memory serves me correctly, her name is Jillian Brannon."

Chief Big D nodded. "Your memory does serve you correctly, Mr. Bowman. That is Jillian Brannon." He paused for effect, and then glanced all around him to let Ricardo know that what he was getting ready to say next was top secret. He leaned closer to Ricardo who was, by now, feeling his own importance and ready for whatever request the Chief had for him. "We have had a break in the case. We have a lead, Mr. Bowman. And we need YOU to help find him."

Ricardo was already nodding his head enthusiastically in compliance. "Yes, sir, Chief, whatever you need sir. What do you want me to do?"

Chief Big D studied his face for a few seconds then stood up straight again. "Well, the truth be told, I need that banquet room tomorrow, and I need you to be responsible for keeping any information that you receive from us or anyone who will be in that room tomorrow away from your employees and away from the press. Absolutely NO ONE can know anything about this, or we run the risk of losing our suspect. You are literally our only hope this community has of finding the killer responsible for Jillian Brannon's murder. It's up to you, sir. Do you think you have what it takes?"

If the Star Spangled Banner suddenly began playing in the background, it wouldn't have made Ricardo Bowman feel anymore patriotic and willing to do his duty to his community and Chief Big D. He literally almost saluted the Chief as he struggled to answer. "Yes, sir! No problem, sir!"

Chief Big D folded his arms and stared hard at the hotel manager who stood at attention as if he were in basic training. When he was confident that he had made his point and that the man was worthy of being trusted, he took the chance and gave him the minimal necessary details to seal the deal. "Ok, Ricardo. Here's the deal. And remember, you must keep your mouth shut and do not let any of your employees know what is going on."

Ricardo quickly nodded.

"We are going to stage an art display in that banquet room tomorrow. It's not real. None of it is real. We will need you at various times to come into the banquet room on cue and welcome people to

186

your hotel as they view the paintings. This will lend legitimacy to the event. Some people there will know it is staged, others will not."

Ricardo was confused. He thought there would be more to it than that. "Is that all you need me to do? Are you sure?"

Chief Big D nodded seriously. "Forgive me if I can't tell you anymore details, like I said, it's top secret. But, Ricardo, make no mistake about it. Your role, as minimal as it sounds, will be one of the most important roles of them all. You just don't know it yet. There are two more things that I need."

Excited, Ricardo eagerly nodded.

"First, I need you to walk me through the hotel and point out each security camera, and make sure they are all working. If we get our guy tomorrow, I need those security cameras to catch him. Second, I need a block of about ten rooms for surveillance, work areas and accommodations for several people coming in from out of town."

Ricardo beamed at the Chief and at Hank and Melissa. "You got it! Follow me."

"Actually, there are some things that I need to discuss with Detective Jordan and Melissa. We will meet you in a few minutes back in the front lobby."

Ricardo nodded and scurried away back to the front desk to do a manual check on the security systems.

Chief Big D finally joined Hank and Melissa on the couch. At any other time, the situation with Ricardo would have been comical, but nothing else was on their minds except Judith. "Melissa? Are you ready to make the call?"

Melissa glanced down at her notes. On the way home from Louisiana, with permission from Chief Big D, she had taken the advice of Clover Fontaine and called Benjamin Preston, the art gallery dealer, for help. When Melissa told him the details of what was found on the paintings, he had been truly horrified. Jumping at the chance to help, Benjamin had readily agreed and was already en route to Orange Beach. Now all she had to do was to call Roy Fontaine and surprise him with the news. Her story was that Benjamin had called her and left a note with her secretary earlier that week, and that her secretary had failed to tell her about the show until late this afternoon. Her call to Roy would be merely out of courtesy. "Yes, I am ready." She opened her cell phone and dialed The Artist's number.

"Hello?"

Cringing at the familiar voice that use to excite her so much, Melissa answered eagerly. "Hi, this is Melissa. Sorry to have called you so late, but I wanted to let you know about two exciting things."

"Yes?"

"First, my client loved the painting that you did for him. I have his check right here, and I will personally cash it and wire the money to an account for you, as always. Second, and it's a little late notice, thanks to my secretary, but as a courteous gesture, I wanted to let you know that your former agent Benjamin Preston in Shreveport, Louisiana, called earlier this week to inform me that he, along with some of your biggest fans, are putting on a display show of your former paintings, some dating back all the way to when he was your agent. He invited me of course, but I can't attend on such short notice. The flight to Pensacola would be enormously expensive, and I have other clients that I have meetings with to..."

"Pensacola, Florida?"

Melissa rustled her notes for effect. "Yeah, hold on, and I will double check the note my secretary left. Uhmm, yes, the nearest airport would be Pensacola, Florida. The show is actually on the Gulf Coast in a small beach town named Orange Shores, no, sorry, Orange Beach." Melissa, Hank and Chief Big D held their breath.

"Never heard of the town."

Melissa silently exhaled. "Me neither. But, if Benjamin Preston is in charge of it, I am sure it will be nice! My secretary scribbled down where it will be, and I can hardly make it out, but I think it says Perdido Lodge. Either way, I can't just hop on a plane and be there tomorrow on such short notice. I will call Benjamin later this week and ask him how it went."

"The show is tomorrow?"

"Yes, unfortunately. Anyway, my client got the painting, and he loved it." Melissa cringed before she said her next words. "The girl on the swing is beautiful!" Hank stood up and walked away from the conversation as tears welled up in his eyes.

"Melissa, I will contact you with a routing number to a new account tomorrow. Goodnight."

The call was ended exactly how Melissa had anticipated: short and to the point. The Artist was extremely consistent. She just hoped that she had been convincing enough to make him take the bait. She placed her cell phone back in her purse and walked past the piano where Hank was watching the moon light glow on the waves outside. "I'm so sorry, Hank. I was just trying to..."

Hank held up his hand. "Melissa, there is no need to be sorry. I know what you were doing." He let his hand fall down to his side and gave her a nod. "You did great, Melissa. You really did."

Chief Big D circled them and patted Melissa lightly on the back. "Good job, Melissa. Are y'all ready to check out the details of the banquet room and the surveillance? We have a lot of work to do before tomorrow."

The three walked through the piano room toward the front desk where Ricardo was waiting for them with the smile and determination of a man on a mission. None of them were prepared for the phone call that came next. As the front desk phone rang, Ricardo excused himself and answered the front desk, slightly irritated at the interruption. "Thank you for calling the Perdido Pass Lodge. This is Ricardo Bowman, how may I help you?" Ricardo's face paled immediately as he listened to the caller.

"What time does the showing of The Artist's paintings start tomorrow?"

Ricardo look wild eyed at Chief Big D, who was not paying attention, and wrung his hand helplessly in the air. "Yes, sir, I will check that for you. Hold, please." He quickly placed the caller on hold and asked frantically to the three who were chatting behind the desk. "Uhm, does anyone know about this yet? There is a man asking what time the show will take place?"

Melissa's mouth fell open. He had taken the bait! "Oh My God!" She looked incredulously at Chief Big D and Hank who were equally as astonished. "We haven't even gotten that far!"

Chief Big D raised his hand. "Okay, quickly! What would be the best time? I say noon."

Horrified at the prospect of that being too late, Hank added, "Noon at the LATEST!"

Chief Big D ignored Hank and looked at Melissa, the only person who had any experience in putting something like this together.

She nodded her head quickly. "Noon. Yes, it can be done." She looked at Ricardo. "Tell the caller the show will begin at twelve noon, with light refreshments and hors d'oeuvres mid-afternoon."

Ricardo tried to stop his hands from shaking as he did not want to appear weak in front of Chief Big D. He took a deep breath and picked the receiver back up. "Sorry for your wait, sir. The schedule for the show is set for twelve noon with light refreshments and hors d'oeuvres mid-afternoon."

"Who is hosting the show?"

Ricardo bit his lip nervously and rustled through some paperwork on his desk. "Please hold, sir while I look for that information." He quickly asked Melissa, "Quick, who is hosting? Who is hosting the show?"

Melissa placed both hands on the desk and spoke clearly, "Benjamin Preston. Tell him Benjamin Preston is hosting the show."

Ricardo nervously said the name to himself before returning to the caller. "Ah, yes, sir, I see here that a Mr. Benjamin Preston is hosting the show tomorrow." The call went dead. Ricardo quickly placed the phone down as if it were a snake ready to bite him. "Was that him? Was that your guy that just called?"

Chief Big D shook his head. "Probably not, Ricardo, but I want you to know that you did one hell of a job! Keep up the good work." He centered his attention on Hank and Melissa. "We're going to get him, Hank. He will be here tomorrow. I've got a good feeling!"

Chapter Forty Three

Unsure of how he felt about the news from Melissa, Roy Fontaine stared down at his cell phone beside the bed. Once again she had interrupted his plans for Judith with news that triggered his pride and arrogance. Of all the cities in the entire United States to have a display of his work, Benjamin Preston, his very first agent, had chosen the very small town of Orange Beach; the town he had fled to after Hurricane Katrina? The town in which the body of Jillian Brannon had been found murdered in the sand dunes on the beach? The town in which a beloved doctor had recently gone missing but failed to make the news? Something did not seem right, yet, when he had called the Perdido Pass Lodge to confirm, the receptionist had seemed so ordinary. And, Melissa, his agent, had acted so nonchalantly about the entire thing when she had called him to let him know that the client had received his painting. Had he been this successful in life at being anonymous and obscure that all of this was just fate and chance? Roy Fontaine scratched his head in confusion as he wondered about the possibilities. If the show was a trap, then there was a huge piece of the puzzle missing. For one, how in the world would Detective Hank Jordan ever link Judith's disappearance to him, Melissa, and his former agent Benjamin Preston? Even if by some tiny chance the detective caught a glimpse of a painting that he had used Jillian's face in, Roy was sure that it would have gone completely unnoticed. Besides, those paintings had been shipped directly to Melissa in New York, a long way from Alabama. And Detective Jordan certainly did not strike Roy as a fan of art. Still, something wasn't right. Suddenly, Roy shot straight up from the bed. He thought of the fact that he mailed the painting to Melissa from Gulf Shores and slammed his fist down on the bedside table; his cell phone came crashing down on the hardwood floor and splintered into pieces. Still unable to convince himself this was all a set up, the fact that he had made the mistake of mailing a painting so close to home made him curse loudly. Somewhere in the back of his mind, he had known he would come to regret it, and now he did.

Judith cowered on the floor, protecting her face from the flying splinters of the cell phone. She was keenly aware of two things; Roy had mentioned Pensacola, Florida, and there was a display of The Artist's paintings tomorrow. Roy glared down at her and yelled as loud as he could. "Tell me NOW, Doctor! Why are you not all over the news?" He threw his leg backward and kicked her swiftly in the side. "Why?"

Judith gasped for air and held her sides tightly to stop the pain. With amazing effort, she managed to reply, "I don't know! I don't know!"

Disgusted with her now that Melissa had called, and unable to concentrate on what he had planned for the night, Roy paced back and forth across the bedroom. The more he paced, the calmer he grew. With each step he took, his pride and ego crept back up to normal levels and overtook his uncertainty. He began thinking again about the possibilities that it could be, in fact, by chance alone. The more he wondered, the less threatening the situation became.

For at least an hour, Judith watched him through slanted eyes walk the bedroom floor. She observed him talk to himself, mumble inaudibly, then shake his head violently at whatever thought filtered through his mind that he didn't agree with. She literally watched the entire process of a madman trying to convince himself that he was completely invincible, and that whatever was going on was truly coincidental. She tried to make herself as small and unseen as possible as she lay on the cold floor in the remains of the splintered cell phone.

At last, Roy finished his tantrum and became totally silent and still. His eyes flickered with an evil fire that raged and grew within him as he rounded the bed and found Judith still cowered on the floor. He grabbed the leash with an animalistic strength and pulled her across the floor of his bedroom into the dark hallway. He was walking so fast that Judith could not manage to stand up in time to walk. Her body flailed across the uneven wooden floor planks as she tried to stand. The collar was so tight around her neck from the strain that it choked her unmercifully. Her knees and thighs scraped across several nail heads that had worked their way up from the wood, but each time she tried to scream out in pain the collar would completely cut her off. Finally, after she was dragged violently back through the hallway, her body came to rest on the linoleum floor of the kitchen. She harshly sucked in air against the tight strap of the collar to catch her breath and balance as Roy left her unattended for the moment. One of the nail heads had ripped through her right thigh and left a trail of blood across the linoleum floor. Judith was too weak to pick herself up from the floor. Her body, void of nourishment and feeling the exhausting effects of the drugs, was completely spent. Giving up, she lay face down on the linoleum and stared at Roy Fontaine's foot from a side view for a moment before blackness took over. She passed out at his feet.

Minutes later, Judith felt water flow over her back, and then suddenly it registered in her brain that is was scalding hot water. Then she heard the familiar voice. "Oh, no you don't!" Roy picked her up from the floor and carried her limp body to the dining room table. Before her was a plate of food that Roy had prepared for her. She was dizzy and unable to focus on what was on the plate, but she could smell that it was food. The familiar fishy smell wafted up toward her while her eyes adjusted. It was sardines and crackers again. She didn't care. She had to eat. She worried that she was dying. Her head lolled around from sheer lack of being able to hold it upright, so Roy force fed her the tiny fish. She chewed the food as best she could and swallowed the water that he put to her mouth. Finally, after about thirty minutes, she felt better. Her vision had completely returned, and she was able to hold her head up on her own. The gash in her thigh had stopped bleeding and for the moment, she couldn't feel any pain.

Roy went to the kitchen and continued to prepare for what he had planned for the night. He wasn't worried about Judith trying to escape. He knew that she could barely hold up her own head, much less run anywhere, and besides, she would never figure out how to get out of the locked doors before he shocked some sense into her. Lost in thought about the display of his artwork, Roy absentmindedly began to prepare his paints and brushes. The more he thought about it, the more he wanted to slip in and see his old paintings. Curiosity was killing him as he replayed Melissa's words in his head. Supposedly, his biggest fans would be there showcasing their collections of his life's work. There would be so many paintings there that he had not seen in many years. The faces of so many women would be smiling from the canvases. If he went to the show, it would almost be like a reunion. Then again, if he went to the show, he would run the risk of having to talk to someone in conversation, and he was anything but social. He wasn't worried about anyone recognizing him, because no one knew who the Artist was. Still, the reason no one knew who the Artist was, was only because he had always been so private and unsocial.

Roy struggled with the decision of whether to go or not. As he swirled his paints together in a red plastic Solo cup, the temptation became too strong to ignore. By the time he was ready to paint, the decision had been made. Roy Fontaine would be attending Benjamin Preston's display. As for the details of his disguise, he would work them out in his head as he worked with Judith. Tonight would have been the night he would end her life, but now those plans had changed. He would just have to be satisfied with posing her for awhile, then putting her to sleep. He swirled the last of the paints together with Jillian Brannon's rotting fingers, carefully washed them and returned them to their resting place in the freezer.

Judith was right where he had left her at the dining room table. Roy smiled as he noticed that her head was bowed submissively as he entered the room. In truth, Judith held her head down so she wouldn't have to see the faces of the dead women that beckoned to her from the walls. She looked up at Roy without moving her head and saw that he was carrying a tray full of paints and brushes.

"Dr. Esther, I trust that you got enough to eat? Did you enjoy your dinner?"

Judith nodded weakly and stared back down at the floor.

"Good, we have a long night ahead of us. Lots of work to do, so, shall we?" He cut his eyes over to the entrance to the hallway.

Using the table for support, Judith slowly pulled herself up to a standing position and limped toward the hallway. Each step was more painful than the last, but she managed to at last reach the dreaded dark hallway.

"Stop right there." Roy bent down to place the tray on the floor and picked up Judith's leash that had trailed behind her. "Here is what we are going to do. You will be posed in a certain position, and I am going to paint you on this wall."

Judith began trembling with fear. This was it. She was finally being added to the wall of death, the wall of blood and guts and headless women. She shook violently as he slowly took up the slack in her leash.

Roy watched the ultimate fear sweep over her face and forced himself to ignore it. He had seen that look on so many women's faces over the years, yet it never failed to excite him. It was the look they gave him right before he took their lives, and it was truly irreplaceable. He couldn't kill Judith tonight the way he wanted to, so he had to ignore what he believed to be her begging him to do so. He jerked the leash to grab her attention and snap her out of her "deer in headlights" look. "Calm down, Dr. Esther, I am not ready to kill you yet. You will know it when I am. Trust me. I need you to go and get the stool from your bedroom while I retrieve a lantern and some rope. I am never far behind you, Doctor, so please remember that. When you return, place the stool here in the middle of the hallway and stand beside it."

Confused and terrified, Judith turned and limped down the hallway towards her bedroom. She did as she was told, cursing herself for not being daring enough to defy him and try to escape. The stool on which he had sat gleefully watching her hallucinate earlier was beside the bed. She didn't have the strength to lift it, so she pushed it across the floor instead. The dull sound of the wooden legs scraping across the wooden floor sent chills up her back as she managed to maneuver it through the doorway. The pain from her wounds had worsened, slowing her steps dramatically. By the time she returned to the hallway, Roy was already there, waiting patiently with black rope in his hands and a lantern to help the lack of proper lighting. He made no move to help her. He just stood there watching her limp pathetically toward him while feebly pushing the stool across the floor. When she finally arrived he took the stool from her and placed it on the floor upside down so all four of the stool's legs shot upright toward the ceiling.

"Dr. Esther, please stand inside the legs of the stool."

Judith bent over to rest her hands on the tops of two of the legs for support and stepped into the middle of the stool. There was barely enough room for both of her feet but she managed to squeeze into it. Then he began to strategically wrap and bind her to the legs of the stool with the rope. Fifteen minutes of complicated knots later, she was bound to the stool in an upright position so that she could not move. The stool helped steady her, but if she was unable to maintain her balance she would crash face first into the wall. Her arms were crossed behind her and tied tightly and securely to two of the legs. She wasn't going anywhere any time soon, and she knew it. Bitter tears slipped from her swollen eyes and down her cheeks, seeping into the black rope that cut through her open mouth.

Satisfied with the morbid results, Roy got to work. It wasn't the wall that he painted her on, but the back of the door that closed off the hallway. She cringed as she listened to the door groan and squeak as he shut it closed. Roy threw himself into his work, feverishly sweeping his brushes across the wooden canvas, as Judith watched herself materialize onto the door. The more he painted the more Judith felt like she was staring into a mirror. The pain in her legs had subsided due to the tight rope, and for that Judith was thankful. She dared not think about maintaining her position for fear that her concentration would cause her to lose her balance. Instead, she concentrated on every brush stroke that brought her to life on the back of the door, and couldn't help but be amazed at Roy's talent.

Chapter Forty Four

Benjamin Preston finally arrived at the hotel. Shaken to the core from the phone call he had received from Melissa about the Artist, he felt like he was floating through the entrance instead of walking. Melissa was waiting for him in the lobby and hurried over to greet him when she saw him appear. Chief Big D and Hank were close behind her. After the introductions were made, Chief Big D escorted Benjamin to the front desk where Ricardo was busy testing the security cameras.

Chief Big D leaned over the desk to see the computer screens that showed the views of the security cameras. "Ricardo, this is Benjamin Preston."

Ricardo politely smiled at him. "Ah, yes, the host of the art display tomorrow. I will get you checked in immediately." He began typing away at the computer as Chief Big D conversed with Benjamin.

"We can't thank you enough for coming here on such short notice under such strange circumstances, Mr. Preston. We will talk privately as soon as you get checked in."

"Thank you very much." Benjamin handed Ricardo a credit card, but he refused to accept it.

"Mr. Preston, there will be no charge." Ricardo handed him two key cards, and stood up to escort them to his room, but Chief Big D put a hand up to stop him.

"That will be alright, Ricardo. I can take care of him from here. I need you to keep checking those cameras to make sure they are all working properly." Chief Big D swept a hand toward the elevators. "Mr. Preston, after you."

Benjamin took his luggage, and walked toward the elevators while Chief Big D, Hank and Melissa followed close behind. As soon as the elevator door slid closed, he asked the group, "The hotel manager doesn't know much, does he?"

They shook their heads in unison. Melissa responded, "He only knows that there is an art display staged to catch Jillian Brannon's murderer, and nothing more."

Benjamin shook his head in amazement. "My God, who would have ever thought that The Artist is a serial killer? The whole way over here, I kept seeing the faces of all those women in the paintings. What a creepy feeling."

Melissa felt uneasy and uncomfortable, as she had yet to be completely truthful about the whole situation. She hadn't told Benjamin about Judith, and the real reason for such urgency that he be in Orange Beach. As soon as he mentioned the women's faces, she heard the sad long breath that Hank exhaled. After what seemed like an eternity, the elevator finally came to a stop on the third floor. They exited and walked to the hotel room. When everyone had filed into the room and Benjamin had a chance to sit down, Melissa broke the news about Judith to him. Hank stood at the far window as she relayed the information to Benjamin. He sat in horror, glancing back and forth from Melissa to Hank as he listened to the details.

"Oh My God, Melissa! And Detective Jordan, I am so very sorry! I, uh, I don't know what to say!"

Hank pushed away from the window and faced the man. "Thank you, Mr. Preston, but right now, I do not need pity; I just need your help." He stuttered through tears and pinched the bridge of his nose to stop from crying. "Right now, I need your help to find Judith."

Benjamin stood up immediately and pushed his sleeves up. "I will do whatever you need me to do. Anything! Where do we start?"

Melissa held up her hand. "We need to get back to the lab and get those paintings. I have to create some sort of display for each one. Benjamin, that's where you come in. Just do what you have been doing for so long. I need a brief description of each painting to display. Also, Clover is there as well working with a sketch artist to help put a face to The Artist, and I am sure that she would like to see you after all that she has been through so far."

Benjamin nodded quickly. "No problem at all, Melissa. I am ready."

They left the room in a hurry and were back at the lab in no time. Chief Big D led Benjamin down a hallway to a small room where Clover sat. The face that had begun to materialize on the sketch pad was not yet finished, and Clover was badly in need of a break. She was relieved to see a familiar face and clung to Benjamin as he hugged her. Benjamin sat down beside the frail woman and took her hands in his.

"Clover, all those years. You must have known."

Surprised that she had more tears to shed, she wiped away one that trickled down her cheek. "I didn't want to know, Benjamin. I just didn't want to know, so I refused to allow myself to see it."

Benjamin let go of her hands and stood up. Chief Big D stepped into the room. "Mrs. Clover, do you need a break?"

Clover nodded quickly. "Yes."

"Ok, come with us. If we are going to be able to pull this off, we need you to be with us every step of the way."

Marcus Donnarumma and Hillary had been put in charge of gathering trustworthy people to attend the show the following day, and the conference room was bustling with people. When Chief Big D walked into the room, everyone fell silent in anticipation of what he would say. Behind him appeared Hank, Melissa and Benjamin who was escorting Clover from the room where she had sat with a sketch artist.

Chief Big D ushered them into the room and introduced them to everyone as Hank wove his way through the crowd of people. Many reached out to touch him or pat him on the back as he walked silently through the room. On the table and propped up against the walls were the paintings recovered from Clover's storage unit, and Benjamin gasped at the collection.

"How many paintings are we talking about?"

Melissa answered his question. "Fifty two to be exact. There are more, but we couldn't haul them all. They are still in her storage unit in Bogalusa. We have as many as we need to pull off a legitimate show, and, I have spoken with him already."

Benjamin's mouth dropped open. "What? Him? As in The Artist? Do you think he will come? Do you think he will take the bait?"

Melissa was full of hope. "The Artist has already called the hotel to confirm that the show will take place. I honestly believe that the temptation will be too much for him to ignore. I think he will be here."

Benjamin shook his head again, amazed at everything that has transpired since Melissa's phone call. "Unbelievable! This is truly unbelievable!"

Melissa nodded sadly. "And you know what else? We know The Artist's name. Do you still want to know what it is, after all these years of wondering? I wish I had never heard it now."

Benjamin's heart raced with anticipation that he could not contain. "What is it?"

Melissa took a deep breath and stared into Benjamin's eyes. "His name is Roy Fontaine."

Benjamin slowly repeated the monster's name as chill bumps spread across the back of his neck. "Ok, where do I start? I need a computer and a room to study these paintings."

Chief Big D nodded and escorted him to a room down the hall. "I will have someone bring you five paintings at a time. That way the room will not be crowded. Is that ok?"

Benjamin nodded quickly and sat down at the desk in front of a flat screen computer monitor as the paintings were brought in. He recognized the first one immediately from years ago; instead of wondering who The Artist was as he always did, he wondered for the first time who the smiling woman in the painting was, and he shivered with fear. He reached out to touch the face in the painting and quickly recoiled, wringing his hands furiously in the air before wiping them on he sides of his pants. He shuddered as he remembered what Melissa had told him over the phone, 'the Artist mixed blood into his paint.'

As Benjamin studied the paintings and typed descriptions of each one, Clover sat shivering in the cold room down the hallway, recalling from memory every detail of the monster that she had brought into the world years ago in the swamps of Louisiana. Wondering what would happen in the next twenty four hours, she wept bitterly as she spoke to the sketch artist about her son's eyes, his skin tone, and the shape of his nose and jaw line. A small part of her wanted him to run far away and never look back, and she hated herself for wishing it.

Chapter Forty Five

Hank Jordan sat silently at the table as people hurried in and out of the room. Unable to focus on anything else, his mind was consumed with images of Judith's face. He thought of the first time he had met her at the hospital during the investigation of the Morrison murders, and everything that had happened between them since that day. Their life together had been nothing but true love, and he owed so much to her for the happiness that she had given him. He reached into his wallet and pulled out their engagement picture. She had been so happy that day in the studio as they posed in front of the camera. He stared down at her smiling face and wondered if he would ever get the chance to see her alive again. He wondered if the chance to walk down the aisle and marry her had passed him by because Roy Fontaine had somehow crossed their paths. It seemed that in an instant, his life with Judith was over. He thought about Jillian Brannon and the way she had been found laying naked and stabbed in the sand dunes. He remembered the sick feeling with which he had immediately called Judith to tell her he loved her while he processed the crime scene. And now, she was gone. Just as his emotions were ready to overtake him once again, Hillary sat down beside him and folded her hand over his, covering up the picture in the process.

She spoke softly but sternly to him. "Hank, you have to buck up, man. You are stronger than this. Judith is out there waiting for us to find her, and you need to be stronger than this. Keep yourself busy. There is a lot to do before tomorrow." She waited for him to respond, but Hank said nothing. "Caitlin called. The flower arrangements are ready, and I said that I would meet her at the hotel. Do you want to come?"

Hank pulled away from her and returned the picture to his wallet. "Where is Melissa?"

"She is in the back room with Benjamin working on the descriptions of the paintings."

Hank absentmindedly surveyed the room as the mental picture of Judith smiling faded slowly away. "Hill, have you ever truly felt completely helpless? I mean, truly helpless. I don't know what to do. I don't know where to go. I don't know how to feel or what to think." With the look of a haunted and lost man, Hank faced Hillary.

"No, Hank, I haven't, and I hope I am never in the position that you are in right now; but I love Judith too. We all do. And I am not going to give up. She is out there somewhere waiting for us to save her!" Hillary quickly glanced at her watch. "Come with me. You need to get out of here for a while."

Hank let out a painful sigh and dropped his head. "Okay. I'll go, but I do not want to leave Melissa here. She is struggling with this too, you know. They have been best friends since college."

Hillary placed her hand on Hank's arm before turning away. "I'll go get her."

Just then, the sketch artist who had been working with Clover ran through the doorway holding the sketch in the air. Everyone crowded around the table staring down at the picture to catch the first glimpse of who they were trying to capture. Hank hurriedly pushed an officer out of the way to see the result of the sketch and made his way to the table. Roy Fontaine stared back up at him from the sketch pad, and Hank struggled not to rip it into a million pieces. His heart raced as he studied the image. Those eyes, dark and sinister paired with a dark wild shock of hair and sharp jaw line seemed to mock him. In truth, those eyes pierced straight through to Hank's heart and fueled the rage that Hillary had tried to bring forth only minutes before. He needed to be angry. He needed to be strong. This was not the time for tears and heartache. This was the time to slam his fist down, bound and determined, and go find her. Hank's fist came down hard on the table, and everyone fell silent. He looked at each person for the first time since he had arrived, and everyone waited for what he wanted to say to them.

He took a deep breath and pulled the picture again from his wallet and held it up for everyone to see. Not one person hung their head in sadness; each one, man and woman stared hard at the picture and nodded their heads with determination and focus. "I want to take a second to personally thank each and every one of you for helping with this. If I have seemed out of it to you, it is because I am, and I will not apologize for it. I have been struggling with sadness that I wish no one will ever have to feel. But now? After seeing this man's face, I am more than pissed! We will find him! As all of you know, the woman in this picture is my fiancée. She is more than just that. She is a loving and caring doctor to most of your children and a fighter by nature, and I know that she is out there fighting this monster and hanging on to whatever she can to get away from him! We have only one person to thank at this moment in time, and, ironically, it is his own mother. Make her feel welcome at all costs. She is the only link we have to identifying him. I don't want any pity, and I don't want people to be afraid of talking about this in front of me. If I cry, it's because I have to." He scanned the room. "Now let's go find this psychopath!"

Hank turned away from the crowd and walked toward Chief Big D who was standing in the doorway. "Chief, I am going to the hotel with Hillary and Melissa."

Chief Big D shook his hand with a fierce grip. "Jiles just dropped off the posters and flyers. I think we are ready to start putting this show together, Hank. I say, we all load up in vehicles and go to the hotel together. I want that banquet room decorated and ready to go first thing in the morning, and I want those rooms that we have blocked off for surveillance wired and ready. You want to ride over there with me?"

Hank glanced down the hallway and saw Melissa, Hillary and Benjamin Preston walking towards them. "No, Chief, I am going to drive them over."

Chief Big D nodded. No longer did he doubt Hank's ability to handle the situation properly. The fiercely determined gleam in his eyes assured the Chief that he had finally awoken from the shock of the nightmare of Judith's disappearance. "Ok, Hank, we'll meet you over there."

Everyone quickly dispersed from the room and prepared to leave. One by one, the paintings were gathered and placed in crates to be transported to the hotel. Each painting was handled with care and respect as the handlers knew that they were holding the bloody remains of victims who had died at the hands of Roy Fontaine.

Chapter Forty Six

Ricardo Bowman quickly escorted Hank, Melissa and Benjamin into the small banquet room that would hold the art display show the following morning. Soon after their arrival, Caitlin showed up with the flower arrangements, and then the paintings arrived. The room was bustling with a team of people who were being directed by Marcus Donnarumma. His job was to strategically place hidden cameras in the room that would be monitored by Chief Big D and others in the block of rooms that Ricardo had given them for surveillance.

Ricardo ordered his night staff to relocate planted palms and flowering plants from around the outside pool into the banquet room. Coupled with the lavish floral arrangements that Caitlin had put together, by the time they were finished the room had been transformed into a small floral paradise.

Then the paintings arrived. One by one they were placed throughout the room, while Benjamin and Melissa staged the scene with the printed descriptions of each underneath or to the side of the framed paintings. Within thirty minutes, the empty banquet room changed into a beautiful art gallery worthy of praise from any critic in Manhattan. Hank and Ricardo walked to each painting and read each description in detail. Of course Ricardo had no idea of the bloody nightmare that each painting told, and Hank cringed as he watched Ricardo observe them in delight and awe. The painting of Judith, of course, had been left back at the lab along with the first paintings that Melissa had brought to Judith's house and also the crude paintings from Roy's youth that Clover had managed to take with her when she left. Hank forced himself not to think of the image of Judith swinging in that swing and kept moving from picture to picture. He wanted to know every detail, every inch of the banquet room, the hallway, and the entire hotel. Of course he would be in the surveillance room throughout the entire day, but he still wanted to familiarize himself with everything.

By two a.m. everything had been set up; the room was breathtaking. Flyers were placed all over the hotel announcing the event, and the night employees carried on as usual thinking that the staged art show was the real thing. Several of them had ventured into the banquet room to observe the beautiful paintings, but Ricardo shooed them away as if they were not worthy of seeing the paintings, and they left without suspicions.

Finally, Chief Big D asked Ricardo to leave the room and close the doors behind him. From the center of the lavishly decorated room he spoke to the remaining officers and police staff who stood at attention. "Ok, guys, this is it. For those of you who are still in here, good job! Tomorrow, I need each and every one of you to be alert and focused." He held up the sketch of Roy that Clover had helped put together. "Commit this man's face to memory. Dream about him tonight. If he shows up tomorrow, it's up to us to bring him down and save Judith. We cannot afford to miss him. This might be our only shot. After tomorrow, he will be spooked, and we run the risk of him fleeing somewhere else with Judith alive, or leaving her behind dead." Chief Big D nodded at Hank out of respect, and Hank nodded reassuringly back. "Now, you've all got your orders and detailed plans that we went over back at the lab. Does anyone have a question about anything?" The room was silent. "Ok, well, try to get some sleep. I want everyone back here in this room at six o'clock a.m. That will be the last time that you see either myself or Hank until this whole thing is over, but as each of you know, we will be on the premises at all times, and only a radio click away. Goodnight and thank you all for everything you have done."

The crowd dispersed, leaving only Chief Big D, Hank, Melissa, Clover and Benjamin behind. The room was silent for a moment as each person did their last minute checks around the room to make sure everything was as it should be. Satisfied with the final results, Benjamin spoke first.

"So, here we go! I have never been so ready to see this guy in my life, and trust me, it's been a long time coming. I just wish it were under different circumstances." Everyone nodded in agreement. "So, Chief, have you decided yet what role Clover has in all of this?"

Clover spoke up at the mentioning of her name. "I have given it a lot of thought all day long. I will help in any way that I can, but I don't think I should be in that room or the surveillance room. If I see him walk in, I am afraid that I will give everything away." She bit her lip to stop herself from crying. "He's still my son, you know."

Chief Big D unfolded his arms and stared back at Clover. He had no intention of placing her in the banquet room or the surveillance room. He wanted to use her as bait if he had to. "Ma'am, you don't have to worry about that. What I want you to do is simply sit by the pool and look for any signs of him. We'll be watching you the whole time. You will not be anywhere near that room. You okay with that?"

Relieved that she would not be near the room, Clover nodded her head quickly. "Yes, I am fine with that."

"Ok, then. Melissa and Hank, y'all, of course, will be with me. So, if no one has anything to add, I say we go to our rooms and try to rest a little bit before this thing starts. I know it will be difficult, but we need to be alert as possible tomorrow."

Melissa stepped up to Chief Big D and wrapped her arms around him. "Thank you so very much for everything. I, uh, I don't know where to even begin to thank you."

Chief Big D hugged her back while staring at Hank over her shoulder. "Don't thank me yet," he whispered out of Hank's earshot. Melissa nodded and let him go. She knew that there was a slim chance of their plan working yet she forced herself to remain hopeful that Roy would come. Without saying a word, she briefly placed a hand on Hank's arm and stepped into the hallway towards the elevator. Benjamin laced an arm around Clover and followed Melissa.

Hank stood among the paintings in silence for several minutes while Chief Big D stared at him with heartbreak that words could not describe. "Well, Hank, if there is a remote chance that you can sleep, now is the time to do it."

Exhausted, Hank nodded in agreement. "I can't promise you I will sleep much, but I promise I will try. Thanks, Chief, for everything"

The two men looked around the banquet room one last time and exited together. Minutes later, Hank was in his own room. Completely dressed he laid down on top of the comforter, and miraculously cried himself to sleep.

Chapter Forty Seven

Roy Fontaine finished his last brush stroke for the night. It wasn't nearly finished, but he had enough on the door to complete the painting without Judith's help. He placed the paint brush in the Solo cup and popped each one of his knuckles as he admired his work.

Seconds before he finished, Judith could hardly keep her eyes open, and now she couldn't close them. Watching the brush strokes over and over again had been hypnotic and the sound had awakened her senses and fear. With each cracking sound, Judith's heart raced. Her eyes flickered back and forth from her morbid reflection on the door to the monster who had painted it. Throughout the entire time she had been tied to the inside of the stool, she wondered about the art display he had mentioned while he was on the phone. She knew it was tomorrow. Would he go? He had also mentioned Pensacola. Was the art show going to be somewhere in Pensacola? Thinking of the possibility of him leaving her to go to an art show had frightened her to the core. Surely he would not leave her in his house alive. Surely, he would kill her first. Judith was so delirious that she wasn't really thinking about the concept of the art show, but only her impending death. Yet, something that seemed too far away to grasp kept gnawing at her brain. Her thoughts, mixed with fear and trepidation as she watched Roy's every move, kept drifting back to the art show.

Roy Fontaine gathered his paints and brushes and rotting fingers and briefly left the hallway toward the kitchen. Judith allowed her head to sway for the first time and sharply inhaled as her bound body momentarily lost balance. She stared hard at the wall, as if willing it to stay away, and momentarily regained her balance. Her thoughts jumped to Hank. Then to Melissa. Then to the paintings with the blood on them in her apartment. The Luminol. Suddenly, she gasped as an idea struck her. This was no coincidence! The art show! Hank was coming to find her! That had been Melissa on the phone! They were forming a plan to save her. She quickly looked around the hallway as hope rushed through her. Suddenly the hallway started spinning, and she lost her balance. As rigid as a mummy her body and the stool pitched sideways and crashed into the wall. She heard running footsteps but could not turn her face away from the wall. Confused but aware that her mouth was pressed against the dried bloody paint that Roy used, Judith pursed her lips together in horror. She whined and shook as she felt Roy's fingers dig into her flesh to upright her.

Although his thoughts were completely on the art display the following morning, Roy allowed himself to chuckle at Judith's misfortune. He was done with her for the evening and had more important things to attend to. One by one he quickly untied the ropes and allowed her limp body to fall into his arms. After she was completely released he carried her to her bedroom and tied her down again. He knew that there was no need to drug her; she would be asleep within minutes if he left her alone.

He was right. Judith clung to the hope she had felt in the hallway moments before. She clung to the mental picture of Hank rescuing her. She clung to anything she could to fight off sleep, but in the end, she lost her battle. Darkness took over and for a few hours, she would finally get some rest. Roy watched her sleep on the video surveillance monitor until he was sure that she was not pretending. Then he crossed his bedroom to the closet where he kept his clothes and his stash of uniforms and disguises. One thing was for sure: he would have to find the perfect one to blend in tomorrow, just in case this was a set up. His plan was to sneak in just long enough to see his paintings, even if he couldn't view them all, and immediately come back to Judith.

He rummaged through his clothes until he found a navy business suit, but quickly dismissed it. His head was shaved now, so he definitely could not pull off the distinguished traveling businessman. He looked more like a worker on the beach. He remembered a pool maintenance polo shirt and fished through his belongings until he found the bag of uniforms. Folded nicely, in the same plastic it had arrived in, was a powder blue shirt with a pool maintenance logo embroidered on the breast. He smiled a wicked smile as he pulled the shirt from the casing and unfolded it. It was perfect. He could wear it with a pair of khaki shorts, and a baseball hat, no, his FloraBama hat. That would really allow him to blend in. He donned his disguise and looked into the mirror. Upon inspection, he decided not to wear the hat, but a bandana instead. He folded a red bandana, wrapped his bare head in the cloth and was rewarded with the perfect reflection. He looked like any other beach bum/pool guy that worked the local hotels and resorts. He nodded at himself as he turned to each side. The next thing he had to do was make a nameplate for his uniform. He walked to his computer and pulled up a program that he had used so many times before, and thought about what he wanted his name to be. A sly grin spread upon his face as he typed: Brannon. Moments later a sheet of paper popped from the printer. He cut the name out, slid it behind the plastic of a cheap name tag, and pinned it to his shirt. In the mirror he stuck out his hand to himself in a nice gesture.

"Hi. Last name's Brannon. I am here to fix your pool." He nodded back at himself and laughed good naturedly at what he imagined his reflection was asking him. "Why, yes! I AM kin to Jillian! I get that a lot. I was her husband."

He held his hand up to his ear and leaned forward into the mirror, as if he hadn't heard what his reflection had said back to him. Then he shrugged and nodded again, this time more seriously. "Yes, well, at least I still have her fingers."

Moments later he tired of the game and checked on Judith one more time. The monitor showed her sleeping like a baby. He removed his uniform and placed it on the end of his bed before lying down. His last thoughts behind closed eyelids were of him standing in the middle of a large room surrounded by his paintings. All of his beauties were there, clapping for him.

Chapter Forty Eight

Hank dreamed. In his dream he was wading through the marsh of a swamp. The moss hung down from the low limbs of the cypress trees and tickled him on his face as the wind blew. Sinister green eyes watched him from the muddy banks as he sloshed through the stagnant black water. Dogs howled in a safe distance from the impending doom of the swamp. Hank saw one of them slinking along the bank and stopped to stare at it. The dog stared back, but with empty eye sockets. He felt something wet in his pants pocket and pushed his hand in to see what it was. When he fished out two blue eyeballs, he screamed and threw them at the dog. The green eyes on the muddy banks surrounded him but quickly disappeared into wildly splashing water, and Hank glanced all around, ready to fight. Something caught his eye through the trees. He stared into the moss, straining to see what it was. He saw it again. It was blonde hair. Something else caught his attention further down the bank. He swore it was a woman running, but the trees were in the way. Suddenly, there were women running through the trees on all sides of him. He couldn't watch one without jerking his attention to the next one. Blondes, brunettes, redheads. They were everywhere, and then suddenly, they were gone. He shook his head and pressed both hands to his eyes before opening them. Hank began to wade through the water again. What caught his attention next wasn't something he saw, it was something he heard. It was faint laughter. He could hear a woman laughing. He followed the sound as it grew nearer. As he frantically searched for the laughing

212

woman, something in the water began to change; he could feel it. He glanced down and watched the water turn from black to brown. Not wanting to lose the laughter, he raised his head in the direction and kept walking, trying hard to ignore the water. It was blood red now. He could feel against his thighs that it was growing deeper and swirling now, swirling slowly and thickening around his clothes. Every step proved harder and harder as he leaned his body weight against the pull. Suddenly he rounded a bend of trees and the water came rushing by. Frothy bloody rapids carried him toward another stagnant pool, but this time it wasn't surrounded by mossy trees. It was surrounded by a meadow full of wild flowers. He swam away from the swift current and found his footing. In the distance he could see the laughing woman, perched high in the air on a wooden rope swing. When she swung backwards she was over the meadow, but when she swung forwards, she disappeared into the tree line. Hank grabbed at the slippery bank, pulled himself out of the swamp water and ran through the meadow, slinging blood from his arms and legs onto the flowers beneath him. When he finally reached the woman on the swing, he was breathless. He tried to call out to her but nothing came from his mouth. He reached his hand up in the air to catch her skirt but missed just in time to watch her disappear into the trees. He ran, following her, but the moss was too thick. Dropping to all fours he scrambled into the swamp forest until he felt cold water engulf his fingers. The kind of fear that brings panic ripped through his body as he fought the moss above him. He had to see the woman. Where was she? He found an opening in the moss and leaped through it just as her billowing skirt brushed his face. Then the laughter turned into a scream. Those sinister green eyes were waiting for her in the water. They were everywhere. Hank found his voice and screamed to the woman. As she swung by him again she reached out for his hand, but it was too late. An alligator sprung from the water and took off her fingers…

Hank scared himself as he listened to the blood curdling screams erupt from his throat. He fell out of the bed and curled into a fetal position on the floor. The room felt clammy, like the swamp in his dream. There was a knock on the door that connected him to the room where Chief Big D was sleeping.

Boom, boom, boom! " Hank? Are you ok in there? HANK!"

Hank scrambled to the door and opened his side. In only his boxer shorts Chief Big D was towering in the doorway with a gun in his hand ready to shoot. "Whoa, Chief! Man, I am sorry. I had a nightmare. I am fine."

Chief Big D slowly let his hand slide down from the cocked position and let out a relieved sigh. "My God, you scared me, man." He looked back at the alarm clock which read 4:43 a.m. They had managed a little over two hours of sleep. It wasn't much, but it was more than nothing. "You want to go ahead and get showered up? Grab some breakfast before things get started? I don't think I can go back to sleep after hearing you scream like that. Besides, everybody is meeting back in the banquet room at six."

Even if he could, Hank wouldn't dare return to sleep for fear of dreaming that again. He wiped the cold sweat from his face and nodded. "Yeah, Chief. I'll meet you in fifteen."

Chief Big D returned his gun to the bedside table and grunted. "And keep your door open."

Hank stepped into the bathroom and turned the shower on as hot as it could go. He undressed and stepped into the water. He had wanted it to hurt a little, but not that much. He quickly jumped to the side and adjusted the water. He let the hot water run down his face and back, adjusting the water hotter and hotter until he was used to it. Finally, he turned it all the way cold and tilted his face directly into the icy stream. He clenched his muscles and fought the urge to jump from the shower until he was used to the temperature. Then, he quickly shut it off. He had always used this technique when he had to wake up fast. It always worked. He toweled off and dressed quickly without bothering to shave. Not many would see him since he would be in the surveillance room, not that he really cared anyway. Shaving was the last thing on his mind. He knocked on Chief Big D's cracked door. "I'm ready when you are, Chief."

"Come on in, man." Dressed and shaved, Chief Big D was stooped forward putting his shoes on. The hotel chair groaned underneath his heavy frame. "We'll have room service bring us some breakfast to the banquet room before everyone gets there, and then I want you to come on up here and get settled in. You can watch and hear everything from in there anyway. We got some last minute things to do and I don't want you any where near that room. Just in case, you know, he shows up early."

Hank cocked his head slightly to argue. "But, I want to be involved the whole way, Chief."

His face was reddened from the blood flow as he finished tying his shoe. When he straightened up the color began to diminish. "Nope. Hank, that's an order. It is not up for discussion. And besides, I need you to watch everything that is being done from a different perspective, to make sure everything is right."

Hank rolled his eyes and folded his arms. He knew it was a bullshit excuse but didn't argue. "Fine. Let's go."

The two men exited the room and knocked softly on the other hotel room doors. Melissa was the first to appear, dressed and ready. The second was Benjamin. He looked like he stepped right out of the classiest art affair that Manhattan could ever offer, completely out of place where he was. Chief nodded; it was a good thing. Lastly came Clover. As if she wasn't frail looking enough, the woman seemed to have aged ten years in two hours. Everyone knew without a shadow of a doubt that this woman had not slept one second. She staggered into the hallway and turned her back to the crowd as she slowly pulled her door shut. Melissa thought about saying good morning to her, but stopped herself. For Clover, there would be nothing good about it.

Silently, the team headed toward the elevators to begin the last minute and final preparations for their waiting game. No one knew what to expect, what to fear, or exactly what to look for. All they had was a piece of paper with a face on it that was conjured up by the memory of an old woman who hadn't seen it for decades, and a room full of beautiful bloody bait.

Chapter Forty Nine

Chief Big D found Ricardo behind the desk. His face was puffy from lack of sleep, but he was otherwise attentive and ready to please. "Good morning, Chief! Where do we begin?"

Chief Big D scratched his head as he surveyed the lobby for anything unusual. "Ricardo, how about we start with something to eat? Can you have someone bring us a little something to the banquet room? Nothing we have to sit down and eat. Maybe just some bagels or something? And some coffee, definitely some coffee."

"Can't catch the bad guys without a little caffeine, huh?" Ricardo picked up the phone and pressed a number.

Chief Big D rolled his eyes and walked everyone into the banquet room. It was just as beautiful as they had left it three hours ago. He closed the doors behind them so no one could see in. Melissa started making her rounds to check and make sure that the descriptions were all in the right place. She knew they were but wanted to keep herself busy. Her stomach growled with hunger, but she didn't feel like eating. She didn't want to be alone, but didn't feel like talking to anyone.

Clover sat restlessly in a chair near the entrance. She didn't want to go near the paintings that she had taken so much pride in all those years. She stared at the floor in silence like she had in her hotel room for the past three hours, and thought about what she was going to do, or how she would feel if she saw her son for the first time after leaving him so long ago. In her heart she knew that he was evil. She had always just wanted to hold him and feel him holding her back. Even as

216

a child he showed no comfort in her arms. She wondered if age had softened him some, if that maybe before they took him away he would reach his hands out to her, ask her to hold him. How could anyone capable of painting such beautiful paintings, such loving heart warming scenes, be incapable of love? She didn't know the answer. She had never known the answer. She simply ran away from it. There was nowhere to go now.

Chief Big D and Hank were going over possible scenarios when the food arrived. Shortly after, policeman from the station and the trusted accomplices started to quickly file into the banquet room. It was a buzz for a while as people drank coffee and shoved pastries into their mouths. At seven a.m. sharp, almost an hour after everyone had arrived, Chief Big D called everyone to attention.

"Alright guys, let's take it down a notch. I trust that everyone has gotten some food and coffee in their systems by now, so let's get down to business." Chief Big D hitched his pants up and took a deep breath. It made him look seven feet tall, and everyone fell silent. "We all got our jobs to do today, inside and outside this room. We all know what this monster looks like according to the sketch provided to us last night." He scanned the room and held up the sketch. "Now, I don't give a damn who the person is that you stop! If he even remotely looks like the man on this piece of paper, you stop him, detain him quickly and get on the radio. People, I need you to have hawk eyes. Now, I am not saying to be haphazard because we don't want to bring unwanted attention to this, so be prudent, discreet and careful. But I also want to make sure that if this guy comes, we catch him."

Everyone nodded except for Clover who seemed almost comatose in her corner.

Chief Big D continued. "I trust all of you! You are good at what you do, even you rookies. But we have never had to deal with something like this, so I'm just gonna say again, be careful. I do not want the press tipped off, not now anyway." He looked down at the floor for a second and lifted his head back up to the crowd as if he was preparing to say something crushing. "I am gonna say one last thing. I don't care if there are some of you out there who don't pray or believe in God. I really don't. But today, everyone in this room is gonna pray! You are gonna pray for the safe return of Doctor Judith Esther, pray for the capture of Roy Fontaine, pray for all of the women who lost their lives to him, and last but not least, you are going to pray for his mother Clover. After we pray, we wait."

All eyes turned to Clover. She sat wide eyed in the chair, aware for the first time of what was going on. She felt a mixture of being saved and being damned as the hunters of her son gathered around her in support.

In his mind Hank talked to Judith as Chief Big D led the prayer. "I'm coming, baby. Just hold on a little while longer. I'm coming." He was still mumbling words to her as Chief Big D ended the prayer and led him and Melissa out into the lobby. They signaled to Ricardo that everything was in place. From the elevator they watched as two police officers dressed as hotel employees joined Ricardo at the front desk, and then they disappeared behind the closing doors, en route to their surveillance station.

Chapter Fifty

Roy Fontaine stretched his arms into the air at 10:15 a.m. He yawned, sat straight up and glanced at the monitor for a glimpse of his sleeping beauty. Clad in Jillian Brannon's dirty yellow bikini, there she lay in all her glory, still asleep. The last time he had looked at his clock was around four a.m. Six hours of sleep was more than he needed to feel refreshed, and Roy felt wonderful. Today was his day. Everyday was his day as far as he was concerned, but today was special. In a few hours his name and his artwork would be applauded, revered, and honored. Some of his most proud collectors would be there, showing off their prized masterpieces, bragging to the next that theirs was nicer. He had to witness it, if only for a moment. Obviously he couldn't be gone too long, for he had a pending appointment with the Doctor.

He looked at his uniform and smiled. Such thought process he put into the details of his life! Such wisdom he had acquired through his experience in life. While he was busy admiring himself, a thought suddenly occurred to him. At first he was angry with himself for not thinking of it beforehand, but then he chuckled as if he was wise beyond his years: of course he would have eventually thought of it. Why? Because he was the definition of clever! He hadn't thought of the fact that the art display would most assuredly take place inside the lodge when he chose an outside uniform. He frowned at the prospect of not having a uniform good enough to blend in. Pool maintenance uniforms didn't necessarily have to match. Hotels usually employ contract workers for those types of jobs. However, in-house employees have regimented matching uniforms.

He sprang out of bed to the computer and Googled the Perdido Pass Lodge. The website displayed numerous tabs along with photos of the lodge. He found what he was looking for and clicked the mouse on 'STAFF'. First was the front desk staff, all smiles, in front of a fountain. Then came the entertainers standing in front of the piano. He scrolled down until he found housekeeping. Normal khaki uniforms as usual. He zoomed in on the photo and saw the Perdido Pass Lodge emblem on the shirt and smiled at his cunningness. He opened a desk drawer and searched through boxes of paper until he found the right one: iron-on transfers. Using his mouse he cut and pasted the logo into Paint, cleaned it up, loaded a sheet of transfer paper into his printer and walked toward his closet. He found a cotton short sleeve khaki shirt, pants to match, and a black belt and hat to match the man in the photo. By the time he left the closet, the transfer was waiting in the output tray of the printer. Pleased with the results, he returned to the closet and retrieved his iron and ironing board. Carefully, he cut out the logo from the transfer paper and placed it onto the shirt, glancing back and forth from the computer monitor to make sure it was exactly like the man in the photo. He pressed the iron down for the exact number of seconds the package instructed, whistling while he worked. The result was an exact match. True, it was not embroidered like the real uniforms, but from his experience in life, no one but he would notice such benign details. Next, he starched and ironed both shirt and pants, and hung them on hangers.

He hadn't abandoned his pool maintenance uniform. He would start off in that, do some surveillance, and if everything was clear, he would return to his van and change into his housekeeping uniform. Better to be prepared for anything. When in doubt, he always reminded himself that 'prevention is better than cure.'

Judith heard noises but didn't dare open her eyes. When she had first woken, her thoughts had been cloudy, and she had opened her eyes for a split second. It took only that long for her to realize that she should shut her eyes again. As she lay there listening to her captor walk around in another part of the house, she remembered the revelation she had come to before falling over into the wall in the hallway. She concentrated on breathing deeply and slowly to keep her eyes from twitching underneath her eyelids. If he was observing her closely it would give away her attempt at feigning sleep. For the first time since he had kidnapped her, Judith felt awake. The six hours of sleep were not nearly enough, but it was enough to clear her mind. The effects of the drugs had completely worn off, and she felt aware of all of her surroundings. She was aware of a printer working somewhere in the house. She heard every whistle that came from Roy's mouth and every foot step he took across the creaking wooden floors. During her captivity, she began to understand how important it was to be able to listen to her surroundings. It was just as important as being able to see. For the first time in her life she had an insight to what it felt like to be blind, as she had kept her eyes closed for a majority of the time while in his house. She had seen things that no one should witness. Photographs of mutilated bodies, screams of anguish and tortured pain captured forever in time, her own blood mixed into The Artist's paint. She knew that if she ever came out of this alive, she would be tortured by the memories of what she had seen in this house.

She willed herself to stop thinking about the horror of her situation. She knew she couldn't escape. But if Hank and Melissa, and no doubt the entire police force of Orange Beach and Gulf Shores, were out there trying to find her, then she would lay there in silence and give herself up to hope and faith. She prayed to God that Roy Fontaine was going to the art display. She prayed over and over again, acutely aware of his footsteps growing closer to her room. And then, he came to her.

Steady, Judith, keep your eyes closed. Don't twitch. Make yourself convince him.

As the door creaked open, she allowed her jaw to sag open slightly. She breathed in and out in time with her pulse. She thought of Hank, her mother, the children she cared for, anything that would take her mind off of him staring down at her. She could smell his rancid morning breath and feel the piercing glare of his evil eyes. Whatever she was doing was working. She sensed him backing up away from the bed. She also sensed him trying to trick her by opening the door and slowly shutting it. She didn't move. Her bottom jaw remained slightly relaxed, her breathing steady, in and out. When he finally did leave, she still did not let herself move. The only thing she couldn't control was the one tear that had managed to stay at bay until it could no longer remain caged. It trickled down her cheek as slowly as it could, as if it too, were trying to be careful.

Roy was pleased that she was still sleeping. No doubt she would wake up while he was gone, but where was she going to go? She could scream but no one would hear her. He walked into the bathroom and turned on his shower. There was one thing he had to take care of before he left and that was to clean up his head. There were a couple of patches of almost shaven hair that he had missed on the back of his head. He hadn't seen them yet, but he could feel them. He had to look neatly shaven to pull off the part of a beach bum employee at the Perdido Pass Lodge. He plugged some clippers into the wall socket and carefully worked his entire head. When he was finished, he used a handheld mirror to inspect his handiwork. There were still a couple of scabs left from where he had cut himself but they were only small nicks.

He stepped into the shower and bathed quickly. The show started at noon and he wanted to make sure he got there before anyone else did. Toweling off while walking into his bedroom, Roy could hardly contain his excitement. Not only because of the showing of his work, but thinking about Judith as well. He had spent a great deal of time in planning her death, and he was absolutely sure now of the way he would kill her. It had been a very long time since he had been able to spend this much time with a beauty, not to mention the fact that he wouldn't have to hurry to kill her and leave the scene. No. He could prolong it for however long he wanted; those were the best kind.

Completely dried he grabbed the pool maintenance shirt, pulled it over his bald head and down his torso. Then he stepped into the shorts. Paying much attention to the details of his bandana, he carefully folded it and pressed it around his forehead, tying it neatly at the base of his neck. The bandana had been one of his favorites while roaming the streets of New Orleans and picking off the prostitutes of Bourbon Street. It was faded and worn and perfect for what he needed. Next came the name tag. He pinned it on haphazardly because any other pool maintenance employee would have done the same thing. It was crooked, slanting down to the left. Finally he observed himself in the mirror. He had made a fine transition into Brannon the pool guy. He nodded curtly at himself and headed for the garage with his other uniform. Once inside he lifted the top off of a storage container and rummaged through an assortment of magnetic stickers for his van. Halfway through he found one for a generic cleaning company and stuck it on the side of the van. The time was 11:30a.m. Thirty minutes to snoop around, and he was more than ready. He backed out of the long driveway and used the remote control to close the garage door. Carefully looking through the foliage in all directions to make sure that no one saw him leave, he backed out into the road, put the van in drive and drove away in the direction of the lodge.

The little girl on the pink bicycle was scared to death. Her mother had forbid her to leave her street after having only learned how to ride several weeks ago. When she heard the garage door across the street begin to open she had darted into the bushes of a neighbor's house so that no one could tell her mother that she had broken the rules. After the van was gone, she broke free from the bushes that hid her and pedaled fast to get to her street again. Her heart didn't stop racing until she was safely back on her street and sliding into the gravel driveway of her parent's house.

Chapter Fifty One

Roy Fontaine turned onto the beach highway and drove towards the Perdido Pass Lodge. He had only been to the lodge once, but he knew enough about the layout to know where he should park. On the left hand side of the road was a BP gas station with two patrol cars parked side by side, and as he passed them, he glanced down to make sure he wasn't speeding. Relieved that he was not, Roy drove past with a smile as if he had gotten away with a bank robbery. Today was a special day and nothing would ruin it. Ahead he saw the big coral sign for the Perdido Pass Lodge on the right. Slowing down a bit, he craned his neck to gaze into the parking lot as he drove past. Nothing was out of the ordinary as far as he could see, and to his delightful surprise, he caught a glimpse of several white service vans parked in the rear of the parking lot. He drove past the entrance and kept driving down the beach road until he came to the Alabama Point Bridge. He exited the beach highway to the underpass and parked briefly beside a group of old men fishing the pass. From the rearview mirror he checked his appearance. Sweat had soaked into the bandana around his forehead, giving him the appearance that he had been working on all morning. He double checked his house keeping uniform and made sure that he had his black belt and hat and then hung the uniform back on the rack behind the passengers seat. This was it. It was time. He would park his van beside the others and quickly enter the rear of the lodge as nonchalantly as he could. The pool would be his first destination. The sun reflecting off the scales of a gutted bait fish caught his eye as he watched the fisherman cast it into the rushing waters of the Perdido Pass. Slowly, Roy put the van in drive again, drove under the bridge to the other side of the beach highway, and put his plan into motion. He turned left into the Perdido Pass Lodge, found the group of service vans in the rear of the left parking lot and coasted right into a parking space between two of the vans. It took less than ten seconds for him to see a crude pathway through the sea oats and sand to the back side of the lodge, and less than five minutes to reach the public beach access that led to the pool deck. Standing on the beach to the side of the lodge he hesitated. He didn't know why, but he did. Something didn't feel right, so he stared at the lodge and waited.

The waiting game had begun. Hank, Melissa and Chief Big D sat nervously in the hotel room that had been transformed into a surveillance station. Several other police officers, including Gulf Shore's finest, accompanied them as well. All eyes were glued to the monitors as they waited for any sign of The Artist. They watched the monitor of the banquet room closely as Marcus Donnarumma and Hillary waited to open the doors for the event. Acting as an assistant, Hillary was dressed like a runway model and stood beside Benjamin Preston with a clipboard in hand. Poised at the door to greet the guests, Marcus was dressed in a black suit and wire rimmed glasses. At straight up twelve p.m., he nodded to the hidden camera above the entrance and opened up the double doors to the banquet room.

The flyers about the art display around the lodge had caught the attention of several guests. Most of them were elderly, grandparents who preferred this type of activity over baking in the hot sun with their children and screaming grandchildren. They were waiting patiently for the doors to open. Mixed among them were people that Chief Big D and others had rounded up for the event. One by one the art lovers filed into the banquet hall to see the paintings of The Artist. Marcus greeted each person as they walked past.

Chief Big D nodded in the surveillance room. So far, so good.

Clover sat in the shade of a palm tree by a wooden bridge that arched over the main pool. She was in the direct view of a security camera that was being monitored by everyone in the surveillance room. Chief Big D had instructed her not to look at the camera, but she couldn't help but glance at it occasionally. She was a nervous wreck, although not nearly as bad as she had been when she had first walked out there. The sun had slightly thawed her nerves and left her wondering when the last time her face had felt sunshine. It had been years ago, with her husband. Her thoughts wandered from her murderous son to her dead husband, and for a while, she forgot about the camera, the paintings, her son, and daydreamed about the life she had finally found but lost.

Roy Fontaine's epiphany never came to explain why he had felt the urge to hesitate moments before. But he didn't feel it anymore. The lodge and the guests around the pool displayed no danger to him, so he walked calmly through the white sand to one of the wooden ramps that led to the pool. He reached into his pocket and fished out a pair of Ray Ban knockoffs and briskly walked the planks to the outer concrete. Along the far wall was a maintenance door that had been left ajar. Holding his head up with confidence and purpose so as not to draw any unwanted attention, he walked to the door and slipped inside to look for anything that would help him blend in better. On the far back wall were shelves and compartments. Roy searched through them quickly until he found what he wanted, an old chlorine test kit. Suddenly the door slammed shut, sealing him into the noisy room. He ran past the pumps and reached out to the knob, hoping that he wasn't locked in from the inside. The knob turned and he laughed with relief. He waited a minute before he opened it, took a deep breath and walked out into the sun. There were a total of four pools, all connected to each other with a main pool in the center. From the main pool the view was directly into the hotel. Unfortunately for Roy though, the sun light was reflecting off the glass windows, making it impossible to see into the lodge. So, he rounded the main pool to find a better view point and found the left entrance way to the wooden bridge that arched over the main pool. A pool attendant carrying an empty service tray was crossing the bridge toward him and Roy had no choice but to wave at him in a friendly manner and prepare for conversation. "Hey there, man!"

The pool attendant stopped to make idle chat but was too interested in a tanned bikini-clad teenager floating in the pool to pay any real attention to Roy. He stared at the long legged girl as he answered. "How's it goin', man? Checking the water?"

Roy smiled and sucked on his teeth as he rocked back and forth on his feet. "Yep, that time o' the day, man." He followed the attendants gaze to the girl in the pool and felt a ripple in his gut. In a split second he had fantasized in complete detail how he would kill her.

Not wanting to leave his perfect view point, the attendant kept the small talk going. "Man, she is hot! How old do you think she is? Sixteen? Seventeen?"

The two men didn't notice a woman coming their way until they heard her say, "Excuse me" in order to pass them.

Still watching the young girl, Roy and the attendant simultaneously answered, "Sorry about that," and let the woman pass.

From the surveillance room Chief Big D watched the female officer on the bridge pass the pool employees and step off the bridge to where Clover was sitting under the palm tree. The woman sat beside Clover and gave Chief Big D the sign that everything was ok. He switched his attention to a monitor in the front lobby.

"How are you feeling Clover? Do you need anything?"

Clover shook her head at the woman. She did not know the woman's name but knew she was one of the police officers involved in the set up.

Roy Fontaine was leaning on the end of the bridge when he heard the woman who had just passed speak to the old woman in the chair on the other side. He hadn't heard the name Clover in a very long time. It was his mother's middle name, but she never used it. He continued to stare at the teenager along with the pool attendant until he heard the next words.

"Your paintings sure are drawing some attention in there, Clover. I must admit, your son, for what it's worth, is a very talented, man. I looked at all fifty two of them."

Every joint in Roy's body stiffened. Every man, woman and child surrounding him disappeared. The churning water in the pool came to a stagnant rest, and the sun rays turned icy against his skin. In an instant, a rage that Roy had never known before ignited with such severity that he immediately grew dizzy. In an instant he knew. In just

227

one instant, he knew that his mother was alive after all these years. In a flash he understood that she was probably responsible for buying most of his paintings and that most of his life, the way he had always known it to be, had been a farce. The sounds came rushing back slowly. He heard the attendant say something to someone. He turned just in time to watch the woman walk back across the bridge. Blinking with both eyes he held onto the railing of the bridge and slowly rolled his head in the direction of the woman named Clover. There she sat, wrinkled and weathered, gray hair flying in the wind around her face and whipping across a pair of bright blue eyes that matched the pool water beside her. He wanted to leap over the side and rip those eyes from their sockets, tear her to pieces with his bare hands, but he couldn't move. He was paralyzed with rage and disbelief. After a minute had passed, the attendant beside him, still completely unaware of anything but the girl, decided that he better keep on moving, after all, he was working. He grabbed the service tray from the ledge and walked away. "See ya, man," he called out to Roy.

Roy knew that he had to act fast, but he didn't know what to do. His thoughts raced through his head as he struggled on what the next move should be. Was this all a set up? Could all of this really be at the hands of his own mother? Cameras! There had to be cameras. Look! No, don't look. Act normal. Damn, where did that attendant go? Pool kit. Test the water. Hurry!

He carefully turned around away from the bridge around to where his mother was sitting. Several feet away from her was a pool drain. He didn't want to get too close to her in case someone was watching, so he walked to the drain and bent down on his knees and stared at the water. He had no idea what he was doing, but he had seen someone check chlorine levels from a pool before. He opened the kit and found the vial for the water. When he bent over to fill the vial with pool water, he cautiously looked over at his mother's face. His own face filled with blood as he struggled to keep his lips from quivering and snarling. The sight of her made him want to explode with anger. He forced himself to act out the chlorine test, and then walked away from her toward the beach. One thing was certain: his mother was coming with him. He had to get back to the van and figure out how. Backtracking the way he came in, he found the sand and hurried back to the parking lot.

Chapter Fifty Two

Hank fidgeted in his seat. His eye sockets hurt from glancing back and forth from monitor to monitor, and his head ached from the building pressure and restlessness. He pulled out the picture of Judith for comfort and ran his finger across her face just as a peculiar looking man stepped onto the scene in the banquet room. He was pale and thin with a head full of dark hair. Hank sat up in his chair and pointed him out to the others in the room. By then Marcus Donnarumma had already noticed him and was signaling to the camera above the doorway. All eyes were on the man as he circled the paintings, inspecting them one by one with one hand on his chin. He read each description and studied each painting with what appeared to be genuine curiosity. Chief Big D held up the sketch of Roy Fontaine and studied the similarities. They were striking. He called Marcus' cell phone.

"Alright Marcus, we are watching him. Lay low for now. Let him walk around, and when he leaves we will be waiting in the front lobby. Just keep an eye on him for right now."

It was 1:30p.m., and this was the first person who even remotely resembled anything about the sketch. Everyone held their breath as they watched the man slowly make his way through the paintings one by one.

When Roy reached the van he almost tore off the sliding door when he opened it. Once inside, he slammed the door shut and bit down on a stray piece of rope on the floor to keep from screaming to the top of his lungs. He bit down until it hurt. Pain was what he wanted to feel. After he calmed down enough to think straight, he concentrated on his breathing and closed his eyes. It was time to put together a master plan in a very short period of time. He opened his eyes and glanced over at the uniform that he had ripped off the rack when he had entered the van. It lay crumpled on the floor but it was still fairly unwrinkled. He stared at the ensemble long enough to know that it would be too big, but that it would have to work. Next, he thought of his mother and all the times that he had ever manipulated her when he was growing up. It didn't take much to control her with fear, but that was then and this was now. When he had studied her face at the pool, he saw the look of raw fear on her face, so he would just have to trust his instincts.

There was an assortment of trash on the floorboard of the van that had been there since he purchased it. There were flattened convenience store paper bags, and old empty cigarette box, and a crushed Mountain Dew can. Looking around he saw a piece of black plastic sticking out from underneath the passenger seat. He tugged on it until it came loose. It was perfect for what he needed. He grabbed the housekeeping uniform, the belt and hat and shoved it into the old black trash bag. He looked around the parking lot to make sure no one was running through it trying to find him, opened the door and headed quickly back to the pathway through the dunes. Once around the building, he took the ramp and walked toward the main pool. There was no turning back now. Even if he wanted to, he couldn't stop himself. He was fueled by a deep hatred that controlled his every move. How dare her!

Chief Big D took a second to glance over at the monitor to check on Clover. She was sitting in the same position that she had been all afternoon, and everything else looked normal. The same people who were out there before were still there. He turned his attention back to the strange man in the banquet room.

Roy rounded the corner and found the female restroom on the side of the cabana where the pool attendants ordered their drinks. Directly behind the cabana was a drop off of no more than two feet. Below it was the sand and a clear pathway to the side of the building where his van was parked. From there he could clearly see his mother sitting under the palm tree. He knocked on the door of the restroom to make sure no one was in there. When no one answered he slipped into the bathroom and walked into a stall where he hung the uniform, belt and hat on the back of the door. Acting fast, he slowly opened the bathroom door and peaked outside. With the black plastic bag in hand, he walked hurriedly to the pool drain near his mother. This time he crouched down on her side of the drain, opened it and pretended to collect the trash from it. He raised his head slightly so she could see his face, and with a calm and eerie voice, he spoke to her for the first time since she left all those years ago.

"If you look up or signal anyone in any way, I will kill you instantly. Stare at the pool, and listen to me. When I finish cleaning this drain, I am going to stand up and walk to the back of the cabana. Then you will get up and go to the bathroom where you will find a housekeeping uniform hanging on the door. Put it on and make it fit. Hide your hair underneath the hat, step outside and walk to the backside of the cabana. I will be watching you every step of the way, mother."

Clover stared at the pool through blinding tears. She wanted to look at him so badly.

Hank glanced over at the monitor to check on Clover. Everything seemed normal. She was still sitting in the same position, although he couldn't see her face for the pool guy cleaning the drain. He quickly glanced at all the other monitors before turning his attention back on the man. Frustration was building and he wanted to charge into the banquet room and tackle the man. He knew he had to wait. The muscles in his legs twitched with anticipation.

Roy fished out the remains of dead flowers from the drain and placed them in the bag. "Answer my question by tapping your foot slightly. Is someone watching you right now?"

Clover moved her foot slowly.

"Will they come looking for you if you go to the bathroom?"

She couldn't stop the tears from coming and her frail frame jerked slightly as she fought to catch her breath. She couldn't signal to him that she had been instructed to use the cabana phone to call them when she needed to go to the bathroom, so she attempted to whisper. He listened.

"Call them now. And remember, I will be watching and listening. Go now."

Clover struggled to stand up but for a moment her legs would not hold her up. She shook uncontrollably as her son finished the drain and walked away. With nervous eyes she dared to glance all around her before she was able to walk to the cabana. On the way she wiped her face as best she could and asked the girl behind the counter to dial the room number that she was instructed to use.

The phone rang in the room and everyone jumped in their seats. Searching the monitors before they answered it, they saw that it was Clover. Chief Big D answered the phone on the fifth ring. "Clover? Everything ok?" He watched the monitor showing the man in the banquet room while he talked to her.

She inhaled a deep breath and answered as steadily as she could, trying not to show any emotion. "I need to go to the restroom."

Chief Big D put a hand over the phone and said to everyone, "Just a bathroom break." He returned to Clover, "Ok, go ahead. We are watching you." He watched Clover return the phone to the cabana girl and walk to the bathroom door. He made sure no one followed her in and then returned to watch the man in the banquet room. Everyone in the room was getting antsy. Minute by minute, the man seemed to be just a normal average tourist with a love for art. Still he had to be questioned. He glanced back over to the monitor to see if Clover was finished, but she was still in the bathroom.

Clover walked to the first stall, opened it, and practically fell into the toilet. Her legs were shaking so bad that she had to sit for a moment to gather her thoughts. The cabana bathroom was stifling hot. The only ventilation was a flap vent on the back wall near the ceiling. The stringent odor of bathroom cleanser and urine filtered through her nose and made her gag. She remembered him telling her to hurry. If she didn't, he would surely come in there and kill her and get away. Then she heard her name through the flap vent. He was saying it as if

232

he were sweetly calling to a dog that had run off. "Cloooooover. Where are you?"

She cringed and sobbed through tears as she pulled off her clothes and put the uniform on. Trying her best to hurry and make the outfit work, she pulled the belt tight around her waist and under cuffed the pants. Raking her trembling fingers through her damp grey hair, she fashioned it into a makeshift bun and pulled the black hat on. There were strays that didn't get caught up in the bun so she pushed them under the lid of the cap and quickly exited the stall. The mirror gave her a cold goodbye as she glanced at her reflection before leaving the bathroom. As instructed, she stepped out of the bathroom and into the shade of the cabana. For a fleeting moment she dared to stare straight into the camera, but when she glanced to the back of the cabana, she could see part of his blue shirt, and knew that he was waiting for her. She took a deep ragged breath, rounded the corner and jumped off the two foot ledge to where her son was waiting for her. Minutes later she was politely escorted into the van, at which time her legs buckled beneath her. Roy caught her before her knees hit the pavement and quickly threw her into the van.

The sudden movement on Clover's monitor caught Hank's attention. But when he saw the housekeeper exit the bathroom, he returned to the other monitors. After a couple of minutes of glancing back and forth, he began to worry. The strange man in the banquet room was just finishing the last of the paintings, so everyone's attention had been on him. Curious as to how much time had passed since Clover went into the bathroom, he tapped on Chief Big D's shoulder. "How long has she been in there?"

Chief Big D studied the monitor. "Too long. But she is old. I am watching for her. I saw the housekeeper come out. She should be out any minute now." Chief tapped his pen up and down on the table, getting ready to call Marcus and the boys in the lobby. He watched as the strange man clasped his hands together and headed for the doors of the banquet room. It was time. He radioed for everyone to get in position. Hank could sit no longer. He shot up out of the chair and watched nervously as the man exited the room. Another monitor showed three men casually walk up to the man, flash their badges and escort him into the office behind the front desk. Chief Big D glanced from monitor to monitor as they waited on the word back from the office. His cell phone rang and everyone held their breath.

"It's not him. We are positive."

Chief addressed the room. "It's not him, guys." Then he addressed the caller. "Hold him anyway until I can get down there."

Suddenly the door opened and Hank bolted out of the room. Everyone called out to him to stop. Chief Big D ran after him but lost him on the stairs. He grabbed his radio and yelled to the officers, "Hank's lost it! He's coming after him! Stop him before he gets to the office!"

Marcus Donnarumma ran from the banquet room to help thwart Hank from getting to the guy. As he ran down the short hallway and into the lobby, something outside by the pool caught his attention. He ran to the window in time to see Hank finish crossing the bridge in the direction of the cabana. Marcus radioed Chief Big, "Chief! He's not after the guy! He is running to the pool cabana! Look at the monitor."

Chief Big D ran back into the surveillance room and checked the monitor just as Hank disappeared into the bathroom. He sighed in relief until he saw what Hank was carrying in his hands when he exited. "My God, Marcus follow him!" He looked back at everyone who was staring pale faced at the monitor. "My God! He's got Clover!" They watched as Hank threw the clothes down on the concrete and ran out of sight to the back of the cabana. Marcus was close behind him. Chief Big D yelled, "Where are they headed? What camera will show them?"

One of the officers in the room checked the map and yelled back, "The left parking lot. They are headed to the left parking lot!" One monitor covered both parking lots, and switched every couple of seconds back and forth. The officer tapped some keys on a keyboard so that the monitor would show only the left side parking lot. Everyone watched as Hank ran from vehicle to vehicle. Marcus finally caught up with him, and on the monitor it appeared that they were arguing back and forth. Finally Marcus radioed in. He yelled frantically into the receiver, "Back it up! Back up the tape! Hurry!"

The officer quickly performed a five minute back up on the surveillance tape of the left parking lot. Melissa chewed her fingers nervously as she watched in silence. Nothing. No movement. No cars. A minute ticked by. Two minutes. There! A man in a blue shirt and a housekeeper getting into a white van! Chief Big D leaned in to study the scene and his mouth dropped open. He slammed his fist down on the table and yelled, "Son of a bitch! That's the pool guy! No!"

The room erupted in radio calls and flying paper while Chief Big D, Melissa, and Hillary ran from the room to the hallway. They were in the parking lot in less than five minutes. Hank was spinning around with his hands to his temples as Melissa and Hillary tried to calm him down. Seconds later Chief Big D got a phone call from the officer who had backed up the tape. They had a license plate number for the van. Minutes later they had an address. It was a house in Gulf Shores on Twenty Second Street. Chief Big D grabbed Hank, shoved him into his SUV and sped out onto the Beach Highway toward Gulf Shores. By the time they arrived, Gulf Shore's police had surrounded the house. Chief Big D jumped from the driver's seat and barreled over to the officer who was yelling through a microphone at the residents in the house. There were two old and rusted white work vans and a pick up truck parked in the driveway. Suddenly, a very hung over looking man appeared in the doorway with his hands in the air. It didn't take long for them to find out that he wasn't Roy Fontaine. He was an unemployed construction worker with a serious drinking problem who had sold the van to a man months ago. His house was searched thoroughly while Hank sat silently in the passenger seat of Chief's SUV. He had given up hope.

Chapter Fifty Three

The police scanner buzzed with the BOLO of the white van. Caitlin had left the florist early and was sitting in the kitchen while her two children watched television in the living room. She was exhausted from making the flower arrangements for the art display at the Perdido Pass Lodge. Her fingers ached as she soaked them in Epsom salt to sooth her arthritis. Although she didn't know all the details about what was going on, she knew that her sister Hillary was at the Perdido Pass Lodge, and she knew enough to worry about her. She hated listening to the stupid police scanner, but she always turned it on if she knew that Hillary was on a hot case.

Suddenly her twelve year old son Sebastian came bursting into the room screaming, "Mom! Mom! Chelsea rode her bike on the other street! She left the street, Mom!"

Chelsea was hot on his heels to stop him from telling on her. "Sebastian, don't!" she yelled while tugging on his shirt.

Caitlin sighed and wiped her hands on a dish towel. She did not feel like reprimanding her children right now, but rules were rules, and she had to punish her. She stood up from the table with her hands on her hips and stared down at her daughter who was now cowering by the table. "Chelsea? Did you leave the street? Don't lie to me! Tell me the truth!"

The little girl shot a hateful look toward her brother and finally nodded. "Yes, ma'am."

Sebastian folded his arms over his stomach and eagerly gave out more information. "She almost got ran over by a man in a white van too!"

Chelsea punched him in the arm and shrieked back at him in anger, "You said you wouldn't tell!"

Sebastian stuck his tongue out at her until Caitlin reached out and swatted him on the arm. She had heard enough from both of them. "Both of you! To your rooms! Now!"

Sebastian protested. "But, Mom!"

"I said NOW! Caitlin, no bicycle for a week! Now both of you, go, and don't come out until dinner!"

She sat back down at the kitchen table and rubbed her temples. A stress headache was fast coming as she kneaded her head with her sore fingers. Finally, she got up and retrieved a bottle of aspirin from a cabinet, swallowed two of them and chased them with a glass of water from the sink. From the refrigerator she grabbed a package of hamburger meat and placed it on the counter beside a box of Hamburger Helper. No effort on her part would be going into dinner tonight. She bent down to the lower cabinet to search for a skillet when suddenly she stopped dead in her tracks. A chill spread up her spine as she slowly stood up. Did she hear her son correctly in that a man in a white van almost ran over Chelsea? She stood at the counter processing the conversation cautiously, wondering if she should be concerned. There were, of course, hundreds of white service vans on the island, but none that she could ever recall seeing in her neighborhood. She placed a throbbing hand over her mouth and stared at the stairs leading up to the children's bedroom. There was definitely a BOLO out for a white van, the license plate numbers she couldn't remember. She had to call it in. She tilted her head toward the ceiling as if her answer would be found there. Finally, she walked up the stairs and into her daughter's bedroom where she lay crying on the bed.

Caitlin stood in the doorway watching Chelsea sob until the child realized that she was there and turned face down into the pillow. "Chelsea, sit up."

Chelsea lifted her head from the pillow and faced her mother.

Caitlin walked to the bed and sat beside her. "Chelsea, is it true that a man in a white van almost hit you today?"

The little girl, terrified if her answer would land her in more trouble, sat motionless on the bed.

"Chelsea, you are not going to get in anymore trouble. But I need you to tell me the truth. It's important."

Wiping away a tear from her red cheek, Chelsea nodded. "Yes, ma'am."

"Ok. Tell me what happened." She knew many of the people who lived in or had rental houses in and around her neighborhood, so before she called in accusing or alerting, she wanted to make sure it wasn't someone she knew.

Chelsea sat straight up in the bed and pointed out of her bedroom window. "I rode down that way to the end of the street and then I turned left toward the bay. When I got to the end of the road, I turned around and came back. But then I heard a garage door opening, and," she looked down at the bed, humiliated that she had disobeyed her mother, "I didn't want anyone to tell on me so I hid in some bushes. The man backed out onto the street and almost hit me. But then he drove away, and I came straight home."

"Did you see what the man looked like?"

Chelsea shook her head. "No, ma'am. But he was wearing a red doo-rag."

Caitlin knew that was slang for bandana. It was a popular thing for kids to wear at the beach. She stared out of the window debating what to do. Finally she decided that she would drive by the house first before she called it in. "C'mon with me. I want you to show me which house the man came out of." Chelsea looked hesitant, as if she could sense more punishment, like having to apologize to the man. Caitlin saw the look on her daughter's face. "I already told you that you weren't going to get into any more trouble. Now, come, show me where."

She yelled down the hallway to her son's bedroom. "Sebastian, we will be right back! Stay in your room!"

He peeked his head out of the door and started to protest that he wanted to go, but thought better of it and shut the door again.

Caitlin drove her daughter to the end of the street and turned left. She slowed down when she heard her daughter say, "There!"

"Are you sure that's the house, Chelsea?"

The little girl nodded and pointed to the left, "There's the bushes I was hiding in, with the pink flowers."

Caitlin stared at the house. It looked empty and boarded up, like many of the rental or vacation homes in Orange Beach whose owners

238

used it once or twice a year. Something about the house was spooky, and she decided to call Hillary. She was sure it would amount to nothing, but still, there was an active and urgent BOLO. She made a u-turn in the road and dialed Hillary's number on her cell phone. It went to voice mail. "Hey Hill, it's Cate. Listen, I am sure it's nothing, but Chelsea saw a man in a white van earlier today, and well, just call me. It's a long story." She hung up and placed the phone in her purse but had to fish it out as soon as she turned in her driveway. It was Hillary. "Hello?"

Hillary spoke very fast into the phone. "Hey Cate, sorry, things are crazy down here. Can I call you later?"

"Did you listen to my message?"

"Uh, no, hold on," Silence, "Ok, sorry, I had to answer that. What was the message?" She was almost out of breath.

"Chelsea saw a man in a white van today while she was riding on her bike, and I thought I would call you about it."

"Yeah, she and about everyone else in Orange Beach and Gulf Shores has seen a man in a white van. It's an absolute nightmare at the station. Did she say what he looked like? Damn, hold on, I have to take this, sorry."

Caitlin waited patiently for Hillary to return to the phone. Several minutes later she returned.

"Ok, sorry, did she get a description?"

"Not really. All she saw was that he was wearing a red bandana, or doo-rag as she calls them. I made her take me to where…"

Hillary quickly interrupted her. "What? Did you say red bandana?"

Caitlin bit her lip, uncertain if that was good or bad. "Yeah, a red bandana. And she showed me his house."

Hillary ignored the other phones ringing and people running around. Word had quickly spread across the island by way of "coconut telegraph" about the search for the white van. They had taken dozens of calls about a white van and male driver, but none of them had been reported wearing a red bandana, the same as the pool guy from the lodge. "Ok, Caitlin? Are you at home?"

"Yes."

"Stay there. I will be there in about ten minutes." She hung up before Caitlin could ask any questions.

Chapter Fifty Four

Judith nearly vomited when she heard the garage door open and close. He was back to finish her. She did dry heave when she heard the sickening cries of another woman reverberating throughout the house. At some point while he was gone she had developed a fever, no doubt from the uncleaned wounds she had sustained, and her head felt like it was splitting open like a rotten melon. The woman cried out over and over in pain while Roy threw things around the house and yelled incoherently. She heard glass break and what she thought was a chair being thrown across the room. Every second was worse than Hell, lying there listening but not knowing what would happen next. And then they came, the footsteps charging towards her doorway accompanied by more screams of pain. The door flew open and Judith couldn't stop herself from looking up at what was coming for her. What she saw was clearly not what she had expected. Instead of an unfortunate young buxom woman screaming, it was an elderly haggard grey haired woman in an oversized housekeeping uniform. With a face gorged with blood and anger, Roy threw the old woman into the room hard enough to crack bones and slammed the door shut behind him.

Clover grew silent and still but acutely aware of the situation. Seconds before her son threw her across the room, she made eye contact with Judith, Detective Hank's fiancée, who was tied to the bed. Now she cowered against the foot of the bed and said nothing. Slamming his feet down hard against the wood floor, Roy crossed the room and stared down at Judith. With one hand he grabbed a fistful of Clover's hair and pulled her up to him so that she could see his beauty.

"Doctor Esther," he said between clenched jaws, "Meet my mother, Irene." He thrusted his mother's face closer to Judith while the two women stared hopelessly at each other. Both feared imminent death, but strangely, were relieved in some small way that they wouldn't die alone. It was the smallest of comforts, but the only one they had.

Roy was outraged and confused. Before he killed his mother, he wanted to know in exact detail how they found him. He wanted to know everything that took place after he kidnapped Judith. And he wanted to record it so he could watch it over and over and over again so that he could learn from his mistakes. He let go of Clover, and she crumpled to the floor. Disgusted at himself and her, he left the room to plan.

When the door slammed shut, neither woman said a word for several minutes. What was the use of talking when they only had minutes to live? Sobbing, with her face tilted toward the box springs, Clover sat awkwardly against the bed while Judith prayed with her eyes closed. Finally, Judith broke the silence. "Irene?" she whispered. "Irene?"

Clover stared at the door and listened to her son thrash around the house. She pulled on the side on the bed for support and managed to upright herself. She had seen all of the gruesome paintings and photos of the headless, mutilated and dismembered bodies in her son's house. The last thing she wanted to do was get to know this woman minutes before they both died, but she did the only right thing she could do. She stood up, leaned over the bed, and grasped one of Judith's hands in hers. "Yes, Judith, I am here," she said between choked breaths.

Judith swallowed her own tears in between gasps and whispered back. "You know who I am, don't you?"

Clover nodded in silence.

"You met my fiancé? Hank?"

Clover squeezed her hand and nodded again while attempting to wipe the tears away. She looked away at the door, forever ready for her son to come in and take their lives.

Judith swallowed and tried to smile. Her lips were cracked and bleeding, but she couldn't feel them. "Is he coming for me?"

Clover let out a painful sob and smiled back at her. Her voice cracked as she spoke. "He's trying, honey. He's trying."

Judith whispered, "Thank you," closed her eyes again and continued to pray.

Clover continued to stare at the door while holding her hand. She looked around the room for anything she could use as a weapon. She knew that her son would kill her and this women, but she would be damned if she didn't try and stop him. She turned her back briefly to the door to inspect the bedside table. She knew there would be nothing in the drawer to help her, but she opened it anyway. Sure enough, it was empty. When she heard something make a clinking noise as she shut the drawer, she stopped and turned quickly toward the door. Frozen in a position of fright, she listened. When she heard nothing else, she continued to close the drawer, when she heard it again. This time, she realized that the sound was coming from inside the drawer. Carefully, she stood up and put her hand into the drawer, feeling around all the way to the back. Suddenly she found the sound maker. Her fingers told her exactly what she was touching, and her heartbeat sped up. She heard her son stomping through another part of the house and hesitated to move.

Judith heard the key also, but it didn't immediately register what it was. She weakly turned her head to see what Clover was doing, and shock spread over her face when she saw her standing there holding a key in the air, as if frozen in time.

Clover glanced at the key and then to a restraint on Judith's arm. Carefully, she inserted the key and turned it. Both women held their breath until they heard a pop and click as the restraint fell open.

Chapter Fifty Five

Hank, Hillary and Melissa fishtailed into Caitlin's driveway, throwing gravel in the air as the vehicle came to an abrupt stop. Chief Big D was on the way from Gulf Shores after being called to a suspicious residence down Fort Morgan Road. Manpower was extremely low due to the volumes of calls they had received after putting out the BOLO, but backup was due in the next ten minutes. Caitlin was in the driveway waiting for them.

Hank turned to Melissa who was seated in the middle of his truck. "Melissa. This is extremely important or I wouldn't ask you to do this. Catlin needs to show us where this house is. Can you stay?"

Melissa stopped him. "Of course I will. I will wait here for you to come back."

Hillary let her out and slid over to the middle so Caitlin could jump in. Careful not to peel out of her driveway, he followed Caitlin's directions to the house. He drove by slowly and stared at the house. The hair on the back of his neck stood up as he searched the property with his eyes. "Something's not right about this house, Hill."

Unaware that she had instinctively placed her hand on her gun, she nodded. "I agree. Drive Caitlin back down to the end of her street, and we will come back on foot."

Hank turned around in a driveway a couple of houses down the street and passed the house again. It seemed completely deserted, but Chelsea had sworn it was the same house she saw the man leaving from. Then he saw fresh tire tracks in the dirt beside the mailbox, as if the van had missed the driveway on more than one occasion. He pointed out what he saw to Hillary, and she craned her neck over him to see.

Hillary nervously leaned back against the seat and turned to her sister. "When he parks the truck, get out and run back to your house. I am turning off my radio, and my cell phone will be on silent. Get back to the house as fast as you can and call the station. Tell them I said to hurry. Something is definitely not right!"

Caitlin nodded nervously and asked nothing. Before Hank could even place the truck in park, she bolted from the passenger seat and ran at break neck speed down the road to her house. Hank came to a full stop in an overgrown driveway of a small house that was obviously used once or twice a year. He and Hillary quickly got out of the truck and ran through the back yard of the house which spilled out onto the street of the house in question . They crossed the street quickly and ran through back yards until they reached the house. Slightly out of breath, they breathed slowly in and out before moving in. The overgrown back yard was covered with pine needles and briars, and patches of sand sprinkled the yard. There was a sliding glass door on the back of the house, but it was covered on the inside by wooden boards, as were all the windows, as if preparing for an incoming hurricane.

Hank crept onto the grass but froze when he heard something. It was a muffled sound, but he thought it sounded like broken glass. He wasn't even sure it had come from the house. He looked back at Hillary and knew that she had heard it too. They waited and listened but heard nothing more. As quietly as they could, with pine needles endlessly crunching under their feet, they snuck around the entire house, checking each window. They found the same thing in each one, wood. Then they heard something else, and this time they knew it was coming from inside the house. They ran quickly to the neighbor's yard and Hillary called Chief Big D. "Where are you? Chief, there is something definitely wrong with this house! You need to get here quick!"

Chief Big D's big black SUV was roaring down Canal Road at ninety miles an hour, weaving in and out of traffic. "I am on my way, Hill! I am about five minutes away!"

Chapter Fifty Six

Clover unlocked the last restraint, and Judith sprang to the end of the bed. The sudden movement made her dizzy, but she shook it off as quickly as she could. She slid off the bed and limped to the window while Clover watched. She moved the heavy curtains to the side and found soundproof padding that was securely adhered to the wooden frame of the window. She dug a fingernail underneath the padding and wiggled it slightly to see how difficult it would be to loosen it; it proved surprisingly easy as her finger pried a corner up to the next level. What she found next was disappointing. The window had been boarded up with wood. There would be no way to loosen the wood without a hammer to pry up the nails. Judith quickly scanned the room for something that would work, but found absolutely nothing.

Roy Fontaine circled his room in a panic. He had been in panic mode since he left the lodge with his mother, and he was not very familiar with the feeling of it. He had switched on the television earlier to check the local news and still nothing about him or Judith's disappearance. In the midst of his panicked thought process, a different idea came to him, and he stopped to ponder the possibility of what kind of set up the art show was exactly. Was it a set up by the police or was there a chance that it was simply a set up by Benjamin Preston to find out who The Artist really was and expose him to the public. He had never even thought to ask his mother; he just assumed it was a set up by the police. If he had been listening to a police scanner he would have known by now that the police were searching for his van. He remembered what his mother had whispered to him about having to call "them" in case she needed to go to the bathroom, but she never said who they were, and he never asked. He found some sort of consolation in this idea, and it calmed him down enough to stop pacing and start focusing. Once again, his ego began to cloud his perceptions.

He heard something squeaking in the distance, somewhere in the house. At first it sounded like a mouse, and he tilted his neck to listen more carefully. Then he heard a scratching noise. He crossed the room to his computer, moved the mouse so he could see into Judith's bedroom and was shocked. Shocked at what he saw, and shocked at himself for being so stupid. The camera didn't show the whole room, and the women were nowhere to be seen, but he knew where they were. They were scratching at the wood that boarded the window. Laughing as loud as he could to make sure they heard him, he continued to watch the screen to see if they would scurry back into position before he got to the room. They did not. So he laughed louder.

Hank decided to circle the house again. One window in particular had caught his attention more than the others. It was a decorative window that had a fake stained glass lining. Some of the lining had peeled away, exposing wood. It stood out from the others which only showed wooden planks. He crept up beside the window and listened. At first he heard nothing, but then he heard a kind of scratching noise against the wood behind it. He whispered into a window pain. "Is there someone in there?" No one spoke back to him, but the scratching sound continued. Hank's heart began to pound as he listened to the noise. He quickly stepped around the house within Hillary's view and motioned for her to join him. When she reached the window he put a finger to his mouth and signaled for her to listen to the window pane. Her eyes grew wide as she heard the sounds as well.

Roy snuck down his hallway of death on tip toes so he could surprise the women. Then he would ask his mother about the details of the art show. From there, he would begin his work. He reached the door and listened quietly. The women weren't talking, just desperately trying to escape. He quietly turned the knob and sprang into the room to catch them off guard. Judith let out a blood curdling scream as she flailed her fists against the wooden planks.

Hank, who had his ear to one of the window panes, fell backwards into Hillary when he heard the scream. He had never heard her scream before, but he knew it was Judith. He up righted himself quickly and turned to Hillary. They had to act, and they had no time to wait for back up. It was obvious that the women were in this room. Hank ran to the front of the house and looked at the garage door. It was old and worn down, so it was possible that he could manually lift it. He tried and it budged a little. Hillary stopped him when she heard the metal whine against his pull. "Hank," she desperately cried through whispers, "He will hear this!"

Running out of time and frantic to get in the house, Hank had to struggle to keep his wits. Hillary was right. They needed grease, oil, something to stop the door from making a sound. Hillary ran back to the neighbor's yard out of ear shot from whoever could be in the house and called her sister who answered on the first ring. "Caitlin. Hurry! Uhm, do you have any, uh, oil, or oh! WD40? Do you have that?"

Caitlin stuttered. "Yes, yes, I do!"

"Bring it now! Hurry! I will meet you at the end of the street!" Hillary dashed through the yards and by the time she made it to the street, Caitlin was pulling up with the can of WD40. She passed it quickly to Hillary who made a mad dash back down the road to Hank. On the way she called Chief Big D who was turning off Canal Road and heading in their direction. "Chief, we are going in! Can't explain! Stay back!" Before the Chief could say anything, she flipped the phone shut and turned the ringer off.

Hank was crying and clenching his fists when she got back to him. He grabbed the door again and pulled up. Each time he did, Hillary squatted and sprayed both sides. Inch by inch the garage door slowly came up. Hank was straining so hard that the veins were throbbing in his neck and forehead. Finally, he raised it enough for both of them to slide under, which they did quietly and very carefully. The white van sat parked in the dark garage. Hank pressed his gun against his chest, snuck up to the driver's window, and quickly pointed the gun inside the van. Nothing. He turned his body toward the door to the house and motioned Hillary to follow. When he reached for the door knob and turned it, he almost lost all control; it was locked. Hillary was already searching for something to pick it. Finding nothing, she slipped her hand into her pocket and fished a credit card out of her wallet. With one hand she steadied Hank and motioned him away from the door. Shaking with fear Hank stepped away and put his trust in his partner.

Hillary slipped the credit card between the door and the frame, wiggled it a little bit until it went down further, jiggled it a couple of times, then turned the door knob at just the right moment. They heard more screams from within the house, and through blinding tears Hank cautiously opened the door. They crept into the first room they could find, the dining room. Hank stopped short and put out an arm to stop Hillary. Their eyes were glued to the far wall past the dining room table where a woman's face was painted. They recognized her instantly. It was Jillian Brannon. More screaming, from the other end of the house in the direction of the window with the fake stained glass. Hank and Hillary took baby steps toward a dark hallway. Once in, they allowed their eyes to adjust to the low lighting. What they saw froze them with fear. Painted corpses, photos of mutilated bodies, and blood baths along the baseboards. Hank turned to Hillary who was behind him. They felt like they were going up against the Devil himself. Hank forced one small footstep after another until he reached the doorway at the end of the hallway. He could hear a man shouting and screaming and a woman crying. This time it didn't sound like Judith. This time it was Clover. Hank steadied himself and looked at Hillary. They raised their guns into firing position and on the count of three, Hank kicked the door in.

The surprised look on Roy Fontaine's face was irreplaceable, and so was Hank's. Roy's left hand held a knife to her Judith's neck, while his right arm pinned her body tight against his. Clover was on the floor on hands and knees begging him not to do it.

Roy snarled like a wild beast. Spit frothed in the corners of his mouth as his eyes locked into Hank's stare. With her gun raised and pointed at Roy, Hillary walked slowly into the room and stood beside Clover. There were no time for tears, and Hank held Roy's stare with a burning passion. Heavy footsteps were heard in the back of the house, and Hank knew it was Chief Big D.

"Put the knife down, Roy! It's over!"

Roy sneered and moved Judith's head to cover his own, leaving only one eye exposed. He sunk the knife deeper into Judith's neck, drawing a droplet of blood. It trickled down her chest and soaked into Jillian's soiled yellow bikini.

Hank held his stare and continued to speak to Roy. "Put it down. It's over. Other police are in this house as we speak. Put the knife down."

Roy spoke, his voice muffled by Judith's hair. "Do you know who I am?"

Hank steadied himself. "You are The Artist. I know all about your work. Put the knife down."

Roy let out a sickening laugh that made Hank cringe, but he held still. "But do you know who I really am? You have never seen my true art. My real masterpieces."

Hank wanted this to continue. He wanted him to talk. "I saw some of your more private works in the hallway. Is that what you are talking about?"

Roy shook the point of the knife a little deeper. "You have no idea."

Footsteps down the hallway. Hank had to act fast to keep anyone from entering the room. "Chief, is that you?"

With his back pressed up against the morbid wall, Chief Big D called out. "Yeah, Hank. It's me. Everything alright in there?"

"Yep, just stay in the hallway, Chief."

Chief Big D cursed under his breath, held the gun up to his chest, and listened.

Roy spoke next. "I must say that I am impressed with you. Too bad you are going to spend the rest of your life without the Doctor. She has become my most prized beauty. It's an honor to die while slitting her throat, just so you know."

Hank made the mistake of making eye contact with Judith for the first time. His hand began to shake, as did his voice. "Don't do it, man. Please."

Chief Big D had heard enough. He stepped into the room with his gun raised. Roy tightly grabbed the handle of the knife with his fist to finish his master plan. Hillary acted faster than he did. While he talked with Hank, inch by inch she had moved around Clover until she was on the opposite side. Now she lunged forward with a clear shot of Roy's left shoulder. She took the chance and pulled the trigger as Roy plunged the tip of the knife into Judith's neck. Roy's arm jerked and spasmed as he tried to control it, and Judith fell forward with her hands on her neck to stop the bleeding. Hank rushed to move Judith away from Roy while Chief Big D charged him with the fury of hell. When

Roy tried to take his own life with his other arm, Chief Big D shot him in the other shoulder, rendering him unable to control the knife. He screamed in fury as Big D tackled him to the floor. "No! No! You can't do this to me! I AM THE ARTIST!"

Hillary radioed for an ambulance as Hank picked Judith up from the floor and ran with her through the house. He kicked open the door to the garage and found the button to open it from the inside. When he reached the driveway he could hear the sirens coming down Canal Road. He knelt down in the front yard and cradled her in his arms. He was crying so hard that he could barely speak. "Hang on, baby. Hang, on. They're coming. Hang in there. Stay with me!"

Judith's body was too hot. Hank could feel her growing hotter by the second as he wrapped his shirt around the wound in her neck. He rocked her back and forth in his arms as he pressed his hand to the wound. Caitlin's car came to a screeching halt in front of the house. Melissa bolted from the car and ran to Hank and Judith. Sobbing with grief she fell to the ground and wrapped her arms around her friend. Judith drifted in and out of consciousness as Hank and Melissa cried over her body.

Chapter Fifty Seven

Clover rocked back and forth in her hotel room as she watched the television. In less than a week since his capture, her son had been linked to more than forty murders in five different states. Most of them were of known prostitutes in New Orleans whose cases had grown more than cold over the years.

She had been allowed to keep only one of the paintings from Roy's youth. From her collection, she had chosen a crude painting of the swamp, one of his first ones from the very first paint set she had bought him. Today she held it to her chest while she rocked and waited for the phone call. It finally came. After she answered the phone, she rode the elevator down to the lobby and got into the unmarked car that was waiting for her.

Hillary got out of the driver's seat and opened the door for Clover. She helped her into the car and drove away from the hotel. Neither had much to say to each other. By now, Hillary was accustomed to Clover's quiet nature. Ten minutes later she pulled into a parking spot outside the hospital and helped Clover walk. They rode the elevator to the third floor toward room 324. Hillary knocked softly and Hank came to the door to let them in. Clover stepped past Hillary and Hank and gingerly walked up to the side of Judith's hospital bed. She reached out for Judith's hand, found it and said nothing. The tears that flowed down both of their cheeks said enough, and finally, Irene Clover Fontaine let her son go.

Dressed and ready to go home, Judith smiled at Clover and gave her a hug. "I am so happy that you waited to go back home so I could tell you in person how sorry I am that this has happened to you, and also how thankful I am at the same time. I know in my heart that he would have killed me if you hadn't done what you did to help Hank find me." Judith wiped a tear from her cheek and leaned over to hug Clover. She whispered into her ear, "Thank you. Thank you for saving me."

Clover hugged her back and choked on her words, "Your welcome. Goodbye, Judith." Clover shook hands with everyone in the room and followed Hillary back down to the car that was escorting her to the airport.

Hank pushed the wheelchair over to the side of the bed, but Judith shook her head. "I'm going to use the crutches, baby. I'll be fine."

Hank smiled at her and fought back tears of joy. Bruised, stitched up and bandaged, she was still the most beautiful woman he had ever known in his life.

Melissa joined him as they helped Judith out of the bed. She and Hank had stayed by Judith's side since she had arrived at the hospital three long days ago. When she had first seen the blood flowing from Judith's neck outside the house, she had been sure that her friend would die. There had been so much blood, or so it appeared at the time. But when she had arrived at the hospital, the emergency room had found that her arteries had been missed by the blade and no permanent damage past a scar would occur. The other injuries, as ghastly as they had looked, would heal over time as well.

Judith steadied herself and smiled at Melissa. "Well, that was one hell of a vacation!" The humor was needed to heal, and everyone accepted it in their own way as they slowly walked out of the room. Everyone was waiting for her in the waiting room. The hospital was filled with balloons, flowers and people eagerly waiting to see Judith. When she finally appeared through the doorway, the crowd went wild. Most were crying and clapping their hands, including Chief Big D and Marcus Donnarumma.

Hank wasted no time getting her into the truck. Melissa leaned in and gave her friend a long hug. "I'll be back in a week."

Judith nodded her head. "Thank, you, Melissa. I love you more than you will ever know."

Hank hugged Melissa too and motioned to Marcus Donnarumma that she was ready to go to the airport, and then slid into the truck beside Judith. He held her hand tightly as he drove her home and wondered how she could ever truly heal from the trauma of her experience. When he pulled into the driveway, Judith made a motion toward the crutches. Hank shook his head and jumped quickly from the truck and ran to her side. Carefully and slowly he picked her up in his arms and carried her up the steps to the door. Judith let her head fall into his arm and exhaled slowly.

When he reached the door, he held her tighter. "Judith, I was so scared that I would never get the chance to do this."

She lifted her head up from his shoulder and smiled with tears in her eyes as he carried her over the threshold.